BORN FOR LOVE

LOVE

THE EARL'S CHOICE

By

S.K. Snyder

Contents

AUTHOR'S NOTE

This novel is a work of pure fiction created entirely from imagination and dreams of the author. The Peerage titles are taken from the 14th through the early 19th century, along with English surnames. A considerable amount of research for historical accuracy surrounding events, fashion, sport, pleasure, and circumstances in general was completed to bring life to the fictional characters, who were created and developed in my own imagination. Many of the fictional locations are based loosely on actual castles, country estates and London venues popular during the historical Regency Era and many remain British landmarks. Any resemblance to actual living or dead persons is entirely coincidental.

1

DEDICATION

**To all the lives lost on the Sea Horse, Melville &
Boadicea. May you rest in Peace.**

15 January 1816, the ships Sea Horse and Lord Melville left
the Ports of Ramsgate. Five companies of troops were
returning home from the engagement with Napolean and his
troops in France, along with their families and private citizens,
including thirty-three women and eight children. They were
joined by the Boadicea carrying troops and civilians, including
thirty-four women and children of the 82nd Regiment of Foot,
Prince of Wale's Volunteers. At 11:00 on 28 January 1816, the
ships departed west along the English Channel and entered the
Irish Sea at 5 pm.

The following day the weather deteriorated throughout the
morning and afternoon. The Kinsale Head was dangerous and
rocky; the Kinsale lights must be located. The lights were never
seen, and the plan was abandoned. With sails down, the Sea
Horse was left to the mercy of the strong winds, flood tides
and heavy sea running. The sea was making breaches over her
from bow to stern. At ten minutes past twelve, she struck
Tramore Bay. The vessel took ground less than a mile from the
coast. But the sea ran mountains high, and no assistance could
be afforded from shore. Lifeboats were previously washed
away but would have been no benefit in the rough seas. All
hope of escape was lost.

Most remained on the deck, many washed away by every
returning wave. Gallant efforts were made by those with calm
minds and strong fortitudes as the ship broke apart against the
crashing waves.

There were tales of those clinging to ropes, tying themselves
to large portions of wood, trunks and other cargo as the vessel

2

was encompassed by the tempest. The bravery of those who felt their demise inevitable prayed for timely intervention.

Many lives were lost between the three vessels, but the Sea Horse's were many. The wreckage was strewn up and down the Irish coastline. Bodies washed ashore for days and were buried beneath the sands to be remembered where they lay, and the courage endured by all.

CHAPTER 1

February 7, 1816 – Tramore, Ireland

"Is she dead?" Eleanor shrieked.

Michael glimpsed at his wife as he continued to slice through the ropes that held the victim. Eleanor anxiously paced back and forth on the sand, watching her husband's attempts at removing the refuse.

"If we don't bring her inside soon, she will be!" It was the only response he managed while attempting to cut the young girl free.

Minutes earlier, Eleanor had been taking her daily walk down the copper coastline of eastern Ireland. It had been a long day. She loved her work, but needed constant renewal, which she found along the shoreline.

Lost in thought, she was nearly upon the wreckage before noticing the scattered debris. The putrid stench of rot and decay permeated the air, yet something pushed her toward the spoilage with an unexplained urgency.

Reaching the detritus, she discovered more than material carnage. Accustomed to deleterious conditions, she spared no time in attempting to unravel what lay before her.

She pulled away the ravaged material and torn ribbons of fabric secured to a travelling trunk. The small knife she carried had a negligible effect on the thick hemp and flax-twined rope.

Eleanor frantically cleared away the rubbish, demanding her hands to work faster as she uncovered arms and legs tightly fastened to the oversized trunk. She brushed away the dark, matted hair to reveal the face of a young girl. Unable to loosen the bonds that held her securely, she lay her head against the figure, listening for sounds of life. She was convinced she detected a faint heartbeat. There had to be one, must be one, although meagre at best she refused to accept this child for dead.

She glanced up to see her companion strolling down the beach. "Michael, hurry!" Her alarming cry was without panic.

Michael, detecting the insistent tone, shifted his walk into a run. He immediately recognised the limp form. "My God, Eleanor, what the devil... blimey!" Lost for words, he knelt to assist.

He pulled a large knife from the leather sheath at his leg and easily sliced through the wet ropes holding the body to the wooden box.

"I think she's still alive." Eleanor breathed heavily attempting to heave the girl upright.

Michael reached under her, lifting her frail, lifeless body into his arms. He was staring at her face as Eleanor found the strength to stand. "If she is, it's barely. We need to get her to the cottage."

"Since she was tied to the trunk, do you think it might tell us who she is?" Eleanor was wiping the waste from the container.

"It could. We'll send someone to fetch it. Come, if this girl is to survive, we must hurry." Michael began to step quickly up the beach to the opening in the protected brush line.

CHAPTER 2

The frigid winter rains continued taking their toll on London throughout January. By early February, it seemed another wet, cold season had settled in for a lengthy visit to the growing city. Those who remained in Town discovered the only comfort was near a roaring fire, with a warm wrap and a glass of spirits or cup of tea in hand.

Richard Hawthorn was one of those stranded in the frozen city. He had not intended to spend Christmas and the New Year in London, but the past year had been one of those inescapable, like it or not, life-altering events. By the merciless and sarcastic grace of God, Richard found himself without warning, encumbered with a noble title, family responsibilities, and societal obligations he had never sought nor wanted.

The Right Honourable 5th Earl of Gillford was compelled to abandon his solitary and perilous role as a clandestine military special agent for The Crown, capriciously exchanging it for one of sedentary and dull political business in the House of Lords. His life confirming, without doubt, God indeed has a sense of humour.

Richard's uncle, The Right Honourable, 2nd Earl of Gillford, was a prestigious and influential Lord in Parliament whose strengths in the administration and influence in his defence of the Church of England were legendary. Regrettably, despite his power and influence, it did not benefit him in his struggle against the mysterious illness that ultimately claimed his life. His successor, his young and only son, assumed the title at the age of two and twenty. However, his pernicious love of spirits combined with the obsession for wild, untamed horseflesh tragically ended his life soon after the inheritance of it. Passing the earldom to Richard Edward Hawthorn, the 2nd Earl's younger brother.

Richard Edward, already ill with consumption, endured the torment of the disease and title for nearly a year before succumbing to its effects on the lungs. Leaving the earldom, the seat in parliament, and the title in the debauched lap of the carefree Richard Frederick Hawthorn.

The well-born and privileged Corinthian was an expert horseman, pugilist, swordsman, and marksman. At eighteen, he imagined himself well on his way to living a gentleman's leisurely life of debauchery and pleasure. However, when he and three of his closest friends were set down from university after riding their stallions through the dining hall at Cambridge, and God apparently needing another good laugh at his expense, his father announced it was time for him to see the world by way of a purchased commission in his majesty's military.

But once again, luck was with the confident and daring Hawthorn. He was soon recognised for his skills and intrepidity, becoming one of the crown's most successful war spies, living life by his own rules and believing he had had the last laugh.

However, through his death, The Right Honourable, 4th Earl, delivered his final set down. Richard was forced to abandon his reckless and covert lifestyle to assume control of an overlooked earldom, an unoccupied parliament seat, along with two younger female siblings and a bereaved mother.

Sipping a brandy by the fire, Lord Gillford was deliberating the annoyance of his newfound life when he heard the unmistakeable click clack of carriage wheels come to a halt at #6 Upper Brook Street.

His butler soon appeared, announcing, "Lord James Sheffield, my lord." The butler stood stoic in the doorway, awaiting instruction.

Hawthorn was standing at his liquor cabinet, filling two snifters, when his friend entered. "Sheffield, how are you?"

"Aside from feeling half froze to death, could not be better," Sheffield said, entering in his usual gaiety and exuberance, moving toward the warmth of the fire. "I do hope that one of those is intended for a dear companion?"

"This weather is only tolerable for a glass of brandy to soothe the spirit and a roaring blaze to warm the remainder." Gillford poured an additional finger for his guest. "What the devil compels you to venture out on this God-forsaken evening?"

"Insanity, I must be a bit dicked in the knob. Cannot bear the thought of eating alone, even in this dismal weather. I found myself at White's, but it was dull as a cow. Then the cursed carriage was intolerably cold, the bricks futile, and I noticed the address. I figured you to have a warm fire and a good brandy."

"Glad you did. This incessant freezing rain is bloody melancholic. So, how do you go on?" Hawthorn asked, handing him his drink.

"Endeavouring to remain warm and sheltered, primarily." He said, savouring the brandy, "Ah, splendid!" Sheffield reclined in the wingback, placing his glass on the armrest. "I was thinking of heading to Eustace Hall if the rain ever decides to abate." He smirked as if doubtful. "It appears that our dear friend Andovir has risen from the dead. He landed at the estate in Suffolk and expresses his intentions to restore the place."

"Attempting to what? During this season? Good God." Hawthorn remarked, proceeding to the sofa near the fire.

"I ought to have remained at Belmont following Christmas. However," he said, "I assured the earl and countess that I would keep them informed of any meagre information I obtained from him, and the letters are duly delivered in London. But now that he has returned to England, I am

8

inclined to ascertain the truth firsthand before I go discussing his well-being on my next visit to Birkshire. The countess shall surely reprimand me if she discovers that I have been carrying tales.

"I dare say she would. I've been hearing of your visits to Lady Olivia. Should I enter the betting books at White's?" The Earl of Gillford relaxed, placing one hessian atop his knee.

"No, no, do not squander your blunt on it, waste of good coin. If you are inclined to make such a bet, place it on the marriage of Lady Olivia and Lord Andovir. Now that he has returned, I will say within six months if the damn fool regains his senses."

"You are bamming me? Well, damme. Would never have predicted it. I had always been under the impression that she was only the irritating younger sister."

"Indeed, she was! We all thought as much until last year. If you had attended the country party at Birkshire in the spring, you would have witnessed her remarkable metamorphosis, as well as the undeniable chemistry between the two." Sheffield winced a bit before adding, "But alas, Andovir has cut us all out; she only has eyes for him."

"She is lovely. I hope she has recovered; she is quite the incomparable."

"She's coming around," Sheffield added. "I cannot thank you for all you did, no other like her. Truth is, if it were not for her unrelinquished affection for Andovir, I would attempt to secure a future duchess." His eyes cut away from his friend." She was a frightful creature in her youth though, and damme if she didn't frighten the devil out of me. But, by Jove, if she didn't transform into a lovely young woman."

"And here I thought you to be a bachelor until his grace calls you to heel."

"And I'm certain to be if Andovir comes up to scratch. You know how it is, Gill, only one in a lifetime, and she was it. I figure the graces will concern themselves with my two sisters before I'm a bother with the societal expectations of matrimony."

"Good to hear. I saw Worth during Christmas; he is already avoiding Derbyshire. Maybe the three of us should try Andovir's continental tour." Hawthorn suggested.

The door opened, Carson begged his lordship's pardon, an urgent message had arrived, and the messenger was to await a response.

Lord Gillford grimaced, stood, and walked across the parlour, meeting the butler by half. "Hmmm, at this hour, this cannot be good news." Hawthorn broke the wax, but not before recognising the war department seal. In silence, he perused the missive. The contents were brief, but the dispatch was unmistakeable.

"You're looking rather unwell, Gillford. Is it bad…"

"Dreadful accounts Sheffield, quite dreadful. Three military ships and cargo were tragically lost in a devastating wreck off the coast of Ireland. There were women and children aboard and a tremendous loss of life. I report to the department in the morning."

"Report? But you are no longer a part of the war department." Sheffield reminded him.

"No matter, this is serious business. My skills are necessary, and there aren't enough hands to accomplish what must be done." He walked to his desk and scribbled out a quick response, handing it off to Carson. Reminded the butler to offer the messenger a warm cider before his departure.

"You must travel to Ireland?" Sheffield was also standing, watching the seriousness and distress on his friend's face.

"First thing, but I must get a note off to my mother. She is expecting me in a few days, and God only knows of my return." Hawthorn pulled another parchment from his desk, dipped his quill, and began another correspondence.

"Do not concern yourself about a messenger. I'll convey the missive to the countess tomorrow. I will ensure they are in no need of assistance before I return."

Richard glanced up at his friend. The strong bond between his four close friends was evidenced by one of them never having to ask for a need. The other seemed to know and provided it without request. "I dare say, Sheffield, you are a right one, especially considering this ghastly weather. It will calm my mother and Clarice to see a friendly face with the delivery. I had no intentions of being pulled back into this life, but these were noble men." The earl lowered his head, "All survived the slaughter at Waterloo, then to be lost going home and with their families." Richard's voice cracked, "Damn, I have no choice but to take part in the recovery and secure the military secrets, arms, and accoutrements. The cargo consisted of sensitive information. Life is truly unfair, is it not."

"Just so!" Sheffield agreed.

CHAPTER 3

Tramore Fishing Village, Ireland, late February 1816

Eleanor was preparing tea for her patient. The familiar sound of boiling water whistled, and she reached for the kettle. A loud crash sounded from the other side of the cottage. She dropped the teapot, leaving it teetering on the burner. Drying her hands on her apron as she moved quickly through the corridor.

Upon entering the bedchamber, the young girl was seated on the edge of one of the single beds. She had inadvertently knocked over the table, spilling its contents. She looked like a child in an oversized dressing gown, her bare feet dangling over the side. Her long brown locks were tangled and messy, resembling a rat's nest. Balancing on her weak arms, clinging to the mattress, she glanced up at the stranger who had entered.

Eleanor ran to her side, sitting next to her on the bed. "Gracious child, you mustn't try to get up yet. You're as weak as a newborn pup. Let me help you back into bed."

The weak patient could do nothing but allow her caregiver to place her back into bed and cover her with blankets and quilts. She pushed the hair from the young girl's face. When the lass peered up at her, Eleanor was startled by the deep violet-blue eyes before she clamped them closed, complaining of the pain.

"My head, the headache, the headache, it is unbearable." the patient whimpered in a weak voice.

"I imagine, dear, you've been awful ill and need to rest. You 'ave a way to go before you are right again."

Eleanor's steady, sweet voice seemed to calm her patient, and the stiffness of her small body went limp again.

"Pray tell, what were you tryin' to do? Gracious, just get ya where you about fixed up, and you go tryin' to catch your death."

Eleanor was rattling on, then remembered the patient had no idea where she was or with whom she was conversing. She picked up the table, straightened the scattered contents and grabbed the small wicker straight chair from the corner, dragging it across the floor to sit next to the bed. She reached under the blankets, taking the girl's hand in hers, and leaning forward over the girl's face.

"Now don't go a tuckerin' yourself. My name is Eleanor, and I'm with the Catholic mission. I'm the one who found ya…"

"Found me?" the young girl muttered haggardly, still keeping her eyes shut and wincing a bit from the pain in her head.

"Yea found ya on the beach, not in no good way neither. But we brung you to safety 'ere, and the doc seen ya an figures you are on the mend but won't be good as new for a bit."

"Where am I?"

"Like I say, a Catholic Mission."

Trying to struggle to raise her head, she opened her eyes and tried to focus on Eleanor's face.

"Now, now, just lay back and don't be a strainin' yourself. You need to save your strength till you're better."

The young girl turned her head so she could peer at the lady treating her so kindly. Things were very unsettled in her brain, but she did not recognise the woman. She was coming around enough to perceive her body was weak and her mind… what was wrong with her mind… something was, but she was too tired to think, oh she was tired.

13

"Begging your pardon, your name was… I cannot remember."

"Aww child, that's understandable, nuthin' to concern yourself, it's Eleanor."

"Eleanor, that is right, I am sorry."

"Naw, don't be fussin' about that." Eleanor hesitated, then asked the question she had been longing to for weeks. "What might your name be, child?"

The girl's eyes blinked rapidly as she licked her quivering lips. Eleanor observed her chest heaving up and down, breathing heavily as if in a state of panic. She sucked her lower lip between her teeth, biting down on it, as she abruptly sat up in the bed and surveyed the room as if searching for answers. Her terrified eyes settled on Eleanor, tears falling to her cheeks, and in a distressing stammer whispered, "I… I don't know."

CHAPTER 4

"General McGinnis, Richard Hawthorn at your service." Lord Gillford entered the office of the commander and stood in front of the large wooden desk piled high with papers and files, all apparently linked to the Sea Horse, Boadicea, and Lord Melville.

"Aww, Hawthorn, it's good to see you. I hated pulling you back into service, but you see how things are."

"Yes, sir! It happens." Hawthorn acknowledged.

The general raised his eyebrows, "I have been informed you have recovered the documents of concern and had a fair bit of trouble doing it."

"Not so much, sir."

"I would venture a man of your stature has little trouble with most things he aims to obtain."

"I appreciate your faith, sir," Hawthorn said, still surveying the files on the desk.

"Relax, and please sit," The general motioned toward the chair.

This was not a good sign for leaving this assignment. It was obvious yet another request was to be asked of him, but he sat anyway.

"It is my understanding you are returning to London within the fortnight?"

"It is my plan, sir." He eyed the general with suspicion.

"Oh, no worries. I'm not to interfere with those plans, but I do have one last request of you."

"Whatever I can do for you, sir." How many times had he heard one last request? He had stopped counting over the last year.

"Don't be so quick to agree, Hawthorn. You might not like this one."

Hawthorn laughed and gave the General a sly grin. "Sir, I can't say I have liked any of the assignments I have ever been dealt."

The general sniggered and assured him it was his own fault. "That's what comes from being the best, Hawthorn. But you can't say you were ever bored."

"No sir, I damn sure can't say that."

McGinnis pulled a file from the bottom of a large stack and handed it to the earl. He opened it and scanned over the pages of doctor reports and statements. He flipped through the thin file, then gazed up at the general.

"A young girl with amnesia, sir? What am I to do with this?"

"I hope you will take her back to England with you."

"Sir, she's a young female!"

"Don't get yourself all worked up in a huff. I understand you're a titled gentleman now. All that muff about nothing. But you won't be taking her alone. One of the elderly ladies here will be travelling as her companion. A Mrs. O'Hara, she is English borne and her husband was stationed here until his death a few months ago. She is ready to return home to her kin in London. She has agreed to chaperone the girl until other arrangements can be made."

"Thank you, sir. There was a time when I would not be as concerned, but my title, along with my uncle's respected seat in parliament, I must be careful to protect the family name, you know."

The general snorted and smiled at Hawthorn, "Being a young man once myself, you're more worried about your bachelor position being threatened than your name. Don't deny it."

"Well, sir, I cannot, but if she has amnesia, it could be a confounded tangle, depending on where she belongs."

"I realise it my boy, and the war department doesn't need a scandal either. But the doctor insists she will not improve unless she returns to England. He is hoping in familiar surroundings, she will remember. Can't be done here, he says. The caregiver and doctor believe she can't be over sixteen or seventeen years of age, and there is much speculation as to who she is."

"Is it certain she came from the Sea Horse, sir?"

"No question of it. She was tied to a military trunk. One we were desperate to find and was one of the first found. But we can't identify her with anyone on the passenger list. Of course, so many were lost off the Sea Horse; Lord only knows who she is."

"And what am I to do with her when I get her to England, sir."

The general coughed and cleared his throat, "I know this is asking a lot, Hawthorn, but we are in a fix, you understand. You will be well compensated for it, I assure you."

Richard took a short, panicked breath. "Sir, you cannot mean…"

"We need you to locate where she belongs. I can assure you it will be the last assignment. God as my witness. We just don't have the skills or ability to deal with this type of situation. With your skills, background, and associations, you can find whatever you need."

"But sir, I have never tried to locate…" Hawthorn stopped short.

17

It sounded ridiculous, even to himself, as he uttered the words. That was all he had done for the military: locate those who did not want to be found and gain information they had in their possession. How difficult could it be to find someone who wished to be found?

"Of course, sir." Resigned to his new mission.

"I knew you would help us one last time. All the information you need is in the file. Where to find the girl, the couple giving her care and Dr Lacy, the attending physician. Everything else, you are the expert, not I."

CHAPTER 5

Richard was glad to be hauling his trunk and valise to the vessel that would return him to England. It hadn't been a tough assignment, but it had been a filthy one. The sand, dirt and sea salt covered everything he touched. It was good to be headed home.

His hackney halted in front of the jetty tavern on Waterford Harbour. The tall clipper ship resting at anchor was alive with activity, preparing for her departure. Richard and Bixby, his valet, alighted from the equipage, motioning for the trunks and portmanteaus to be removed and transferred to the men loading the cargo.

Hawthorn turned toward the tavern to seek out the passengers he would be escorting to London. The doors were propped open, and a large group of stevedores were crowding into the pub, searching for one last ale before they set sail. Once the brawny group cleared the entrance, Richard saw an elderly woman and a frail young girl huddled together on a small wooden bench on the far side of the entryway. The matron was surrounded by trunks and bandboxes, her short, thick limbs swinging nonchalantly while she fanned the humidity away from her face.

The frail lass was wrapped in a grey hooded cloak, clutching a small bag in her lap. Her gaunt features and white knuckles were gripping the one valise as much for safety and protection as anything more. She had refused the military's offer of money but accepted one dress, a pair of shoes, a pair of gloves, a bonnet, and the grey cloak Richard had insisted upon. Assuring him, she preferred to wash the one dress each night. Eleanor had given her a dressing gown, and she insisted that was plenty.

Richard had only met his charge once, but he had run into Mrs O'Hara on several occasions during the final two weeks. A nephew escorting her one afternoon had described the elderly relative as "corky." Richard decided it fit her perfectly. She had no sense of real propriety but was extremely friendly and nurturing, and he was certain she would be a caring companion for the misplaced girl.

"Oh, me lord, yoo hoo! Lord Gillford, ow'er 'ere!" Mrs. O'Hara hailed.

Dear God! She had spotted him strolling up the boarded walk and was now loudly summoning him. Hawthorn gave the lady a small wave, hoping she would not find it necessary to yell across the street at him again. Although he held the title for nearly a year, he had not yet grown comfortable with its use and found it most uncomfortable when blasted across the wharf. He had enjoyed not being addressed as Lord Gillford while in Ireland.

"Good morning, Mrs. O'Hara. How do you go on?" He bowed and greeted his assigned burdens. The widow stood and curtsied, and her companion, without raising her eyes, rose quietly, gave a small curtsy, and slid back onto the bench.

"Oh, I'm a jolly good 'un, me Lord." The matron was one of those souls who was always in good spirits for no reason … just because anything else was just rude.

She smiled at the earl and cocked her head toward the miss to ensure he observed she was not doing well.

"And how is our young miss?" Richard was towering over her as she slowly raised her eyes.

"I am well, my lord. Thank you for asking." She muttered quietly.

"You seem a bit out, are you certain."

"Yes, I am only vexed and hesitant what is to come next. I feel particularly stupid."

Understandably, with no memory, comfort was unattainable. He had been so involved with his assignment that he hadn't thought of her situation until this moment. She had no idea who she was, where she lived, or even her age and was forced to depend on the kindness of strangers. He for the first time, imagined how bewildered she must be.

Kneeling in front of her, he gently lifted her chin. "You are not in the least stupid. You have been through a violent trauma. With the loss of your memory, the physical pains have now turned into emotional ones. I have been assured when you return to England and to all which is familiar, your memory will return."

"Thank you. I pray you are correct, my lord, but..." She choked back a sob, her eyes still lowered.

Oh no, not that, not tears, good God almighty, please, no tears. The earl took her gloved hand in his. "It is all right. Know this, you will be looked after very well until your memory returns, and I will locate your parents and where you belong."

"Is that what you are to do?" She raised her eyes to meet his, and he was struck by the brilliant violet-blue eyes staring back, but their intensity gave way to the longing and anguish that filled them.

Richard repressed his surprise at the deep hue and tried to comfort her. "Yes, as soon as we return to London. I will begin searching for your family."

"Thank you, my lord." She liked him and felt safe with him. She had not realised until this moment how very much that meant to her. She had no memory, but the sense of protection was somehow important.

"But first of all, we need to call you something besides miss. How were you addressed by Mr. and Mrs. McLeary?"

"Only Miss. Eleanor was exceedingly kind and spoke with me extensively but referred only to me as Miss."

"Well, I do not care for it. It's cold and impersonal. Since we are to become familiar and you are in my charge, we need to call you something other than Miss."

She smiled up at him as if that alone would make her feel less isolated.

"Thank you. It does make one feel quite awkward. It is as though those around you are afraid to get too attached. They might catch the amnesia."

Richard laughed, and when he did, she did as well. He squeezed her hand, stood, placing his hands on his hips, cocked his head to one side and declared, "Miss Smith, are you ready to return to England?" She shrugged but agreed, retaining the smile that normally came and went quickly.

The ladies remained on the bench until all the baggage was secured and the final arrangements were made for their cabins. They were sailing aboard a chartered clipper, procured, and arranged by the military. Richard had spent too many years with the war department to rely on logistics going as planned. He motioned for his valet to follow him, and they headed down the boardwalk to find the captain.

Once he was satisfied the cabins, the trunks, portmanteaux, and valises were all secured properly, he and his valet returned to assist the ladies aboard.

"Bixby, I think it would be more appropriate if you helped Miss Smith, and I will escort Mrs. O'Hara."

"Whichever you wish, milord." Bixby nodded.

"It has nothing to do with wish, I said appropriate."

Bixby recognised the earl's signature raised eyebrow and wondered if his lordship might question his decision to take on the fair maiden. He, too, noticed the girl, with no memory was changing. As her health returned, so did her attractiveness.

"Miss Smith, Bixby will help you aboard, and I will escort Mrs. O'Hara."

"Of course, my lord, but I am certain I can manage." The young girl hesitated.

"The quay and gangway are unstable, so I would prefer you had an arm to lean on."

"As you wish!" She slipped her hand through Bixby's extended arm.

Mrs. O'Hara gave the earl her hand, and he helped her from the bench, placing her fingers in the crook of his arm as they made their way to the jetty.

"I gits it, me lord. Afeared the old woman 'ill end up in the brink, I sezs." She lifted her eyes to the earl and gave him a wink.

"Mrs. O'Hara, are you flirting with me?" Richard grinned down at her as they made their way up the gangway.

"It'll be tha' one chance me ew'er gets, gotta make the better of it. Ne're been close to an earl afore."

They both let out a chuckle as he helped her onto the ship. Just as he was about to say something else, they heard Bixby.

"Milord, My Lord, Lord Gillford… hurry!"

The earl and chaperone quickly spun round to see Bixby trying to hold Miss Smith upright. He was uncertain whether she had fainted or was only confused. But Bixby was holding on to a limp dishrag, and they were both about to tumble into the briny waters beneath the pier. Lord Gillford assured Mrs O'Hara was safely aboard, departed the gangway and took several long strides toward his valet. As he reached the two, he saw the terror on the girl's face. She was far from about to swoon, but she was determined not to take another step

23

toward the ship, even if it meant landing in the salty sea. Without a thought, Richard grabbed her about the waist. She was struggling to pull away, but the strength of the earl was no match for her.

"I cannot!" she screamed, "I cannot! I will not!"

The earl twisted her to face him and lifted her where the tips of her boots barely touched the ground. The terrified tears covered her face. He pulled her to his chest and held her tightly. "It is all right; it is all right!"

He motioned to Bixby, "Go on board and assist Mrs O'Hara. Have our items settled for sailing. I am taking Miss Smith back to the tavern. Notify the captain we will be aboard as quickly as possible. Damme, I should have thought of this."

"Yes, my lord. I will bring you any missives needed."

"Thank you, Bixby."

Richard released his hold on the trembling young girl but kept one hand securely on her waist and nudged her back to the security of solid land.

"I am sorry." She sobbed.

"It's all right, really it is. I must apologise for not considering how this might affect you."

"It makes no sense. I do not remember anything. How can I be terrified to board a ship when I do not remember ever being on one." Her small body was trembling.

He led her into the jetty tavern and gently settled her into a chair. He motioned for the owner to bring a glass of brandy as he took the seat next to her. She buried her face in her hands and pressed her fingertips into her forehead and temples.

"Your headache's returned?"

"Yes," she said softly.

"'ere ye are. Git ya anyfin' else guv'nor?"

"No, thank you, this will do for now." Richard tossed him a crown, and the snaggled tooth man grinned, tossing it in the air and catching it swiftly.

"Thank ye, thank ye, indeed!" Swiftly returning with the glass.

Richard took the brandy and lifted it to Miss Smith's lips. "Here, drink this, and you will feel better in a bit."

"What am I going to do? I cannot walk to that ship. I am sorry, I just cannot!"

"You need not worry; just drink this and let me worry about the rest."

She took the glass and sipped the amber liquid. The first sip took her breath away, and she couldn't stop coughing. She stared at him as if he were giving her poison. "My goodness, it burns all the way down my throat."

"I suppose you have never had brandy before?" He should have considered it.

She looked at him strangely and back at the spirit. Then, she tipped her head to one side. "I don't know!"

Richard laughed and shook his head. "It was a silly question, was it not. This is going to be a remarkably interesting journey, Miss Smith."

She forced a smile, but it was not funny to her. "For weeks, it has been my misfortune. The simplest questions are unbeknownst to me, and the manner in which people regard you, as though you are dim-witted or simple-minded. It is extremely distressing. I wish to explain it, but no one can truly understand."

"I believe thing will become easier. And I am confident your family will provide you comfort and support. Once you are reunited, I am certain your memory will swiftly be restored." At least Richard prayed it would. This assignment was the last thing he wanted to linger on. The what-ifs were extremely disturbing.

"Eleanor mentioned I would be staying with you when we return to England. Pray, what does that signify?" She inquired nervously, rolling the snifter between her hands.

"It signifies my mother, and my two sisters will be attending to your well-being whilst I endeavour to locate your family."

There was obvious relief by this answer, as she stared at the glass containing the dreaded liquid. The next few sips went down a bit easier, and she began to relax.

"How is your headache?" The earl asked.

"Better, thank you. It is no longer throbbing; it is more of a dull ache."

Convinced the captain was displeased with the delay, the earl was eager for the brandy to take its effect. A glint formed in her eyes, her posture relaxed, her breathing eased into a more restful rhythm, and her arms lingered on the table. Her laced fingers caressed the tumbler as if it were a precious gift. She raised it one last time to her lips, clutched it firmly with both hands, and tilted her head back to drain the final swig.

Startled, Richard arched his eyebrows in surprise, as Miss Smith's arm dropped with a loud thud onto the table. Her eyes were shut, and her head languidly flopped forward. He observed in astonishment as she slowly raised it, her figure gently swaying, ever so slightly, to and fro. He winced when she slammed her hands to the tabletop steadying herself.

"I do believe I am feeling better." She hiccupped, slowly fluttered her eyelashes, bestowed a charming smile upon him, and giggled.

"I believe I ought to have removed the drink before it was completely consumed." Richard reached for the empty container. She tightened her grip and pulled it closer. He let out a chuckle.

26

"Oh, n-no," she stammered, her speech slightly muddled as she squeezed her eyes shut tightly and then widened them abruptly. "I thi-nk it was j-u-sth the right amount," she hesitated, balanced her elbow on the table and rested her chin in her hand. "In order for me to... to... to..." she lowered her gaze and narrowed her eyes, "what was it?" she paused, "Ooohhhh yes," she stuttered, "board that... that... boat." She emitted another giggle and gave him the most endearing grin.

"You do!" Richard couldn't help but laugh as she struggled to maintain herself upright. He needed her a little intoxicated, but this? He rose and pulled her chair from the small table and offered his arm. With both hands placed on his elbow and forearm, she attempted to rise, only to fall forward, landing limp in his arms. Richard staggard backwards, hastily embracing her to prevent her from meeting the floor face first.

He desired her relaxed, but he also needed her to remain capable of walking onto the vessel with minimal assistance. It appeared he had overestimated her ability to tolerate brandy. He assisted her to stand her upright, but her head floundered backwards, and her bonnet went flying off her head, saved only by the meticulously tied ribbon at her throat. She raised her head and giggled again.

"Miss Smith, I do believe you're foxed!"

"I am?" She hiccupped again and promptly passed out in his arms.

Richard grimaced, leaned forward, effortlessly hoisted her petite frame over his shoulder, her head adorned with a lopsided bonnet and arms dangling down his back. He turned to take his leave, and his eyes met the snaggled tooth barman, who brazenly grinned as he wiped a bar glass clean. The earl only smirked and quickly departed with his baggage slung perfunctorily over his shoulder.

Making his way down the quay with his encumbrance thrown over his shoulder, his gaze was drawn to Bixby and Mrs. O'Hara positioned side by side on the ship's deck. The chaperone's eyes widened, and clamped a hand to her mouth in shock at the unseemly pair approached the gangway.

"Oh my 'eavenly dazs, we ain't gittin' off to a vewy good start, is we?"

"Mrs. O'Hara, I assure you, I did not mean to give her this much brandy. I only meant to calm her."

"Welp, me lord, at leastin' she didn' give you no more troubles, now did she?"

Richard chuckled, "No, at least we can say that."

The widow gave him a grin and motioned for him to follow her. "Bring 'er to 'er room, and I'll take care from 'ere. She'll be good as new tomorrow, she will." The matron led the way to a small cabin with two berths and motioned to one. After Mrs. O'Hara assured him, she could manage from here, he took his leave.

When Hawthorn returned to the deck, he found Bixby seated on one of the rope boxes. As the ship eased out of the Waterford harbour with the tide, he turned to the earl.

"I fear this may be the longest voyage we've ever undertaken, my lord."

The earl cut his valet a sharp glance. "Are you referring to the sail to Ramsgate or our unwanted cargo?"

Bixby looked up at his master and laughed. "Take your pick, sir. It doesn't much matter, now does it?"

"There is a reason we remain bachelors." Lord Gillford stated candidly.

"Amen to that milord, amen to that." The valet agreed.

"I'll bet if we locate that captain, we will find some good brandy."

"If we don't, my lord. I know where the good stuff is hidden in the Earl of Gillford's trunk." Bixby winked at him and grinned.

"That will work, my good man!"

***

One morning, Mrs O'Hara found the earl leaning against the mainmast, his arms crossed, watching the girl. She was leaning against the foremast, staring up at the multiple jibs, then drooping her gaze across the open water.

"It's a sad sight, ain't it, milord?" The woman coaxed.

"I have tried to imagine what it must be like not to know your own name or where you belong. Yet, as terrified as she was to board, she now stands on the deck searching across the waters looking for answers."

"Shez a brav'en, I 'as to say. Ain't so sure I cud of dun it meself."

"I would say she is resolute and determined." Richard adjusted his position, crossing one boot over the other.

"Aye, dat too!" Mrs. O'Hara shook her head and strode away, leaving the earl to study his new responsibility.

Gillford watched the small wisp of a girl struggling to find herself during the journey back to England. She spent her days on deck casting her eyes across the water hoping for a memory to surface.

As she regained strength and colour in her cheeks, Richard noticed the similarity to his sixteen-year-old sister Emily. They both carried a small feminine frame, dark hair, although Emily's was brown where this girl's had a copper hue, which seemed to brighten by the day. Their oval faces were graced with small delicate lips and tiny noses. Where Emily's eyes were hazel, the shade of this young girl's was a striking, almost

29

mesmerizing violet. He found it uncanny how much they favoured one another in frame, structure, and colouring.

He quickly blamed the connection for this new sense of protection growing for her. He needed to find her family. He could not allow himself to develop an attachment. The healthier she became, the more beautiful she appeared, and the more difficult to remain apathetic and indifferent.

He also questioned how he was to move forward with the entire situation. He couldn't just dump her off to her parents and wash his hands of her? She trusted him and was becoming more attached to Mrs. O'Hara. She felt safe and comfortable. He made promises to watch over her but prayed would be able to keep them. He had assured her she was safe, and under his protection. He realised safeguarding her might have many different meanings. The few people she had learnt to trust and depend upon had washed their hands of her. The more he considered it, the more he found abandoning her was not an option.

Something else was needling Richard. There was more to this situation, but what? And why did it matter? The war department had given him instruction to locate her family and return her to them, but that sounded a bit too simple.

He wasn't certain if it was his clandestine background or the attachment he was forming, but something was not quite right. Why had she not been on the passenger list? Why didn't any of the survivors recognise her or even know she was aboard or with whom? The more he pondered it, the more misgivings he had. Was she running away? If so, from what or who? Of course, the War Department had no interest in such information. As he reflected upon it, he had been the best dupe for them to wash their hands of her.

The closer they came to Ramsgate, the more he was convinced locating her family was not enough. Who knew what kind of people they were? They might just jerk her from his custody, and there would be nothing he could do to stop it.

Good Lord, he was concerned for her, and her trust was important to him.

What had happened to him over the past year? A year ago, he had no responsibilities, little care for himself and none for anyone else. He could not afford to do so. He took risks in the service to The Crown that could easily end his career, his life, and the life of those around him. Now, he had a title, a place in parliament and four females who entrusted their very existence to him. Bloody hell, he hardly recognised the man he had become and this feeling of responsibility; he disliked it exceedingly. But, deep inside, the gentleman he was raised to be, lurked in the darkness. He would not let these ladies down. This one, in particular needed him as much as the other three, maybe more.

***

After their arrival at Ramsgate and everyone was settled in with the Clancy's at the Inn, Richard took an afternoon stroll along the harbour overlooking the sea. How odd it was going to be not returning here as frequently. He would miss the exhilaration of his years in the military. He disliked his new reality, with two sisters aged twenty and sixteen years old. He must find them suitable matches, which included nights spent amidst the Ton, along with days arguing with pompous, powerful old men. Half of them wanted England to remain unchanged, and the other wished to fast-forward her into the industrial future. He also needed to find a way to bring his mother back to the living and move past the loss of his father.

As his mind wandered regarding where his life was headed, he was glad he had this last contract from the department to ease him into his new responsibilities. One foot in the future and one foot in the past.

As he approached the inn, he noticed Mrs. O'Hara with Mrs. Clancy and poor Miss Smith sitting on the bench in front. What a sad little creature she was. The more he discovered of her, the less he could figure how and why she had been on the

31

Sea Horse. Someone who cared for her profoundly and knew there was no hope remaining on the crumbling ship had tied her to that important military trunk. Whoever it was knew what was in it. Meaning they were most likely in service to the Crown in some ranked capacity. Even so, it was a miracle she had survived.

At daybreak the following morning, several sleepy travellers took their seats in or on the Gillford crested coach to begin their journey to London. Richard closed the heavy curtain next to him, nestled himself into the crushed velvet corner and dozed off. Bixby opened a periodical as the light was just enough to read, and Mrs. O'Hara pulled out her knitting.

Miss Smith rested her elbow on the edge of the window, stared at the passing landscape and watched the sunrise. She had no idea what awaited her in London, but she could not escape the apprehension that suddenly swept over her. She wished she could recall something of her past. As the well-sprung coach rambled along, a sense of melancholy overwhelmed her. Not at all certain why, but she had a dreadful feeling she was headed in the wrong direction.

.

CHAPTER 6

After one excessively long day of travel the large carriage swayed through the London streets, and everyone was ready to come to a halt. Although the weather was cooler than normal, the coach remained stuffy, even with the windows open. Richard wished he had informed his coachman to pony his gelding. But at last, they were finally nearing Mayfair.

The wheels slowed, and the house was coming into view. The earl's thoughts were on how to approach his mother and sisters. He had written how it would be, but putting words to parchment was never quite the same. He was bringing a stranger with a curious affliction in their home. He hoped she would understand; he prayed they all would.

The coach came to a standstill at #6 Upper Brook Street in the late evening hour, and the footman let down the steps. Richard alighted and peered up at the four stories of imposing house that had become his home over the last year. At moments such as these, he had to shake his mind loose, assuring himself it was not a dream. He was indeed The 5th Earl of Gillford, with all its shackles and chains. Damn his careless cousin, the young fool! He turned his attention back to the present and handed down the female standing at the equipage door.

"Is this your house?" Miss Smith gazed at the four stories of brick and stone with the grand entry, trying to prevent her mouth from gaping.

"Yes, it is home to my mother, sisters, and myself. Come, I am sure they are waiting for us in the drawing room. It is not time for dinner, and once introductions are made, Emily and Clarice can escort you to your room. As they approached the top step, the door opened, and they were greeted by a stoic servant.

"My lord!" The butler nodded, backed away and as his lordship entered, received his hat and coat.

"Carson. It is good to be home. I hope all is well?" Richard gave him a stare with one raised eyebrow, which begged for an honest answer. He was met with a matching arch of his butler's. It was unfortunate; he knew what that gesture entailed.

"Everything is now in order. The countess and your sisters are in the blue saloon."

"I suppose that is the best I could hope for after months away."

Taking their coats and hats, the butler agreed. "Yes, sir."

Turning to his charge, "this is Miss Smith. Clarice informed you of her arrival?"

"Yes, my lord and accommodations have been readied. She was placed in the room adjoining Lady Emily at her insistence."

"I am neither surprised nor have I objections. I'm certain my sister is looking forward to having a guest her own age."

"Indeed, she is! She speaks of nothing else."

"Also, can you ensure Mrs. Blair provides Mrs. O'Hara a room as well? She will be with us a few days until I find Miss Smith another chaperone."

"Yes, my lord."

His ward stood by quietly as the earl gave direction to his staff. When he turned back to her, the apprehension of her countenance was plain, she was pale, her lower lip sucked inward with her teeth clamped tightly to it.

"It is going to be all right and tight. I dare say my sisters are at the height of excitement, awaiting to greet you. They have been in the country for the last few months attending to our mother, and to have someone closer to their age to associate has caused considerable expectation."

"Are they aware of my absurd situation? I would not be excited to meet such a plagued person."

"On the contrary, I anticipate my sister Emily intends to provide you with every stimulation to prod your memory."

He took her elbow and led her up the staircase.

"She will, I am certain, have a thousand places to escort you, with the excuse that you may remember being there before."

"Oh dear!"

"Do not fret. I will do what I can to keep her from overtiring you. But it will not be easy."

As they reached the top step, Miss Smith straightened her shoulders and made every attempt to make herself look as presentable as possible after a long day of travel in a drab grey dress. Noticing her anxiety, he patted her hand and then opened the drawing room doors.

Three ladies were drawing needles and threads through tightly held cloth. Heads bobbed up in surprise, the two younger girls dropping their hoops, leaping to their feet, and advancing on the newcomers. The older lady gently lay hers on her lap.

"Girls, girls, for propriety's sake, remember your manners."

As expected, the two young ladies paid no heed to their mama and prattled their way through introductions. Miss Smith matched names to faces, noticing how pretty they all were, including her guardian's mother, who gave her son the most endearing smile. The family resemblance was easily seen between the four, all with chestnut brown hair and hazel eyes. The first-born sister was quite tall, nearly the same height as her brother. The younger sister was nearly the same as herself.

She stood to the side and just behind the earl as he welcomed the embraces of the two excited siblings.

"Oh Richard, it is so good to have you home." Clarice easily kissed him on the cheek.

"Thank goodness you are home." Sounded the voice of the youngest. "It has been absolutely dreadful with you away. Mama and Clarice have bound me to the house, insisting I must wait for your return to run about." She held on to his right arm and embraced it in a hug.

The earl wrapped an arm around each. "I am certain, above all things, you have been treated like a prisoner in my absence, my dearest." He cut his eyes to Clarice, who shot him a coy smile as if to say, yes, and you can thank me later.

Emily, undaunted by the mockery, turned to their guest, taking her hand. "I have been so anxious to meet you. First, you must call me Emily, as I am certain we are to be the best of friends. I especially have been waiting, as my brother says you are closer to my age. He, of course, told us a little about your horrid experience, and I am so pleased you are healthy again. I cannot wait to assist you in any way possible to help you regain your memory. I know if we..."

"Emily!" Her sister snapped and directed her gaze to their guest. "I do apologise for my sister's rudeness. She does have better breeding than she appears to own. And please, do call me Clarice. Neither of us is accustomed to formalities, so please, do be comfortable whilst you stay with us."

The younger sibling was miffed and offended by the interruption of her welcome, which she considered warm and friendly and looked to Richard for support.

"I must agree with Clarice. Miss Smith has had a long trip from Ramsgate, and the last thing she needs is to be overwhelmed by an overly excited little chit." He grinned as he attempted to give her a bit of a set-down. He had no experience in overseeing a young girl of sixteen, and she was living proof.

"At least let me introduce mama, then I will allow you to show Miss Smith to her room. I understand you have chosen the one next to your own."

"Oh, absolutely! I did not want her to be uncomfortable, and she can bother me any time of the day or night, as it has an adjoining door, you know. I am sure it will be strange for her at first to be in a place she's never been, and I do not mind at all being awakened in the middle of the night or really anytime, just in case she needs something, you know, at first, or even later, with her memory only just returning. I do not wish to be rude, but it is what you told us, is it not."

Richard took a deep breath as his sister continued to prattle on and on, as she was known to do. Why had she not been taught to hold her tongue and say only what she meant, as was Clarice and his mama? But in that regard, many times, their lack of words in an explanation left one nearly as confused as Emily's loquaciousness.

He shifted his attention to Miss Smith, smiling politely. He had warned her and was relieved she was not in the least offended. He took her by the arm, pulled her away from the duo, and guided her toward his mother.

"Well, I never!" blurted Emily, "That was very rude, Richard, when we were having a conversation."

He glanced over his shoulder at his youngest sibling, "No, my little one, a conversation is an exchange of thoughts and news between two people, and I do believe you were the only one involved in the discourse."

Emily put her hands on her hips but was quickly drawn backward by Clarice when she started toward the couple making their way further into the room. The elder shushed her sister, reminding her to mind her manners and allow for introductions.

Richard presented Miss Smith to his mother. She curtsied gracefully. "Lady Gillford. It is a pleasure; I hope I am not an intrusion into your home."

The countess smiled and took her hand, motioning her to sit, brushing the curl of reddish-brown hair that had fallen across her brow. "You are most certainly not an intrusion, my dear. What a lovely child you are. Let me look at you." She lifted the girl's chin and seemed to be studying her face.

Richard found this quite odd. Since his father's death, his mother had shown little interest in her own girls over the past few months. In fact, she had shown little interest in anything or anyone. Now, she was perusing this young girl's face with such fascination he could not decide what to make of it. His mother released the girl's chin, but not her hand and turned to her son.

"Richard, she is charming. There is something familiar about her. My mind is so confused, I cannot induce my memory to come to me, but I assure you I will."

She turned her attention back to Miss Smith. "It is no longer my home, but on my account, you are welcome to remain here as long as you like." She patted her hand and released it. Then, she looked up at her son. "I think our guest would like to wash up for dinner. Maybe you should have Emily take her upstairs."

Her youngest daughter was instantly at her side, happy to escort her new friend away from the drawing room. The earl took his little sister by the arm and gave her a sombre stare. "Do not wear on, Miss Smith. She has had a long day. Show her to the room and leave her some time alone."

"Yes, I will, I promise. But must we call her Miss Smith? It sounds so very cold."

Richard glanced at his charge, and she only smiled, giving him no indication of her position on the matter. But Emily clearly wanted to make the girl feel welcome.

"So, what do you suggest? Then we will ask for her judgment."

"Well…" She placed her arm at her waist and rested her opposing elbow on her open palm, tapping her cheek with a forefinger.

"Since she has grown used to Miss Smith, what if we call her Missy?"

She looked around for approval and received a demure smile and nod of acceptance. Richard snickered, shrugging his shoulders, "Then Missy it is."

How simple it was to make young ladies happy, it seemed. They both were pleased with the new adjustment, and the earl could only shake his head in amusement. He looked back at his mother, who appeared entertained by his lack of understanding of the importance of such a small thing. The three headed towards the door, giggling and chatting, his sisters deciding they both should escort their new guest to her room.

The earl shook his head, satisfied he had made the right choice in bringing the young girl to his mother and sisters. He moved to withdraw, only to be halted by his mother's voice.

"Richard, wait!" The countess implored. "Come sit with me a moment. Then you can change for dinner."

"Of course. I am sorry for the sudden disorder, but it could not be helped."

"That does not signify in the least. I want to speak with you about her."

"Oh!" He was taken aback and made his way to his mother's side. "Is something amiss?"

"Not at all! In fact, something is remarkably familiar about her. I cannot place it, but it is as if I have seen her. No, not her exactly, but one who favours her considerably. You have absolutely no information about her?"

"Unfortunately, I do not. But Mother, does she not seem of quality and consequence? And she reminds me of Emily."

"No, that's not it. It is something entirely different. Indeed, I do agree with you. She carries herself well, and the way she sits and holds herself, I have no doubt she has been trained since birth. Someone is missing that child, Richard. You must find her family."

"I will do so, but first she needs a doctor and then I will go to Bow Street. Surely, if she is being sought after, they will have some information of it."

"Bear in mind, if she is of the first circle, Bow Street may not have been contacted. The Ton and scandal, you know. The family may have retained a private contract."

"Just so, but it would most assuredly be a runner, and the magistrate can learn of it. I intend to have a private meeting with Sir Childs. I can't lay my finger on it or exactly say, but something is not quite right with the whole of it." He paused. "She was not on the Sea Horse passenger list."

"She wasn't?" Lady Gillford looked curiously at her son.

"No. Please keep this information between us. I have not disclosed it, even to her."

"How can you be certain she was indeed on that particular one? Several ships were lost during those few days. It was all the gossip in London."

"She was tied to a military trunk, which was without doubt from the Sea Horse. Whoever bound her to it believed she stood a better chance of surviving and being found. They were assured the military would search until that particular trunk was located."

"So, you think she was taken aboard the ship without anyone's knowledge other than her escort."

"It is a possibility. There are more questions than answers for now. In one of the military's stories, she may have been betrothed to one of the sailors or at least wished to be and was taken to Ireland to be married. But the reality of it, we do not know. Until I find more clues, the only thing, I alone believe, whoever tied her to that trunk was of significance to her."

"That poor child. It must be horrid not to have any memory at all."

"None, that is why I must find a good doctor first thing tomorrow. I have contacts, and I will seek them at White's later tonight."

"After dinner." His mother stated firmly.

"Yes, mother." He laughed and took her hand. "I will dine with you and only take my leave after I have my brood of hens settled for the evening."

His mother attempted to jerk her hand from him in mocking disgust, but he held it firm as a grin spread across his face. She returned one of the same.

"It must be most disagreeable for you to have a houseful of females, especially three now, under the age of one and twenty. What a good man you are, my son. A lot has been left on your shoulders in such a short time. You are managing it well, and I have been absolutely no help to you recently, but I intend to remedy that."

"Do not worry yourself. The past year has been exceedingly difficult for you."

"Yes, I willed myself to die along with your father many times, and it did not take. So now, I must get back to the living. It is apparent it is not my time."

"No, indeed, it is not! Your family needs you." He bent and kissed her on the cheek, "And I am very glad to hear of your new persuasion."

"Something intrigues me about this new mystery of yours. It has given me a spark. I cannot explain it, but I feel as if I know this girl. I am not saying I know her, but possibly her mama or grandmama. Perhaps it is silly, but as soon as I saw her face, something swelled inside me. A memory, I only need to recall it. Now go, make yourself ready for dinner and do not keep us waiting with your dandy preparations."

He laughed and kissed her once more on the cheek and took his leave.

CHAPTER 7

Emily did not allow Missy a respite. As soon as she readied herself for dinner, she lightly scratched on their adjoining door and slowly opened it when she heard Missy's welcome, poking her head in.

"My brother instructed me to leave you in peace. But I cannot. I just cannot. I hope I'm not intruding. Oh, please say I am not."

"Of course you are not! He has been exceedingly thoughtful and considerate. Please, do come in."

Emily came inside and plopped down on the bed watching Leslie at the vanity.

"And he does not understand girls of our years, I am afraid. He was much older and off to school by the time Clarice and I were of any age of significance."

"He did share that with me." Missy said, twisting her hair into a knot at her nape.

Clad in the same sombre grey wool as when she arrived, Emily glanced around the room, wondering whether the young lady had another. Finding only a small valise in her possession, she leapt from the bed.

"Come to my room. Let us find you a gown. You would feel more comfortable if you were able to change."

"Oh no, you must not. Do not go to the trouble. I..."

"Nonsense! It will be the most fun. I cannot imagine what you have been through, so I will not begin to do so. But I beg of you, let me do this. I am always being told how selfish I am, never thinking of anyone's comfort but my very own, and I tell you truly, I am not. So please, I have gowns I think will look much nicer on you than on me. Come, come."

Emily would not accept otherwise. She took her new friend by the arm and hastened her into the adjoining room. When she flung open her closet door, Missy gasped at the overflow of frocks in every colour and shape.

"You see, I told you so." Emily swept through the dresses, searching for particulars. She removed a pale blue satin, holding it up to her new friend. "This one! It is beautiful, and with your eyes, it will be perfect. I am sure it will fit."

Missy stared at the gown. It was indeed the prettiest garment she had seen... since well... ever. She had no memory of laying eyes on such a gown. It was the strangest sensation, it was as though something inside her knew it was exceptional, but the fog wrapped around her mind wouldn't let her through it.

Shaking those thoughts from her head, she returned to Emily and the offering. "It is beautiful. But I should not, I really should not."

The want in Missy's countenance was evident and Emily insisted on her accepting it and began unbuttoning her grey frock.

She had to admit, she wanted more than anything to fit in at dinner. She felt quite out of place, even though everyone had been extraordinarily kind since her arrival.

The younger sister rang for her lady's maid, and once the dress was properly fitted, the maid twisted her hair into curls with ringlets down the nape of her neck and each side of her face. The gown had a chaste neckline and the pale shade of blue indeed complimented her violet-blue eyes.

"Oh, you look beautiful! I am so excited." Emily clapped her hands together and giggled with delight. "Let someone say I am selfish tonight! I beg them to try. You are enchanting. I have created a porcelain doll, with Regina's help, of course. Is she not the best with hair?"

Missy faced the mirror unable to believe the image in the glass. She became noticeably quiet, and her face paled.

Emily scanned her visage. "Are you well?"

"Oh, yes, I'm sorry." Snapping from her fog, "It was only… appearing… so vastly different. It was as if a thought or memory or something, I couldn't quite grasp it."

"You see, I was right. We will put your life back to rights again, and your memory will soon return. I am sure of it. I told Mama I would help you remember, and now that I have met you, I can think of nothing more I had rather do."

The girls locked arms and headed to the staircase. As they approached the entrance to the drawing-room, Emily tugged on Missy's arm, bringing them both to a halt. The youngest Hawthorn cleared her throat, and all heads turned toward the door. Silence blanketed the room. With a satisfied smile, she stepped away from her new friend as all eyes took in the transformation.

Stunned and overlooked, the countess dropped to her seat, taking two sharp, short breaths. It was as though she had seen a ghost but could not draw forth a clear image. Clarice was the first to speak.

"Oh my, how very lovely you look. What a perfect choice, Emily."

"Is she not beautiful?" The young Miss Hawthorn was incredibly pleased with her creation as if she had conjured up a dream.

Just as Richard found his voice, Carson appeared and announced dinner. Clarice and Emily, already at Missy's side, escorted her to the dining room, leaving the earl dumbfounded. Before he could catch his breath, his mother took his arm.

"We must find out who this child is, Richard. I know that face, and when I saw her in that gown, I was shaken. But it has been some time, my foggy mind is searching relentlessly."

"Well, there is no doubt she is gently bred and from a family of consequence, but whose?" His mind was now more determined than ever to begin his investigation.

**

Later that evening, Richard made his way to #37 St. James Street, working through the mysterious pieces of his latest assignment. His mother's initial reaction to the girl, and then again after she was properly dressed, had vexed him more than ever. How and why would a young lady of propriety board a military ship so covertly? There was more to this than a mere runaway marriage. His gut was telling him so. He would need to play this one under the rose, at least until he had more information.

If she were in trouble, he could be placing her in danger by publicly and openly displaying her, especially with no memory. He had survived by his instincts, and this was no time to disregard them.

Sheffield and Worthington were seated in a quiet corner when Richard entered White's. He made his way to join them, greeting other gentlemen along the way. It was apparent his absence had been noticed, along with the knowledge of his whereabouts to the site of the Sea Horse disaster. When he reached the table, Sheffield shrugged his shoulders. "I didn't put the oars in; I've been out of London most of the time you were gone."

"Weren't me because I had no idea what you were about until yesterday." Worthington followed.

"No one is accusing either of you. The Sea Horse disaster was in all the papers, and the need to prittle-prattle about it is evident."

"Glad you made it back to town before the end of the season, but this damn chilly rain needs to go away. Sick of it."

"Sheffield, are you ever satisfied with the weather?" Gillford made himself comfortable and motioned for a brandy.

"If it ain't fit for riding, hunting or both, no, I am not!" Then chuckled.

The three caught up, and Richard was surprised to learn of Andovir and Olivia's wedding which had taken place whilst he was in Ireland.

"Should have made that wager before I left." He raised his glass to the marquess.

"They are off to Suffolks, but he swears he'll be at Belmont for the hunt; I'm not placing any blunt on it." Sheffield turned the conversation back to his friend's latest adventure. "Well, did you finally rid yourself of the war department? You said that was to be your last assignment."

Richard hesitated, his friend laughed and cocked his head, knowing the answer by the delay. "What have you gotten into this time? You will never be done with that damnable department."

"Can't say you haven't got a point. But this time…" he drew a long breath and exhaled, "damme if it's not the most ridiculous yet intriguing assignment I have ever undertaken. It is one of the reasons I am here. Do either of you know a good doctor?"

Worth and Sheff cut their eyes at one another in curious amusement. Both wondered if their friend had taken leave of his senses. The military was filled with doctors, and he needed them to find another.

"And not just any doctor. I am looking for a special one of sorts."

Now they sat up and leaned forward, casually observing their friend with concern.

"What kind of special?" Worthington asked.

Richard moved in toward his friends and, although not whispering, quietly ejaculated, "A head doctor."

"You're bamming me." Sheffield tipped back in his chair, "Don't believe a word of it and if you do need one, good God, man, what went on over there?"

"Not for me, you idiot."

"Then why the secrecy? I thought for a minute there we might have to visit you at Bedlam."

"Nothing as serious as that. What the bloody hell has been going on with the two of you? Must be a damn dead bore if you have to start imagining I am to end up in Bedlam."

"What do you expect? You come in here after we are well on our way to being foxed, talking about being touched in the head."

All three leaned back in their chairs, and Richard downed his brandy, deciding he had come in with his brain waterlogged. They had a good laugh, and he filled them in on his situation.

His two friends decided things were actually worse than if it had been his own brain in need of a doctor. Who wanted or needed a female with real head problems? They were enough trouble when they didn't have any brains at all.

Noticeably offended, Richard still believed, his overprotectiveness was due only to the resemblance to Emily. But there had been a change in his regard toward the girl, especially after his mother's interest. They hadn't seen her, so how were they to know, everything about her made it impossible not to get involved.

Neither knew of a doctor with any amnesia experience, but Worthington had a name of one who frequently volunteered at the Bedlam hospital. Richard decided to consult him, if for no other reason but to obtain a name that was familiar with the symptoms.

It was not yet 2 am, still early for this set, but Richard's trip from Ramsgate had been tiresome, and he called it a night, tucking into his waistcoat the name he was given. He set out down St. James, leaving his two friends to greet the morning light without him.

As he walked up the steps of #6 Upper Brooks Street, there were candles burning in the drawing room. Handing his hat and gloves to Carson, he inquired about the light.

"It is Lady Emily and Miss Smith, my lord. We've had a bit of excitement."

Richard didn't wait for more information. He bolted to the staircase taking them two at a time, bursting into the drawing room. Missy was seated on the settee, while his sister was coaxing her to drink from a snifter of brandy.

"What the bloody hell is going on, Emily? And what are you doing with that damn brandy?" He was marching toward them when he witnessed the girls grabbing at their dressing gowns and wrapping the loose material around them.

"Stop, you big ape!" his sister snapped. "Sit down and do not come one step closer. Neither of us is dressed properly."

Richard, stunned at the outburst, halted. "And why the hell not? What on earth prompted you to come downstairs clothed in nothing but your sleeping gowns?" Suddenly, he observed their bare feet. "And bare feet. My God, are you both determined to catch your death."

Missy latched onto the snifter with two hands as she began to tremble. Emily wrapped her arms around her.

"Now, look what you've done. And I just settled her from the nightmare. She nearly fell down the stairs had I not prevented it. What an arse you can be."

49

His little sister's language shocked him to attention, and belatedly, he became aware of the situation. "A nightmare?"

He turned to Missy, who was shivering. He grabbed a wrap that had been left draped across his mother's chair. Still holding tightly to the spirits, he placed it around her shoulders and crossed it in front of her. When he pulled it tight, he froze and knelt down removing the snifter, and set it on the nearby table.

"What is that?" Richard was staring at her décolleté area.

She tightened the wrap around her and now that he had stopped yelling, she had stopped shivering. "W-what?" she murmured.

"That necklace. Is it Emily's?" glancing at his sister, who shook her head.

Missy clutched the necklace. "This?"

The earl nodded.

"I was wearing it when I was found on the beach."

"You never mentioned it."

"I never thought it important. Dr Lacy found no one in Waterford who was able to open it."

"It does appear to be a locket." He said, observing the delicate trinket.

"They thought so too but attempts to open it failed. They returned it to me, and I have not removed it again. I forgot it, except..." She wrapped her fingers around the gold oval pendant.

"Except?" Richard measured her hesitance. She seemed to be trying to remember something that would not come.

"It seems important. I am not at all certain why, but I did not want to remove it, and it is as though I'm lost without it. It is comforting when I am confused. Is that not odd?"

"No. It is not odd at all. Might I inspect it?"

"Yes, of course." She moved to the edge of the settee and allowed him access to the clasp.

He removed the piece and studied it, especially around the thin rim. There was definitely an appearance of two pieces meshed together. He picked up his quizzing glass and focused again on the seam.

His audience was watching him intently. Noticing their heads moving back and forth in unison as he rotated the locket, Richard laughed.

"What now?" Emily the first to take offence jerked back in earnest.

"Nothing, it was only the seriousness of your visage. It was a bit amusing, that is all."

They rolled their eyes peeked at one another and giggled, which satisfied Emily that Missy had calmed with her brother's presence.

With renewed interest, Missy watched Richard study the locket. "Do you think it opens?"

"I do. Can I take it with me to Rundell & Bridge tomorrow. I trust them to attempt it and they may have information regarding the piece itself."

"As long as it is returned. For an unknown reason, it is dear to me. It seems to be the only link to my past, although I have no sense of its meaning."

"Of course! I will bring it to you as soon as I return." Richard smiled at her reassuringly.

"Very well. If it does open, maybe it will solve some of the mystery of who I am."

"Just so. Now, do you believe you can go to sleep," he glanced at his sister, "Both of you?"

"I hope so. It was most unexpected. I have not had a nightmare since the first weeks of my recovery."

"And thank God, I heard her. She was at the top of the stairs when I found her." Emily added frightfully.

"Maybe you should lock your hallway door and leave the adjoining one to Emily's room unlocked. That will keep you from wandering the hallway without her notice."

"What a wonderful idea. I sleep ever so lightly, you know." His sister agreed.

"Only if you think it would be best. I do not wish to be any trouble."

"You will not." Richard paused. "Of course, had you fallen down the stairs, the entire house would be turned up." He smiled and nodded for them to be off.

Missy smiled at his jest and clearly saw the reasoning behind his concern. She was certain she would have no further nightmares, at least not tonight.

The girls headed up the steps with linked arms. Richard sat on the ottoman and twirled the gold piece over and over in his hand, finishing off the half-empty glass of brandy, which had been stranded on the nearby table.

CHAPTER 8

The following morning, Richard rose early. He was still on the War Department payroll and had a vast amount to accomplish. It would take some time to get accustomed to society hours. Especially those of his male friends and acquaintances of going to bed at dawn and not rising until after noon.

Today required finding a doctor for Miss Smith. If the nightmares were starting again, it could be dangerous. Regaining her memory had become even more important. He needed to speak with Dr Hanover.

However, he was desperate to open the locket, it consumed him, it was his only clue. He had assumed for weeks nothing of importance had been found with the girl. Richard must discover its significance before revealing too much information to anyone. As he sat with coffee and biscuits at the breakfast table, he retrieved the gold piece from his waistcoat. It looked incredibly old, or maybe it was just the result of the briny waters off the Irish coastline. At least he could learn that from the jeweller.

He remembered the first time he saw Missy. The sun and sea had burned and dried her skin, and she was so ill from the days without food and water. The exposure had mottled her body. The only other time he visited her before leaving, she still appeared haggard and much older than her suspected years. By the time they set sail to England, she had made drastic improvements. Since returning to London, her complexion had taken on a creamy peach colour, her drab brown hair had softened, with hints of copper which grew brighter each day.

The improvements in her overall physical health were seen daily. Those violet-blue eyes sparkled and were more mesmerizing than when he had first been checked by the unique colour.

She had taken his breath away the previous night at dinner in his sister's satin gown. Everything about her vociferated good-breeding and upper society and the locket could be an important key. He would go to Rundell & Bridge straightaway.

The earl finished his light breakfast and left the house before anyone had stirred. Anxious to try his newly acquired matched greys, a purchase made prior to departing for Ireland, he left word for his personal groom to have them readied. He had several stops and requested Jonathon to accompany him.

Carson helped him on with his coat, hat, and gloves and was pleased to find the sun shining and his tiger waiting in front, holding the horses.

"Top of de mornin' guv'nor." Jonathon patiently stood at the heads of the high-spirited pair.

Richard settled into his seat and picked up the ribbon and nodded to release the pair. They shook their heads in unison and attempted a small rear, which gave his Tiger enough time leisurely grab the rail and swing himself up to the platform. They were soon off to Ludgate Hill.

The earl pulled up in front of #32, secured his ribbons and leapt from the two-wheeled chaise.

"I am not at all sure how long I will be. You may have to take them around a time or two before I return. Handle those greys as if they were your own." He called to his tiger already at their heads.

"Absolutely, guv'nor!" Jonathan acknowledged as his master step to the walk.

His lordship tipped his hat to a group of ladies passing, who blushed and giggled, then made his way into the jeweller's establishment. With a confident air, along with his top hat, twelve-capped driving coat, and glistening top boots, left no

54

doubt he was a man of quality, and the clerk wasted no time approaching him.

"How may I be of service, my lord?"

"Is Phillip Rundell or John Bridge about? If so, I am in need of a few minutes of their time." Gillford handed the man his card.

Recognising the crest, he escorted the earl to the rear of the establishment. The clerk excused himself and returned quickly with the shop owner, gave a quick nod, and left the two.

Rundell welcomed Richard into his private office, closing the door. "Please, my lord," motioning toward the side-by-side leather chairs adorning it. "How may I be of service?"

Richard pulled the locket from his waistcoat pocket and tossed it on the desk. "I need to know everything you can tell me about this piece."

Rundell looked up at the earl curiously, his pragmatic stare gave no expression. The jeweller picked up the trinket and slowly moved his hand up and down, checking the weight. Picking up a special quizzing glass, he studied it as he slid it through his fingers. His attempt to open it resulting in capitulation, he glanced at the earl. "Have you opened it?"

"No, several efforts have been made with no success. Yet another question: can it be opened without damage?"

"I am not to receive further information?"

"I have little to give." Gillford answered regretfully.

"If it has not been sealed by anything other than time and wear, probably so. Do you wish to try?" He asked, appearing hopeful.

"First, what can you tell me about it?"

"It is an exquisite piece, handmade of heavy gold. It is of an old scroll design. I would say close to one hundred years old. More reason than not, it will not open."

"Could it be of heirloom quality?"

"That it is. It appears to be a commissioned one, as the shape is unusual. No specific markings on the outside, I assume all marks are within the locket."

"Then let us attempt to open it."

"Very well." Phillip Rundell stood and motioned his lordship toward the doorway. The earl followed him to his tooling room.

Inside was a little man with thick spectacles sitting on a stool bent over a raised table positioned against an outside wall with a large window providing a bright workspace.

Rundell handed the man the trinket, and without a word passing between them, the man examined it, carefully rotating it again and again. He picked up a tin bottle with a long, tiny metal spout. He poured a bit of the contents into a glass bowl, then dipped a small brush into it and began coating the edges of the locket, continuing to turn it. He sat quietly as he followed the slick movement of the oil work its way through the years of dirt and grime that had built up in the narrow crevice.

The two gentlemen stood in silence as the skilful man chose one tool after another, sliding each around the crease. He removed it occasionally to wipe away what appeared to be timeless bits of dirt and grime. He chose one last tool with a thin, flat end.

Both men leaned slightly forward over his shoulders as he slid it between the top and bottom parts of ornate gold. The two sides suddenly separated with a slight click. The men exhaled in unison, as if they had been holding their breath for the duration of the man's efforts.

The man gently cleaned the old gold piece, wiping off the oil and polishing it with care. He never moved his body as he soundlessly handed the opened piece to his employer.

"Thank you, Edwin." He only nodded as Rundell passed the locket to Richard. The men left him to his work and returned to the office. The earl surveying the inside of the charm, hoping to reveal anything that might solve the mysteries of the young girl who had captured his attention.

Reticently examining it, Phillip Rundell broke the silence. "Have you found your answers?"

"I am not certain." He handed it to the jeweller and asked if he saw any specific markings.

The jeweller studied the interior and scratched down a few markings, readjusting his quizzing glass several times.

"The two initials in the bottom centre edge, I believe it is RB."

"Does that mean anything to you?" Richard questioned.

"The piece is close to a hundred years old. It could be... wait, let me check, one minute."

He extracted a large book from the small case behind his desk and flipped it open, thumbing through a few pages. Placing a finger to an entry, he peered back at the locket.

"I'm sure it was crafted by the goldsmith, Richard Baily, one of the leading gold craftsmen of the time. It would definitely meet the quality with which he was famous, and it appears to be his plate stamp. I am not at all sure if the engraving was completed at the same time. It could have been added later. That is difficult to know in an adornment of its age."

"Thank you. You have been most helpful. I am in your debt and will await your note?"

"I would not dare do so. Only recall us when you are prepared to make a jewellery acquisition." The man smiled, extending his hand. Richard snapped the locket closed, tucked it away in his waistcoat pocket, shook Mr Rundell's hand, thanked him again, and took his leave.

On the street again, his two greys and curricle were nowhere to be found. He stepped to the smooth stone of the building and leaned a shoulder to wait. A few minutes later, he heard the unmistakable sound of his Tiger whipping the ribbons around the corner, bringing the matched pair to a halt in front of the earl.

Jonathon jumped to the head. "Fine couple a' blood cattl', good bottum. I wuz a 'ittle worr'd 'bout tak'em round, but dey minded 'emselves real good, dey did."

Richard smiled and laughed a bit. "After what I had to give for them, they should have driven themselves around."

"Dey is prime bits of blood, guv'ner, so I'z to guess dey wuz wurth e'fer penny!"

The earl grinned, took his seat, nodded to his groom. As the groom leapt to his position, he released the greys, and they moved out steady and smooth when given their heads.

"I dare say," the earl boasted, "they were only a tad fresh this morning." Satisfied with their behaviour.

"Sur'em wuz. De blast' wead'er bein' wat it is, can't exercise 'em, so I'z sure dey wuz."

Richard loosened the reins as they headed down the Strand. He had to pass Bow Street on the way to his next appointment. He hadn't planned his day properly. But the greys were doing well, the weather was fair, and they needed the exercise. He pulled up to the house on John St., just off Oxford. A small wooden shingle dangled from the porch, indicating Dr Hanover's residence and business.

"Allow me five minutes, Jonathon, then take them around."

Jonathon gave a nod to his Lordship as he made his way up the walk. Steps led to a small, covered porch with a sign on the door directing patients to come inside, so he did so.

Lord Gillford was met by a rather large, middle-aged woman sitting at a small desk, which did nothing to conceal her girth. But when he closed the door and circled back to her, she had a wide, welcoming smile between her chubby cheeks.

"Might I help you, sir? Are you here to consult the doctor? What might be ailing you?"

"I have come to visit Dr Hanover, although I do not feel unwell. I only require, if possible, a brief moment of the good doctor's time."

Richard glanced around, noticing several people sitting in straight-backed chairs which lined the walls of what appeared to have once been a parlour. One lady had a little boy sitting on her lap, and as their eyes met, the woman smiled. He tipped his hat and shifting his attention back to the older woman receiving him.

"I shall inquire if the doctor can spare a moment for you. Please take a seat if it pleases you. I shall return shortly."

She pushed her chair back and exerted considerable effort to support herself. With one hand on the chair and the other on the small desk, she managed to stand. She hurriedly waddled down a nearby hallway and swiftly disappeared through one of the closed doors.

As promised, she returned quickly, making her way back up the hallway. Placing both hands on the desk again for balance to retake her seat, she peered up at him with a grin.

"The second door on your left, he will grant you a moment between his patients. You need not rap on the door; the chambre is empty." She winked at him and plopped down on the chair. She was a little out of breath from her short hike, but she was still smiling. The earl decided she looked like a proud mama and assumed it just might be her son, who owned the establishment.

Richard opened the second portal and slipped inside, walking around the room, surveying its contents. One short table with a writing pad, quill, and ink, two more straight chairs identical to the parlour ones and one long table against the wall, which contained several drawers. On top were flat wooden sticks and several various metal objects of assorted sizes, which he had no desire to ponder their usage. They were a bit terrifying, so he turned his attention elsewhere.

The walls displayed water colourings and sketches of children and adults from young to old. The artist was quite good. He also scanned a certificate, which, on closer inspection, indicated the man of medicine had completed special training in his field at Cambridge. The thought occurred to Richard, he hoped this man had learnt more at the university than he had and chuckled.

"I trust that doesn't reflect poorly on me being a Cambridge man?" The doctor had quietly entered into the room.

"Indeed, no! Cambridge man myself. The chuckle was in hopes you had learnt more than I had done during my tenure."

"I can't say so, but at least they thought I acquired enough knowledge to award me the certificate."

They laughed and met one another with a handshake.

"Jeffery Hanover."

"Richard Hathaway."

"How may I be of service to you, Richard Hathaway?" The doctor gestured toward the two chairs.

"I am unsure if you are able to do so. I was referred to you by a friend who mention you occasional provide services at Bedlam."

"I do volunteer work to assist, but it's a melancholy place, and not the sort anyone would want to make a permanent occupation." He said, sadly shaking his head.

"I understand. I must say I would not desire it."

"What are you seeking information regarding a specific someone or something else?"

"Actually, I am in service to the war department and, for several years, received what I would call the most challenging cases. Not because they are particularly difficult but because they are demanding. This particular case is the guardianship over a young girl from the Sea Horse disaster."

"Such a dreadful and sorrowful occurrence." Hanover lowered and shook his head again.

"Yes, it was. All the soldiers managing to survive battles in France and Belgium, ultimately defeating Napolean at Waterloo, only to have such a useless end to their lives."

"Undeniably."

"In her situation, she has lost her memory and has no recollection of anything prior to being discovered on the beach."

"Nothing at all?" The young doctor appeared surprised.

"Nothing. Neither her name nor her age. We wouldn't even be certain she was off the Sea Horse; except she was tied to a military trunk which no doubt came from that particular ship."

"Hmm, do you want me to take the case or recommend someone?"

"I desire to find someone who is familiar with amnesia, which I understand to be a rather obscure subject matter. However, if you've had a case, that is preferable to none at all."

"I did have one. I also had a professor at Cambridge who found the brain and its emotional function intriguing. But to say I am an expert; the answer would be no. The work I undertake at Bedlam is quite simple. Those whose lives have been impacted by their ability to deal with the situation life has presented them is not part of it." An explanation he hoped Hawthorn understood only referred to medical treatment.

"I am seeking someone who can be trusted to guide us as she regains her memory if she is to do so. What can be done to assist her recovery? Could the trauma of the shipwreck be the cause? Things of that nature."

"The individual under my care did indeed recuperate in time." It's not an extended area, but the mind is intricate, and our understanding of it is limited. It appears that trauma does indeed have an impact, and if the individual has memories they wish to erase, the duration of the healing process is uncertain. In my experience, it is quite unusual that she recalls nothing."

"Privacy is of utmost importance. The department is concerned about her safety, making a public outcry unfeasible."

"I shall be delighted to visit her and assess her situation. I would also like to examine her. Ensure we don't have something physical involved. If she spent a considerable amount of time at sea and her health deteriorated, she may have some deficiencies that require attention."

"Might I implore you to visit my home?"

"Of course, if you believe it is the most suitable."

"I do. Her recuperation showed greater progress in Ireland. She experienced nightmares early on, but they had ceased until we arrived in London. She was apprehensive coming here, and now the nightmares have resurfaced."

"Does she speak during them?"

"The missionaries in Ireland mentioned she only spoke of the wreckage. My sister is the only one who has been by her side here in London. Truthfully, I did not inquire, but my sister will provide what information she is able."

"Good. I shall pay a visit, and if I believe I can help her, I will do so. The only other thing I can mention is that any information you can discover will support her recovery. However, if she senses a threat and is using the amnesia as protection, once you share what you know with her, she may or may not improve. So, we mustn't overwhelm her. I'll converse more on this once I have examined her."

"Thank you. When will you be free to visit with her?"

"I could attend the day after tomorrow if it is convenient, perhaps around eleven?"

"I will ensure everyone is up and about. Would you care to join us for breakfast?"

"A cup of coffee or tea, but I will have long broken my fast."

"I understand. Oh, in addition, I did take a locket to the jeweller today. They managed to open it, and found a name engraved inside. Should I withhold that information from her until your examination?"

"Is it perhaps her name?"

"Possibly."

"If the chance presents itself, use it in a casual manner. Otherwise, withhold the locket until after my examination." Dr Hanover eyed the curiosity and confusion of Richard's countenance. "If she anticipates it might be her name and is prepared, her response will be guarded. However, if you casually address her, she might respond instinctively, not allowing her subconscious to protect herself."

"Much the same as she reacted when I assessed her ability to speak French."

"Exactly. Just as she knows and speaks English. Certain responses are natural, and responses are given without hesitation."

Richard shook the doctor's hand and thanked him again for taking the time to meet with him and for visiting Miss Smith swiftly. They parted with the assurance of meeting again soon.

Richard thanked the woman in the entry for her assistance and exited the house with little doubt the elderly woman was the doctor's mother. Although their statures were completely different, their features were undeniable.

Jonathon was waiting patiently as the earl exited the building. "Jist in time guv'nor. Dem steppers wuz 'bout ta' need 'round agin.' Fidgittin' de wuz'."

"No problem at all, the horses are top priority, you know."

"Th'nk ye' guv'nor. Ne'ber duz 'em good makin' 'em wait long. Where ta now?"

"Bow Street." Richard leapt to the seat of the curricle, took the reins, and nodded to Jonathon. The earl headed the pair down Duke St and let them pick up a fast trot when they turned onto Oxford. The young pair were setting a fast pace in the early afternoon, which was passing quickly.

Richard was ready to be done with his long day. He doubted the Bow Street visit would be lengthy. He had nothing to share with the magistrate and figured if anyone were looking for his ward, after all this time, Sir Childs would need to address it with his runners. If she were from an aristocratic family, as his mother suggested, it would probably be a private commission.

As they approached #3, the earl pulled up the ribbons, and Jonathon jumped down. "Hold them here as long as you're able. I shan't be a moment."

When Richard entered the building, it was quiet, and the front desk was empty. He knew his way, but he was in no hurry. He propped his elbow on the high desk and leaned into it. He reached into his waistcoat pocket and pulled his snuffbox, flipped the top open with his thumb and took a pinch, inhaling lightly. It was a new batch, and although he had used the same mix for years, it was hardier than usual and had a light mint aroma. Just as he was replacing the box, the clerk came around the corner from the hallway and was startled by the large man standing at the desk.

"Sorry, I didn't hear you come in. Ain't been waitin' long, I hope?" The man squinted at the newcomer, and when the earl smiled, the man made the recognition.

"By Jove, Hawthorn hadn't seen you in an age and didn't recognise you. I understand you're a titled gent nowadays. Too good to come 'round much, Aye?"

"You know better, Darcy. I've been in Ireland for some time, and as far as the title business, adjusting to it is has been quite a challenge for me, as well. Never expected it, and bloody well doesn't always sit well, you know."

"Yep, yep, I believes it where you're concerned. I always expected you to turn to running when you were done with the military."

"Figure it that way myself. But one never knows, does one?"

"Seems that's so. What can we do fer ya today?"

"Is Childs in his office?"

"He is. I'd been in the back. Let me make sure he's alone. Never know, these days."

The smaller man, with rounded shoulders, made his way down the hallway to the last door. The earl waited as he knocked and eased it open, then stepped out of sight briefly. He returned to the hallway and motioned Richard to proceed in his direction.

"Good seein' you again, Hawthorn. Guess I should say me lord."

"Not on my account, Darcy." He patted the old man on the back as they passed. Strolling leisurely down the unlit passage, the door remained ajar, but Richard knocked lightly before poking his head inside.

"Come in, come in Hawthorn! This is a surprise. I can't remember the last time I've had the pleasure."

Sir Childs reached across his desk, and the two men met with a hardy handshake.

"Me either, sir! It has been a while."

"Sit. Can I offer you coffee, or I can have Myrtle bring some tea?"

"Neither. I don't figure to be here long. At least not today."

"Hmmm, that sounds familiar. Let me guess, still not released from the war department?"

"Not yet, but I've no cause for grievance. I select and decide what I wish to handle. Again, they have informed me this is my last."

"How many last assignments have you had now?"

"A full year's worth, sir."

"If you don't put your foot down or use that title of yours, you will most assuredly have another year."

"Perhaps, but damme, it is difficult to let go. For myself well as them."

"I've often pondered what I might do myself should I walk out this door. It's all we know, Hawthorn, hunting down miscreants, catching them without harm to oneself, experiencing an adrenalin rush. Can't exist without it." The magistrate shared a grin of satisfaction Richard understood well.

"You mentioned once before there will come a moment, and we must recognise it. It is my moment. Well, it will be when this one is completed. I must consider the well-being of my mother and two sisters."

"Bloody hell! Forgot about your father and didn't realise you had siblings. Sorry to learn of it, he was good man. So, you gained a title you didn't want, care of a parent and two siblings, both sisters."

"Youngest is sixteen."

"Good God!"

"Good God indeed!"

"How may I assist you in completing this one? I know that is why you're here. You never grace us with your presence otherwise. Like most of us, not much of a talker."

"Sadly, I am learning to be. Sisters, you know and not happy about it either. Enough of that. I was given an amnesia case."

"Amnesia? Doesn't sound like a war department special agent assignment?"

Richard chuckled at the thought of the tiny whisp of a girl being a spy.

"It truly is not. Found myself in the wrong place at the wrong time. Ireland, retrieving confidential items from the Sea Horse."

"Hmmm, doesn't appear to be a position I'd like to find myself."

"Wasn't! However, this girl has no memory, was discovered on the beach, not listed among the passengers."

"Are you certain she's off the Sea Horse?"

"Undoubtedly, securely fastened to one of the items we were meant to recover. Then, of course, the war department had to take charge of her. Memory hasn't returned, and since I was returning to England, they asked me to locate her family."

"Doesn't seem like you possess much information."

Richard hesitated to leave anything out when making requests of Sir Morgan Childs, but mistakes could easily happen at this stage. The more he kept to himself, the less chance of an error for now.

"Nothing. Aside from her eloquent English, along with her graceful walk, carriage and natural mannerisms implies she is quality."

"Meaning aristocratic, gentry or wealthy CIT."

"I assume, if so, those families do not wish for scandals, so most likely a private commission."

"Yyeess!" the magistrate replied slowly, wrinkling his nose, and squinting his eyes in contemplation. "Allow me to conduct some research. Did you mention it to Darcy? He may know something."

"Wouldn't think of bypassing you, sir!"

"You're a good man, Hawthorn. I always thought you would be working for me someday. But, as you've discovered, circumstances change."

"Truthfully, I thought so myself!"

The magistrate and Hawthorn stood simultaneously and reached for each other's hands.

"Keep me in informed, and as soon as I find anything, I will dispatch a messenger to you. We can meet here, and I will have any files that may be available."

"Thank you, sir! I have always been able to depend on you."

"I feel the same!"

CHAPTER 9

"Good evening, my lord." Carson reached for the earl's topcoat, easing it off his lordship's shoulders, then relieved him of his hat and gloves.

"Did I miss dinner?" Richard ran his hands through his hair, combing down the chestnut locks that were out of place.

"No, my lord. The countess insisted it be delayed an hour in anticipation of your late arrival."

"Where is everyone?"

"In the blue saloon."

"Everyone?"

"Yes, sir. All four ladies."

"I will change my attire. Tell mother I shan't be long."

"Yes, my lord!"

Richard headed up the staircase, pleased he would not be seen before disposing of the locket in his bedchamber. He had no intention of allowing Leslie, Miss Smith, Missy or whatever her name was, to open it and see the engraving. He wasn't at all certain how he was going to manage revealing its contents. He had to decide how to casually mention it in conversation. Forgetting it in his jacket was a reasonable excuse.

Bixby was shining boots when Richard entered his room. "My Lord, shall I have hot water brought up?"

"No time. It appears the ladies have waited for me. If I am to host them each evening, I require guests. The only male at the table is far too much pressure, even in my own house." He arched an eyebrow and flashed a smile.

"Indeed. The countess insisted it would be improper to proceed with dinner knowing you were to arrive for it."

"I can only imagine the lengthy tutoring my sisters and our guest received from my mother regarding the proprieties of ill-bred manners."

"Yes, sir, she has always been very strict about such things."

"And probably the reason Emily is so rebellious."

"They are daughters of an earl. May he rest in peace, and she is determined they conduct themselves so."

"I believe Clarice values her status, but Emily? She finds it a burden, I fear."

"She'll come around, sir. She is still young, and the alterations to her life…"

"Her life? What of mine? I had meticulously planned every aspect of my life. Moreover, she was brought up a lady, and the title doesn't make it any more difficult."

The visit to Bow Street with Morgan Childs had frustrated Richard. He had imagined himself serving the magistrate and continuing the excitement of a special agent as a Runner. It may not have been a glamorous life, but the adrenaline of hunting and apprehending the reprobates and gaolbirds suited him.

Subsequently, he must endure the lectures of old men who thought far too much of themselves and would take no heed to someone of his youth regarding the future of England. He attended one session of Parliament, and it had been one too many. Why had his cousin been so damned clumsy? Why had the 2nd Earl not born more sons? Why had his father died before recognising he ever held the title? He had already fallen ill, and his cousin had never bothered to make an appearance in the House of Lords.

The seat had remained empty for five years following the death of his uncle. He was a fine man and highly esteemed; Richard had respected the man's influence and power. If only he had lived, even if fate had taken the two, his uncle would have prepared him for the position.

Why did Richard persist in tormenting himself? He had significant knowledge to contribute to parliament if only he had the influence. His military experiences, particularly his assignments, had provided him information few possessed. The vulnerabilities and strengths of his beloved England he had witnessed in his military career. Especially where other countries were concerned and had much to share. Oh well, in time, he would gain the respect and admiration of the position, he hoped.

The valet completed the earl's toilette, sympathising with his master. He too had been impacted; however, he did not regret the dodging of gun fire or running for one's life. "Situations changed rather quickly for all those living under this roof."

"Overlook my rudeness, Bixby. I am weary and had many challenging visits. We have this final assignment, so we shall endeavour to complete it and move on with our boring existence thereafter."

Bixby nodded and helped his lordship into his coat, flicking a few pieces of lint from the shoulder. Richard combed through his hair one last time, then remembered the locket.

"When emptying the pockets, place the contents on my dresser."

"Yes, sir."

When the earl made his appearance, he found all four ladies engrossed in needlework. Each one dressed in a different gem-coloured satin gown. What a pleasing sight; it had been a shame he hadn't thought of inviting friends. Sheffield and Worthington were always good company and liked his French cook. The man prided himself on extravagant multi-course meals, whether a simple family repast or an elaborate dinner party. The conversation did not go in his favour, with a four-to-one ratio against him. It was sure to be another evening of bonnets and fripperies. What the devil were fripperies anyway?

Clearing his throat, he entered the room. "Ladies!" The ladies set aside their needlework and rose to their feet.

"Oh, dear Lord, I beg of you, do not! Mother, I am aware of your efforts to tutor, but I'm much too fatigued to appreciate it. After today, the last thing I wish to be reminded of is my position and title. I remain in service to the War Department. May we not enjoy a relaxing, peaceful evening without all the propriety?"

"Thank God!" Emily agreed without hesitation.

"Emily Grace!" Her mother gasped.

"Oh, mama, you have been fussing at us all day. I am sure Missy is ready to escape this place."

"No, no, please do not say so. I am profoundly grateful to her ladyship." She said softly.

"Thank you." the countess replied, her tone serene but stern, "At least someone appreciates the reminders of courtesy and good manners."

"Missy is just being polite, mama."

"Of which you should take heed, my impetuous sister. It would do you no harm to attempt some decorum. Your manners are beneath your station." Her brother raised an eyebrow indicating the conversation was over.

"I have not enough arms to escort you all to the dining room. Mama, Missy, if I may have the pleasure. My sisters may follow." He glowered at both.

"What did I do?" Clarice barked.

"You smiled." Richard promulgated.

"Oh!" Clarice, more cognisant of her sibling's mood, was aware when to hold her tongue, even when in agreement.

To the earl's relief, dinner was quiet. Emily sulked throughout, not being accustomed to her brother's rebuffs. Clarice, fully aware when he was in a temper, was reticent. His mother and Missy continued their normal intercourse, comfortably sharing experiences in Ireland.

As Richard pondered ways to reveal the name found in the locket, he decided to wait for a more suitable moment than interrupting the girl's meal. She ate like a bird and was still a bit thin.

The customary post-dinner ritual of gentlemen taking port and engaging in political discourse was dispensed. Gillford had previously informed Emily a conversation required two participants, therefore, he withdrew with the ladies to the drawing room, hoping for an opportunity to disclose his findings. However, much to his chagrin, Missy declared her desire to withdraw to her bedchamber for the remainder of the evening.

"So soon, my dear. Are you feeling well?" Lady Gillford's tone exuded motherly concern.

"Yes, ma'am! I am only a tad fatigued."

"She found a book at Hatchard's today; she is eager to read." Emily tittered.

"If that is all, you may read here."

The countess wanted to ensure she was not ill. She was blossoming but still thin, and her constitution remained questionable. There was something about this girl that exasperated her. She felt a strong connection, but why? What was it? Remember she must!

"Thank you, but I would like to burrow into my bed covers and do nothing more than rest."

"Of course, dear!"

She made her excuses to Emily and Clarice, then was interrupted.

"Missy," Richard called.

She swirled to face him. "My lord?"

"Is that a new gown?"

After seeing her in nothing but grey wool for weeks, he couldn't help but admire the change of attire.

"No, my lord. It belonged to Emily. There were a few alterations made. Do you not approve?"

"No, no, I only wanted to comment on how lovely you looked."

"Thank you, my lord!" Her cheeks flushed with colour.

"Missy, the need for protocol extends to you as well. Please, address me as Richard."

"Oh, I would never do so. Such behaviour is most improper, my lord."

"Then call me Hawthorn or Gil, but I implore you, no more, my lord. My days are filled with it."

"Thank you, I will consider it."

Missy wanted nothing more than to remove herself to the privacy of her room. She curtsied to the countess and the earl, who bid her goodnight.

Richard poured a glass of brandy, strolled to the window thinking the girl must have been tired, as she made no mention of the locket. Due to Emily's outburst and his visible agitation, she may have concluded it was not the most opportune time for a reminder.

He owed his sister an apology, but he would issue it tomorrow. She needed to understand she would now be held accountable for all her actions, as the daughter and sister of an earl. She would be formally introduced into society the following year, and she had yet to understand that her behaviour would be heavily scrutinised by the members of the Beau Monde. Her actions would reflect upon the entire family. A lesson he too was learning, no longer the son of a second son. Let her sleep on her indiscretion and receive her apology tomorrow.

"She's a lovely girl." The countess interrupted her son's reflections.

"She is." He sipped his brandy, without looking away from the window.

"You are distressed about something Richard?"

He pivoted from the casement and furrowed his brow. "There is something I cannot quite discern."

"And it's regarding the girl?" the countess said.

"Mmm, yes."

"I have similar feelings, Richard. She is so familiar; something about her I cannot quite place. I am aware I have never laid eyes upon her in particular, but something is remarkable, and I cannot escape it." She remarked, placing her embroidery on her lap.

"I am going to bed, mama!" Emily interrupted. "I purchased a novel today as well, and I wish to begin reading it."

"Which one?" Clarice interjected.

"Emma. It's by the same anonymous author of Pride and Prejudice and Sense and Sensibility."

"Oh, and Mansfield Park, as well. I do want to read it if you would be so kind as to allow it when you have finished."

"We might read together for a while if you wish." Emily felt as though she had an enemy in her brother. She needed to gain the support of her sister.

"You could read it to me." Clarice lay her embroidery aside, and together, they bid their mother and brother goodnight. They were heard chattering all the way up the stairs.

Lady Gillford quietly scrutinised her son's restlessness. "If you wish to go out, I can retire to my room."

"No, mother. I am not going out. There are things I must work through, and White's is not the place for it." He smiled, and she returned the gesture.

She understood too well his propensity to overthink and analyse every problem he encountered. As a child, he overcomplicated even the tiniest issue. But she also believed it had kept him alive in his dangerous assignments for the war department.

"I am not certain how much I wish to share with the doctor. Confidentiality is most important. Sadly, I must remember what I've told and what I've withheld and to whom."

"I have warned you repeatedly, it is dangerous ground to tread, Richard. But you have eventually resolved the issues effectively." His mother picked up her needlework and shifted it nearer to the candle.

Richard refilled his snifter, made his way to his favourite oversized wingback, crossed one boot over his knee and picked up the book he had begun the day before to distract himself from his worry regarding his ward.

Several hours passed before his mother broke the silence. "I seem to have finished this pattern; I believe I shall retire. What hour does the clock indicate? I cannot quite decipher it from this distance."

"Half past one." He quipped, "I suppose it is becoming interesting at White's."

"I would assume so from the stories your papa would tell." His mother grinned.

"I beg your pardon; I am not at all sure why I mentioned it?"

"It's quite all right. I know of things you men find interesting." She snuffed out the candle at her chair, "I will see you tomorrow. Goodnight."

Richard stood as his mother rose to her feet, kissed her cheek, and smiled as she gracefully exited the room. He continued reading for another hour. The low burning flames of the candelabra began to flicker, and he placed the book on the side table.

Finding his drink consumed strolled across the saloon for another but was disquieted by a loud noise coming from the floor above. Setting his glass aside, he proceeded to the hall, where he met a dishevelled Carson.

"My lord, come quickly."

"What's happened?" The earl inquired, advancing toward the butler.

"It's Lady Emily." He said breathlessly.

Brushing past the butler, Richard hurried upstairs taking the steps by twos with Carson close on his heels. As he rounded the corner to the family wing, two footmen were stationed outside Missy's door. He reached for the door but found it locked.

"Emmi, are you all right?" He called to his sister.

"Yes, Richard, but hurry."

He dashed through his sister's chambre and was stunned to find both girls huddled in the corner near the door. Missy was shaking violently and drawn up in the foetal position, attempting to make herself as small as possible. Emily, kneeling just beyond her reach terrified but desperately trying to soothe her friend.

"Oh Richard, she recoils when I try to touch her. She's asleep. It's like the last time, but much worse. Please do something."

"Move back." Grasping Emily's shoulders, she moved to his side, clearly distraught.

"It's pitiful, she's pulling at her hair. I was at a loss as what to do."

"Shh. It will be all right, Emmi. She is safe, and we are going to help her. We need to understand her mumblings if we can."

The earl knelt close but refrained from contact. The mutterings were hushed, and tears were streaming down her cheeks. He focused on her voice and began to hear the whines of a frightened child.

"No, papa, no, oh mama, please, no." she whimpered almost inaudibly.

Attempting to reach for her, Richard was stunned by the strength of her unconscious state. He tried to ignore the flailing arms and bring her closer, but a punch to his jaw made his head snap back, forcing him to readjust himself before being knocked off his feet.

"Don't touch me, please, don't!" Her voice became stronger and louder, swinging at the space in front of her, fighting an unseen adversary.

Disregarding the pummelling, he enveloped her slender arms with his own, drawing her close to him caressing her firmly. He lowered himself to the floor and whispered softly. "Leslie, you are all right. Leslie, it's only a dream." He waited a few moments and whispered again. "You are safe, Leslie."

Her intensity gradually faded away with his continually whispers. He spoke in a soothing tone, softly repeating her name. Her rigid body relaxed, and he quickly rose to his feet, holding her tightly against him. Cradling her in his arms, he headed toward the bed.

Her body collapsed, and she hung like a ragdoll in his embrace. He gently placed her on the counterpane, adjusting her on the pillow, arms by her side. She was soaked in perspiration.

Richard glanced around, searching for his sister. She had risen from her seated position but had not moved from the corner, only staring at the sight of the broken girl. He needed her help, but she was nearly in shock over the situation herself, "Emily, secure some dry and wet cloths and instruct a footman to summon Mrs. Blair. We must ensure she is dry before she catches her death. Hurry!"

She approached the foot of the bed, still in stunned silence, her eyes fixed on her unconscious friend. She seemed to be in a trance, not comprehending the request of her brother until his stern voice broke through her confusion, and she dashed out the door.

Richard removed a sizable handkerchief from his coat pocket and gently wiped Leslie's forehead, carefully brushing away the damp strands of hair from her face. The thin sleeping chemise hugged her body and clung like a second skin. Disgusted with himself for noticing the figure through the sheer, invisible nightgown, he chastised himself for his inability to control the direction of his gaze. She would never forgive such an indiscretion.

Where the hell was his sister? What the bloody hell was taking her so damn long? The longer he was alone with Leslie, the more he wanted to appreciate her voluptuous curves. Good God, he was sick. She was unconscious, covered in sweat, susceptible to catching pneumonia, and he was lusting after her. Thank God, he heard his sister's voice.

"Here, Mrs. Blair." Emily called from the next room.

Richard leapt from the bed and pulled the sheet over Leslie. The moisture quickly saturating the fabric. At the sight of the poor girl, Mrs. Blair gasped. She had a stack of dry towels, quickly dropping them at the foot of the mattress, as she removed the linens. One by one, she covered the girl with the thick cotton towels.

Emily carried a small bucket of water and several smaller pieces of cloth. He seized the vat and cloths, submerging them in the cool liquid before gently wiping Leslie's face, neck, and arms.

"Emmi, find a fresh dressing gown and bring it. Quickly!" He shouted. "Mrs. Blair, this chemise must be removed immediately. I doubt you can accomplish it alone."

The housekeeper was wrapping towels around the child's limbs, soaking up the dampness, and her eyes darted to the earl's, "Beggin' your pardon, my lord?"

The censure from the housekeeper of his presence in the room was quite severe.

"I ought to have woken a maid, but I didn't know," she said frustrated.

Unsure how to proceed, except for her continual wrapping and drying of the young girl's body and limbs, she glanced to the earl. "She requires dry bedding as well. Should we try to rouse her?"

"I know as much and as little as you about these dreadful walking nightmares, Mrs. Blair." He barked, as he gathered and tossed the damp towels into a pile across the room.

The elderly woman, who was a small in stature would never move the girl alone or even with Emily's help, nor could they change the bedding, which was also a necessity.

There was a butler, two footmen, and himself from whom to choose her help. He had to make the decision, so he did.

"Once Emily returns, you and she will dry and remove her clothes. Once she is dressed somewhat properly, I will remove her from the mattress and hold her whilst the two of you change the sheets."

Mrs Blair's eyes shot to the earls with disapproval, disappointment, obduracy and finally, resolution. She saw the acknowledgement in his countenance, and both knew there was not to be a proper answer.

"We have no other choice, Mrs Blair. We cannot wait for a maid to dress and make their way up here. It's impractical and could be too late. Hell, it might well be too late now." The earl begged her to understand.

"Yes, sir, I agree. She is not healthy enough to survive a setback. Please forgive me for not bringing another servant. I had no idea when I was awakened. I dressed so quickly myself."

She was busily replacing wet towels with fresh ones as they both attempted to keep the girl dry and warm.

"Mrs. Blair if you please. Occasionally, unforeseen circumstances arise. I encountered situations during the war where I had to engage in actions that were significantly more inappropriate and morally repugnant than what I am presently dealing."

"But will she think as much when she awakens?" She said still reluctant.

"She must never know!"

"Yes, my lord!"

Emily returned with a cotton dressing gown. Mrs Blair noted the long sleeves and closed neck collar, as she shook it loose from the folds, and it was of thick cotton.

"This will do nicely, Lord Gillford." The housekeeper appeared relieved, "Please take your leave for a moment."

"I will be at the door." He said reluctantly, "Mrs. Blair will need your help, Em."

"Yes, Richard." His sister glanced around the room, unsure.

"You are a good girl," giving her an encouraging smile as he walked from the room but perceived the worry in her eyes.

The elder woman raised Leslie's limp form to a seated position and directed her help to the other side. Between the two, they were able to remove the chemise and wiped the perspiration from her, one washed the other dried.

The patient's hair remained wet and untidy. Emily dashed to the dressing table grabbing a brush, then stroked and twisted the long copper-brown locks into a tight knot while the housekeeper held the girl upright securing the fresh gown.

They called for the earl to come and remove her from the bed. Richard quickly scooped Leslie into his arms as her head settled in the crook of his neck. He moved to the oversized leather chair next to the window, resting her in his lap. The thick cotton did nothing to prevent him from feeling every curve of her bottom. The cradling embrace, the steady breath against his neck, the scent of a woman, oh God, they needed to hurry with those damn bed sheets.

Leslie moaned, slightly moving her body. Richard nearly leapt from the chair. Don't, please, I beg you, his mind willing her to remain still. It was taking every ounce of decency he had not to think about her well-formed shape. His transient thoughts pondered, glancing down at the bare feet dangling from under the nightdress, his eyes sliding upward imagining the soft skin of her legs to the top of her thighs, reaching…

"We are done, my lord. You can bring her." The voice breaking his thoughts.

"Thank God!" he whispered to himself.

"My Lord?" the housekeeper looked at him curiously.

"Nothing." He stepped to the side of the bed and gently laid Leslie into the fresh linens as Mrs. Blair covered her with the sheet and blankets.

He garnered his sister's attention, "Emily, you do understand, Missy must never be told the details of this night. No one should. It must be kept between you, me, and Mrs. Blair. She understands how important keeping the knowledge between the three of us. Do you understand?"

"I think so." The young girl looked at them both with wonder.

Facing his domestic, "Your work here is done. Thank you. I need a moment with my sister."

"Yes, my lord." The older woman turned to the young sibling. "Goodnight, Miss Emily, please heed your brother's words. Goodnight, my lord." She curtsied to them both.

"Goodnight." They replied in unison.

The housekeeper left the room and he circled to his sister.

"Emily, it was inappropriate for me to remain in the room whilst Le… Missy was… was so dishevelled. But we had no choice. You and Mrs Blair were unable accomplish it alone, and we had no time to remove her soaked clothes and sheets. She's not well enough to withstand a chill and another illness. Do you understand?"

"Yes, sir, I do." She was finally calming down from the disturbing incident.

"It would be extremely embarrassing for her, and she would never trust any of us again. We must help her find her memory and her way."

"I understand, Richard, but do you really think we might? She seems so lost, and when she has these nightmares, it is the most horrid thing. I ache for her."

"I am sorry to put you through this. But you have managed it very well, especially for such a young girl who has had little disruption in her life. You are much stronger than I have given you credit. I was proud of you tonight."

Emily ran up to her brother and hugged him tightly. She had seen a side of him she had never known. They both had come to a new understanding of one another. Richard placed his arms around his sister's shoulders as they regarded their sleeping guest.

"I was so frightened for her," she said as she clung to her brother. "She seems so frightened and vulnerable, does she not."

"I fear she is. I am not at all certain what is in her past, but my instincts tell me she is in some kind of trouble, and I must discover it soon. This has turned into the most difficult assignment I have undertaken."

Emily looked up, her youthful eyes studying his. She smiled and squeezed him. "You care for her."

"What?" He whispered and glanced down at her.

"I have seen the way you look at her, Richard. You have feelings for her, whether you choose to admit it or not."

"Of course, I care for her. She is my responsibility, and when I first saw her in Ireland, she reminded me of you. But we know nothing of her, where she is from, her family, nothing."

"That matters not to you." Emily kept her eyes on him.

"She may be betrothed or even married."

"I do not believe she is!" she said adamantly. "We have spent much time talking. I think she has not been around very many men, especially ones of her age."

"What makes you say so?" He glanced at his sister curiously.

"She does not remember her personal history, but general conversations about boys and life, I have more experience than she does and…"

"My dear sister, that is quite enough." Richard broke in, interrupting her. The revelation that his youngest sibling knew anything of men shocked him, and his need to learn more from her diminished instantly. "As the head of this family, that is more information that I wish to hear from you. You should go back to bed; it has been a long night."

"We cannot leave her alone; I won't do it! I agree something has frightened her terribly, and maybe someone was after her, and may be after her still?"

Richard stroked her hair and led her toward her own door.

"You may possibly be correct, but she will not be alone. I am to sit with her awhile. I will take my leave before she wakes. We both can speak with her later in the morning. But remember, you and Mrs. Blair were the only ones in the room when she was changed."

"I remember." Emily hesitated, "I love you; you know. I am glad you are home. I have missed you." she hugged her brother once more. "Goodnight."

"Goodnight, and no more thinking of boys. You are far too young for that nonsense." He furrowed his brow but smiled at his sister.

"Oh Richard, don't be absurd." She kissed his cheek and left for her room.

He reminded her to leave the door ajar, as he sat in the large leather chair, staring at the stranger, lying peacefully at rest. She was growing lovelier every day, and he would have to be a damn fool not to see it. He no longer believed it was the shipwreck that held a grip on her memories. It was something else, and he was convinced whatever happened to her, happened in London.

CHAPTER 10

The sunlight filtered through the window across Leslie's face. She opened her eyes and lowered her chin as she removed her arms from under the covers. Her hand flew to her throat, as the tiny lace from the dressing gown chaffed against her neck. She panicked and threw back the counterpane. The chemise was not her own. She draped her legs off the edge of the bed and turned to peer at the sheets. Fresh linens, fresh counterpane, and pillow. Head in hand, she rubbed her face, then buried her fingers into her temples, a movement becoming far too familiar. Vibrating halos danced around her vision. Why was this happening?

"Why can't I remember?" She rubbed her temples.

She was becoming a burden to the Hawthorns, and they had been exceedingly generous and hospitable. Emily provided her with clothes for every need. Clarice accompanied her on shopping excursions, purchasing items such as combs and even a bonnet. Lady Gillford, my goodness, she was incredibly thoughtful, treating her as if she were one of her own daughters.

Emily reassured her the inconveniences of her amnesia and health difficulties were nothing with which to concern herself. Nevertheless, she was acutely aware of the odd circumstances and if she possessed any memory at all, she would leave. But how foolish? Where would she go? She had no idea where she was other than Mayfair and would likely only find herself meandering around in endless circles. How she despised her situation and dependency on others.

She swung her feet over the side of the bed and slipped gracefully from the tall mattress. When she reached the floor, her knees gave way, and she swiftly grasped the large chair nearby and settled into it. The leather was warm, and she tucked her bare feet underneath the gown, wrapping the extra material around her knees, relishing in its tepidity.

It suddenly occurred to her the smooth hide usually felt cold when first touched. Someone had stayed… after her… her episode. What else could one call it? A nightmare was something that tortured one in their sleep. You awoke frightened and confused but still in your bed. But last night? What happened? It must have been different. She had never awakened with a change of clothes or fresh linens. Who had she inconvenienced last night? Perhaps Bedlam was where she should be. In a padded room with no one to hurt. Bedlam? How did she know of Bedlam? She buried her face in her hands. How was it, she recalled some things and not others? Her head began to ache once more.

After dressing, Leslie made her way to the breakfast room, hoping to see no one. She only wished for chocolate and maybe toast and butter. She quietly opened the door, but the rustle of a newspaper was instantly perceived.

"Good morning." Richard folded and set aside the paper. His eyes followed her, as she moved toward the sideboard.

His countenance was excessively calm, exceedingly affable, exceptionally amicable… it was obvious, he knew.

"Is it?" She questioned softly.

"When the sun is shining in London, it is indeed." He remarked indifferently.

"I suppose." She returned.

She filled her cup with chocolate and placed a small scone on the saucer. She returned to her place, fully conscious he hadn't taken his eyes from her. Uncomfortably, she took her seat and gazed across the table. She had just as soon be forthcoming.

"I am well aware it was not a pleasant night for everyone."

Richard remained silent, hoping to alleviate her concerns, but realised it was useless.

"It's not as though you intended it," he remarked in jest.

"Of course, I did not." She said. "But it changes nothing. I upset the entire household."

"You upset no one! We were only concerned for your well-being."

"Who did I intrude upon?" She asked as she raised her eyes to meet his.

"Only myself, Emily, of course, Mrs. Blair, Carson and two of the footmen."

"Oh, goodness! They were all present?" Her countenance flushed scarlet.

"No, no! The footmen and Carson were outside your door. The men were extinguishing candles and heard Emily's cry for help. The butler informed me in the library and accompanied me up the stairs in case he was needed. Emily and I were the only two in the chamber."

"You said Mrs. Blair?"

"Yes..." Richard hesitated. He had to phrase this delicately so as not to cause her further humiliation.

"We called for her after you were calm. You required your attire changed."

Her face shown a look of mortification. Richard was certain she was breathless.

"You were perspiring profusely and curled in the corner. You would have caught your death had you remained in your clothing..."

"You mean my thin chemise."

"Yes, it was soaked and would not adequately dry enough for you to remain in it." He studied her response as she considered his words. "Mrs. Blair and Emily exchange your clothing and bed sheets. Your hair was wet, and Emily dried it, brushed it, and pulled it back, then wrapped a towel to encourage it to dry."

She lowered her head, then raised only her lashes, "Did you remain in the room?"

"No, of course not!" He said quickly, then gave her a sheepish grin, hoping to induce a smile, "Not that I did not think of it."

It worked, she relaxed and almost smiled. It appeared his roguery lightened her concern.

"You were quite distraught, and it frightened my sister."

Her mind was trying to recall anything from the previous episode. She picked up the silver sugar tongs and selected a cube for her chocolate.

"Leslie, do you remember anything at all from last night?"

Her hand froze, levitating above the table! Richard followed the tongs and the sugar cube as they fell to the table with a clang, and her hand began to quiver and shake. Rapidly withdrawing it to her lap, she began to tremble, and her eyes glazed, as if she might swoon. Richard bolted from his chair and rushed to her side.

Tears were streaming down her cheeks, and her entire body swayed as though she would collapse. He embraced her around the shoulders and pulled her from the chair, cradling her the same as he had the previous night. His boot nudged one of the chairs away from the table. He placed her in his lap, her head resting on his shoulder.

"Damn it, I'm sorry! I should not have. I am so sorry!" Richard stroked her hair, trying to soothe her.

She could feel the warm tears as they fell. She brushed them away and began to settle, raising her head to stare up at him.

"That is my name, is it not?" A slight whimper slipped from her lips as she tried to stop the tears.

"I think so."

"But h-how did you know?"

Regaining her composure, she retook her chair as Richard pulled the pendant from his pocket, placing it on the table before her. She glanced at it, then at him, vexed. He nodded toward the locket.

She lifted it, the neck chain draping through her fingers. Leslie clutched it in her palm, pressing the gold slide at the side. The piece easily opened, revealing the engraving. She traced the tiny, curved writing with her finger.

"My grandmama!" She whispered. "My namesake."

The tears were still trickling down her cheeks as she traced each letter.

"She gave it to me. I cannot remember when, but I have worn it for many years."

She glanced at him, the smile reverting to pain.

"Oh, Richard, why can't I remember. I must remember."

He placed his hand over hers as she closed it around the locket.

"But you are! You remembered your name and your grandmother. It is a start and Dr Hanover will be here tomorrow. Perhaps he can explain what is happening."

"I must look dreadful." She whisked the back of her hand across her cheek.

Taking his handkerchief from his pocket, he wiped her tears, and then handed it to her. "You look beautiful, Leslie."

He lifted her from the chair, gripping both arms just above her elbows, standing closer than he was fully aware he ought. He brushed her hair away and tucked a loose lock behind her ear, lightly tracing his knuckles down her neck before retracting his hand.

Richard knew he should release her, but something wouldn't let him. The scent of lavender filled his nostrils. A fragrance, he was suddenly aware, had been the same each morning since they had boarded the ship in Waterford. He lowered his eyes to hers and saw confusion in them. She was not resisting but was clearly bewildered. He dropped his arms to his side and took a step back.

"Are you feeling well now?" He moved away and stepped toward his chair, no longer making eye contact.

"Yes." She answered softly. He never failed to provide comfort, even in moments of humiliation and embarrassment. He would curl his lips upward ever so slightly, not quite a smile, yet a sensation that overwhelmed her, but with a sense of… of… of what? Security, safety, even without her memory or comprehension, were things she had always longed for.

His touch was tender, his embrace warm. She was protected, even when the discovery of parts of her memory frightened and terrified her; Richard was comforting and dispelled those fears.

In silence, she stared at him. She should go. She was aware her face was stained with tears and her eyes red. She shook her head to clear her thoughts, "I should retire to my chamber and freshen my countenance."

The earl only nodded; his eyes lowered. As she turned towards the door, he briefly lifted his gaze and caught sight of a bit of muslin as she disappeared into the hallway.

What was it about her that urged him to her side so readily, without considering the consequences, simply to comfort her? Had Emily been right; something was happening to him? He did care for her, and last night's behaviour was inappropriate and out of character.

This was an assignment, and if his instincts were correct, there was no room for sentimental attachment. More importantly, he could not risk making an error in judgment because of unguarded emotions. Furthermore, if his sister was correct… she was an innocent… he had wished she was not.

CHAPTER 11

The following day, Dr Hanover firmly grasped the bronze knocker at precisely a quarter past eleven. The butler took the doctor's coat, hat, and gloves and escorted him to the receiving room just off the entry.

The chamber was modest in size yet boasted a grand window overlooking Upper Brook Street. It was adorned with heavy, dark green velvet draperies which had been tied back, allowing a flood of light into the room.

"Lord Gillford and Miss…" Carson paused. What name had been given… "Miss Smith will join you shortly."

Left alone, the caller perused the room brimming with books. He wasn't certain if it was welcoming or only a means to occupy one's time until a haughty aristocrat chose to receive a visitor. There was a floor-to-ceiling bookcase that encompassed one interior wall. As a scholar, he was drawn to books, tracing his forefinger along the exquisitely bound titles. The impressive collection consisted of leatherbound classics of varying subjects which appeared never to have been read.

A diminutive individual dressed in green muslin cautiously entering the room. Withdrawing his attention from the literary prose he faced the petite female with the striking but unusual copper-highlighted brown hair. Closely in her wake was the man he had met two days before.

"I hope we haven't kept you long?"

"No, not at all. I was admiring your collection of reading material."

Smiling at the unspoken quip of noble arrogance in the response; he touched Leslie's elbow pressing her slightly forward.

"Dr Hanover, I am delighted to present Leslie Smith, Leslie, Dr. Hannover" She extended her hand, and the doctor squeezed it lightly, not breaking eye contact.

"It is a pleasure to make your acquaintance."

"Thank you…" She responded quietly.

The doctor dropped her hand and snapped his eyes to his lordship. "Did you say, Leslie?"

"Yes, a discovery made only yesterday."

"It is indeed a pleasure, Miss Smith." He said again.

Her eyes anxiously darted back and forth before finally settling on the doctor's. When Hanover's flick of curiosity and slight squint at the violet blue eyes, it disquieted the earl, who concluded it to be nothing more than his own initial response to them.

He invited everyone to be seated and escorted Leslie to a small settee, as the doctor sat directly across from her.

"Should you require my presence, I shall be in the library. Carson may have…"

"No." Her eyes shot to his pleadingly, "Please, do not leave me." She reached for his hand and gently clutched it in hers.

He squeezed it slightly, "I am certain the doctor wishes to speak with you privately."

"No, I implore you." The persuasive eyes turned to Dr Hanover.

"If you wish for Lord Gillford to remain, I have no objection."

Richard regarded her grasp and beseeching gaze; he would not abandon her with a stranger. Appropriate or not, she viewed him as her protector. Without a word, he took the seat beside her. She slipped her hand deeper into his, clenching it firmly. Amused, he tittered at the death grip of the small, delicate hand before releasing it. Dr Hanover smiled favourably as she drew strength from it.

"You are comfortable with Lord Gillford, are you not?"

Leslie's eyes never wavered from the doctor. "Yes, he has been with me as…" she hesitated, "as long as I can remember and has kept me safe."

"Safe?" Dr Hanover questioned without surprise. "Safe from what?"

She gave him an odd look, "I don't know, but not having your memory is terrifying. One cannot recognise his friends from his enemies; I am secure with him. He would never let anyone harm me."

Her voice so pragmatic the doctor jotted a note of it.

"Do you have adversaries?" He asked curiously.

She looked at him prudently, "I don't know."

Pondering the question and her response, perhaps not in the sense that most perceive an enemy, but somehow, she was positive she did.

"Tell me what you do remember."

Leslie clasped her hands in her lap gathering and working through her conscious thoughts before relaying the details of the only memories she owned.

"I awakened in a small chamber. The McClearys were taking care of me. They discovered me on the beach. Apparently, I had been adrift at sea. I have no memory of it. They claimed me to be delirious; I was in tremendous pain and the mere thought of nourishment, even water left me wretched. It was as though my body and mind were at odds with one another."

"Is that when you first met Lord Gillford?" Dr. Hanover scratched in his pad.

"He arrived shortly afterwards."

"So, you have known him for quite a while."

"Yes," she swayed her head to one side peering at the doctor curiously.

"What do you recall of that meeting with him."

The questions regarding their first meeting, the earl found peculiar. He attempted to disregard it, hoping Hanover only meant to ease Leslie's apprehension and nerves. However, he didn't appreciate the intrusion.

"I cannot summon much of it, but I remember him kind, and I thought…" She stopped abruptly; her cheeks flushed pink as she glanced down.

"Pray, do go on…" Hanover paused his writing, dipped his quill in the small inkwell, awaiting her response.

She hesitated and detected Richard's annoyed countenance. They had never discussed that day, which piqued his interest. He only remembered her deteriorated health and tormented condition.

"I had rather not say."

"Why?" The doctor cocked his head quickly.

Leslie realised he was analysing her hesitation. "It is embarrassing."

Both men regarded one another. She cleared her throat, understanding her silence did not bode well with either.

"Very well!" she gathered her strength, "I believed him to be extraordinary and the most handsome man I had ever laid eyes upon!" She blurted, lowering her head, face bright pink.

Richard derived a mix of shock, along with a bit of self-satisfaction, but remained outwardly stoic.

The doctor, cognisant of his mistake, continued. "So, you are at ease answering my questions in his company."

"Yes."

Lord Gillford, however, was not! He ought to have insisted on departing and considered still doing so. It was now far too late. He shifted uncomfortably in his seat, crossed his leg over his knee, casually surveyed the room, brushed a piece of lent from his tan breeches, then decided it best to ignore this little minx for the moment. More attention needed to be heeded of Dr Hanover. What was he up to?

"What else do you remember?"

"I speak French and appear to have a tremendous amount of knowledge of subjects most women do not. My name is Leslie, and I have a faint memory of my grandmother."

"Pray, why are you so certain?"

"Regarding my name?"

"Yes."

I have been addressed by several names. They were fine and pretty names. But when Rich… I mean his lordship, called me Leslie, somehow, it was familiar. I cannot explain it."

"And you are still comfortable with it."

"Yes."

"Have you experienced London? If so, how was your experience - joyful, sad, fearful, or something different perhaps?"

She hesitated, glimpsed at her lap, then met the doctor's eyes once more.

"I do not care to venture out in London. I am anxious."

"Explain this for me."

"I am unsure if I can do so."

"Try."

Leslie unconsciously rubbed her palms. Richard noted the doctor's close attention to the nervous motion. He casually leaned back, awaiting her response.

The earl regretted he had not regarded Hanover closer from his arrival. The questions had a sense of familiarity and specificity. Had he recognised her? Once again, he had permitted his personal feelings to disrupt the investigation. Typically, he was suspicious of everyone, he could not allow this to persist. Focus, he reminded himself, and returned to the interview.

"I do not trust my instincts." She remarked, "I am not certain I would recognise a threat."

"What kind of threat?"

"If only... I... I do not." Leslie lowered her head, fully aware of how absurd she must sound to anyone who listened to her rambling.

Her discomfort caused the doctor to change the direction of his questions.

"I assume you suffered various injuries from the shipwreck. Can you tell me about them?"

"Many minor ones had healed by the time I awoke. I think..." she paused and sought the earl for confirmation. "My arm was broken and a bone in my leg or my foot?"

"The small bone in the lower leg, but it was not dislodged, and healed quickly," Richard confirmed the reports of the Irish doctor.

"Oh yes. How foolish of me to forget." She tugged at her skirt anxiously. "Also, a few broken ribs, and my inside was unwell. I consumed only a liquid diet for some time. I was refused meat, vegetables, fruit, and even bread."

"I suppose you had many bruises."

"Yes."

"Any on the face or head?"

Richard swiftly removed his boot from his knee and straightened. This was an odd inquiry. Not the head, of course, but why would he ask about the face? Why would it signify? He stared at Hanover and was certain the man was aware of it but paid it no heed and continued to focus on Leslie.

"No, but most of the bruises were gone."

"Do you recall having bruises before?"

Richard moved forward in his seat. This man was no longer asking general inquiries and seemed intent on continuing.

"I do not remember," Leslie stated conclusively, observing Richard had pitched forward and stiffened.

"Very well." The doctor readjusted and moved closer to her.

"Miss Smith, I understand you experience nightmares, and many times leave your bed?"

Leslie lowered her head and whispered. "Yes."

"When was the last occurrence?" He followed her eyes as they met her companion's.

The earl reclined and gave her a slight nod. She inhaled a deep breath and turned to the doctor.

"Two nights ago." She whispered softly.

"Tell me what you recall?"

"I don't remember anything." She sounded embarrassed and frustrated.

"How can you be certain you had one?"

"I... someone changed my clothing, and my bedding."

"Who discovered and assisted you?"

"Yes, Emily. We have adjoining rooms so she can help me."

"And you trust Emily?"

"Yes, she is very dear to me."

"Why did she change your clothes?"

"I… I was perspiring; she was afraid I would take a chill."

"I see."

Leslie's agitation and stress was elevated, and she wished to say no more. Richard believed it to be time to conclude the visit.

"Dr Hanover, are you able to help us, or should we seek another physician?"

The doctor stopped his writing and looked at them. "I would like to try. I would also like to perform an examination, if agreeable."

"Now?" Leslie shrieked!

"What kind of exam?" He directed his gaze to the doctor.

"Only basic." Hanover assured her, "I would like to evaluate your reflexes. Examine your bone structure, especially at the breaks. I want to look into your eyes, ears, and your throat."

She looked to Richard, pleading for a response. Yet she was aware he would not decide on her behalf. They had not discussed the details of the nightmare, but from speaking with Emily, he had been the one to calm her and the one who had stayed through the night. It was his warmth in the chair. He was always there for her comfort and protection. But she had to make this decision.

Unable to bear the thought of being alone with another man, a stranger, she would displease everyone with her next request, but it was the only way she would allow an examination, here in this house or at his office.

"Only if Lord Gillford remains!" She said emphatically.

"Leslie! That would not be appropriate. I cannot."

"It is the only way I will agree to it." She turned back to the doctor, her defiance resolute, "The only way!"

After the exam and interview were completed, the earl accompanied Hanover to the foyer for a private word before his departure.

As Richard headed towards the stairs, Leslie still stood where he had left her, and he was surprised to find her there.

"I thought you would have returned upstairs. I am certain everyone is in the blue drawing room."

"Emily is and was having her breakfast when I came downstairs." She acknowledged; her voice soft and noticeably altered.

She was casually wandering the room, dragging her fingers along the furniture, her eyes lazily half-closed, her long lashes brushing against her cheeks.

What was she doing? Her movements were suggestive, or was it simply his own arousal from observing the examination?

The doctor had raised the hem of her skirt, revealing the delicate shape of her ankles. He had checked her calves to ensure all the bones were in place and healing properly.

All Richard had witnessed were the beautifully shaped limbs and imagined his own hands caressing the tiny ankles and calves, rather than the medicinal coldness of the doctor's. He had instantly chided himself and walked to the window for the remainder of the evaluation.

He shifted his gaze from Leslie as he made his way to the buffet, pouring a drink, and turning to face her.

Leslie gracefully strolled to the door and gently closed it. He raised an eyebrow as she whirled to face him, leaning against the richly polished mahogany while accentuating her posture drawing attention to her breasts. As he lowered his glass onto the table, his expression remained impassive. Yet he found himself exceedingly unsteady. What was she up to?

His mind wandered back to the examination. Hanover had gently held her delicate wrists and ankles, softly massaging them. He turned his gaze to her eyes, cradling her face in his hands. Richard had attempted to avert his stare but failed miserably. The various manipulations and touches had left him unsettled. He reminded himself again, this was a man of healing. However, he had envisioned his own hands stroking the soft skin, rather than Jeffery Hanover's.

He had gleaned her every scent and the touch of her gentle contours. There was a flash of the translucently drenched chemise that revealed her. Admittedly, he had been aroused by it and had burned the site of her in his mind, knowing he would never have another opportunity.

Now, here she stood, leaning alluringly against the door, her arms elegantly placed behind her on the handles. Was she purposely appearing provocative, deliberately seeking to seduce, or was it only his own wayward thoughts?

He stood motionless as she pushed herself away from the wooden panels, easing her way toward him. She drifted across the floor captivating him. What the hell was she doing? What the hell was he doing? He could not permit this. He had years of experience keeping his emotions in check.

"I – I want to know what happened the other night. Please tell me."

She approached him, halting before him, not close enough to touch but near enough to sense the warmth between them.

What in God's name? Was she aware? He forced himself to meet her gaze.

She relied on him to protect her and guide her through the blindness of her memory. He watched as years of composure and emotionless encounters gradually slipped away.

She had never consciously come within his reach. What was she thinking? Had the doctor's visit caused her to remember more, or had it frightened her, and she only sought comfort?

"What do you wish to know?" Richard stilled, not daring to act. The faintest manoeuvre he might do something he would forever regret.

"Everything." She delicately enveloped his wrist, drawing it to her.

Richard stopped breathing.

"You stayed through the night; Emily said it was you. She told me how considerate and kind you were."

Unable to stop the descent into the depths of her eyes, he struggled to maintain his composure. "I remained in the leather chair only to ensure you did not have another nightmare." His voice was unfazed but raspy and trembling.

"I felt the warmth of it, somehow, I assumed it was you. I am not certain how, but I did." Her dark velvet eyelashes brushed her cheeks, her eyes burned into his again. "What else?"

"Nothing." Richard's heart pounded. He must regain control. The soft touch of her hand was driving him mad. For God's sake, she was rubbing her thumb in circles on the inside of his wrist.

She gently placed her hand in his, intertwining their fingers. She brought both hands to her heart and leaned into him, joining their bodies with their interwoven hold.

"I do not believe you." She said softly, "I admitted to the doctor, you took my breath away when I first laid eyes on you, and I meant it. I have wanted to be near you since that day. I am safe and at peace with you."

Richard eased her hand to her side, released it, moved away, and cleared his throat. He was spiralling out of control, this had to stop.

"Leslie, you don't understand what you are saying. What you are feeling is not real. You see me as your rescuer, your protector. I will soon become a man who only does what is asked of him. You are sorting through emotions and anxiety as you regain your memory. When it fully returns, you will no longer have need of me. I shall soon become a part of your past."

"You are wrong." She didn't move, but he sensed her body stiffen in defiance of his rejection.

"You cannot know that." He pivoted to face her. "There could be a husband, a betrothed, a lover. You may only be a child. Hell, you may have a child."

That took them both aback.

"I am not, and there is no one else." She might not have a memory, but there are things a female knows... the heart, the emotions, the unconsciousness of unrealised sentiments. She had none of those things.

"Leslie, you may have been married just before you boarded that ship. You do not remember."

She closed the space between them.

"I don't care. I need you. I am safe with you. You have held me in your arms and gently stroked my hair. Do not tell me you do not have some affection... something."

"What do you remember from the other night Leslie?" His voice was harsh, as fear shot through him. What had she remembered?

"Nothing." His tone startled her.

104

"When did I hold you and stroke your hair?" He was fumbling for balance, now irritated and frustrated. Had she remembered more than she was willing to admit?

"Yesterday morning!" She said, wondering how he could have possibly forgotten. She could not.

At the breakfast table, he had embraced her and good God, pulled her into his lap. He had treated her like a frightened child when he spoke her name. Holy hell, how many inappropriate responses had he committed while attempting to console her? He had lost control; lust was all it could be, and it was winning the battle; this could not happen. Leslie was not the only one lost in denial.

He took her wrist and led her to the settee. He had to regain power over this situation. She had to understand this was a job, and until her past was recovered, her attachment to the Sea Horse resolved, and her reason for escaping London, this was nothing more than his assignment. It had to be.

"I admit, my affection for you has grown, but it is out of my protection of you, and is natural after all this time together. Yours is the same. Until we discover who you are and where you belong, my assignment comes first."

That was the best he could do. She was alone and reaching for purpose, and he was her only lifeline.

A tear ran down her cheek. She couldn't possibly have genuine feelings for him. She had no one or nowhere else to turn. Of course, she had some adoration for him. In her circumstance, powerful sensations were to be expected. But Richard also knew when she regained her memory when she remembered the man she lost at sea, she would be devastated and heartbroken. Then, the affection she had for him would dissolve. He had to remind himself of the tangled situation and protect her tender heart, along with his own.

"Sometimes I forget I have a past." She wiped a tear from her cheek, "As time passes without my memory, this is the only life I have ever known, and you and your family are so incredibly special to me. I have behaved improperly and embarrassed myself, but you are truly all I have."

Unrestrained, he wrapped his arms around her and drew her close. He pressed his face to her hair. He had not paused to consider how isolated and alone she must feel. His family was her only link to the world. This undoubtedly must be his worst nightmare.

CHAPTER 12

Distracted, Richard was mindlessly tapping his spoon against his saucer when a footman stepped to the table to refill his coffee. With a stiff smile, he reclined in his chair watching the dark liquid flow from the silver urn to the Ansley teacup. Why had Dr Hanover requested to see him in private? He was uneasy but the call was unavoidable.

The earl's thoughts were again interrupted when Carson entered the breakfast parlour with the small silver tray, which carried calling cards and messages. Recognising the seal, he immediately broke it and scanned the parchment. Childs had information. He and a runner, who would be in the office at 3 o'clock. They had several files for him… Several?

For God's sake, how many young girls fled their households? That was something he had never considered. Was he on the verge of uncovering details about Leslie and understanding the immature female mind and her vulnerability to it? He forgot Carson was patiently waiting at his side.

"My lord, what shall I convey to the messenger?" The butler inquired.

Shaken from his reflection he lowered the missive. "Do bring me parchment and quill."

The butler immediately presented the paper, inkwell, and quill to his lordship.

"I should have expected as much." He smiled at him. "Not at all certain how I managed without you, my good man," He commented as he scratched a response to Childs.

Receiving the note, Carson bowed without expression, though his soul was touched with pride from the unnecessary and often not-given compliment.

His lordship perused the missive again from Bow Street, slowly reading the words again… several files. It appeared his investigation was moving forward.

He wanted to help Leslie, but he was also aware of the unpleasant truth… locating her family and the return of her memory would take her away from him. He placed both elbows on the table and waved the parchment back and forth, fanning the furrowed brows, planning his day.

Dr. Hanover and St John Street was to be his first destination, then on to see the magistrate for his 3 o'clock. Folding and tucking the letter away in a waistcoat pocket, he returned to his eggs and ham.

***

Dashing upstairs, he found Bixby in his dressing room, polishing a pair of Hessians.

"Good God, man, do you do nothing but polish my boots?"

His valet cast him a baneful visage, then with pompous indignations, remarked, "If his lordship wishes them to serve as a mirror, then indeed I do!" Retorting with a prick to his pride.

"I require breeches and top boots, Bixby. I am off to Bow Street this afternoon. Send a message to Jonathon requesting him to prepare the curricle and greys. He is to accompany me."

The Hessians were set aside, and a footman summoned to take the missive to his lordship's tiger. When Bixby returned to his duties, he had forgotten his wounded ego and gathered boots, tan breeches, white muslin shirt, collar, cuffs, and a dark blue tailcoat with a matching waistcoat.

Richard's bath had been drawn in anticipation of the early departure, enabling him to quickly endure the morning toilette. His cravat tied and his pocket watch confirming it was nearly noon, he must hurry to exit the house before the ladies made their way downstairs.

"I will return in time for dinner; prepare the burgundy jacket. I think I will go to White's afterwards."

"Yes, my lord," his valet answered, brushing lint from the dark blue coat, and observing with pride how easy it was to turn out the earl. His broad shoulders never needed padding and his breeches hugged his muscular thighs, presenting the perfect specimen. It was his first charge, who needed no fillers whatsoever.

Bixby had polished his way into the earl's noble house and coveted the envy of the dandy set's valets for his skills. The pride in his work was becoming legendary now that the Ton had replaced the battlefield. As his employer took his leave, the valet crossed his arms and nodded his head with satisfaction. The perfect Corinthian, he grinned at his work.

Carson met the earl at the door with his multi-capped charcoal grey driving coat, beaver hat, and dark driving gloves. "I suppose we are not going to have a summer this year." Richard said as he slipped his hands into the deerskins and peered out the door, confirming his curricle was waiting.

"Jonathon arrived five minutes ago, my lord."

Richard shook his head slightly; how did Carson Blake guess his every thought and anticipate his every need? He and his wife had served the Hawthorns since he was still in leading strings. But he was dispatched to Eaton at eleven and commissioned into his majesty's service following only a year at Cambridge at the age of seventeen.

Two years prior, when the family moved to Gillford House, the young earl's butler and housekeeper had taken other positions. The Blakes had been with the family too long to dismiss them, and their knowledge of each member was sometimes startling. The old butler seemed to anticipate Richard's wish before the request was made, he gave him smile took his hat then strolled from the door. It was indeed good to be home.

109

"Top a duh mornin' ta ya, guv'nor. W'ere to?" Jonathon called as the earl approached his chaise.

"Back to St. John Street and then to Bow Street." Richard climbed into the curricle, lifted the ribbons to engage the greys and motioned to his Tiger to release their heads.

The youth kept his eyes alert as the large wheel rolled past, nearly grazing the toe of his boot. Grabbing his hold, he swung himself onto is platform. "Spanish faggot today guv'nor, bet'rn a dog's soup 'bout yes'ter-day."

"Absolutely!" Richard laughed at his Tiger's use of Cant. It took him a good while to understand half of what he said. Many times, he agreed without having the slightest notion of what the devil the boy was about.

Today, he assumed Jonathon was referring to the weather, which had finally cleared, and the sun was shining. It had rained for several days in a row, which was normal for this time of the year, but had remained cold, which was not. 1816 was quickly being defined as the year without a summer. Bloody depressing it was.

As he manoeuvred onto St. John, Richard was edgy regarding this meeting. The doctor hadn't given him any hint as to the reason, but it was apparent he did not wish for Leslie to be included.

The elderly, heavy-set woman faithfully at her desk, glanced up and smiled. He heard the chair scrape across the wood. She was trying to stand.

"I do implore you to remain seated, it is not necessary." He said gesturing for her to keep her seat.

"Lord Gillford, it's so good to see you again." She managed to say, the mere attempt left her breathless.

"I believe Dr Hanover is expecting me?"

"Yes, my lord, the second door on your right." Lifting her heavy arm and pointing to the corridor.

"Much obliged!"

Richard made his way down the vestibule, knocking lightly, as he opened the door. Dr Hanover looked up and met the earl halfway across the office. Shaking hands, then motioning for him to join him at the desk.

Sliding the piles of file notes aside, the doctor, leaned forward placing his elbows on the cleared surface.

"I will get straight to the point; we are both very busy men." His lordship nodded in agreement, as he continued. "I am aware you were displeased when I visited Miss Smith. But I had to discern how she perceived your relationship before the accident."

"We had none. I had only met her through my assignment by the war department."

The doctor reclined in his chair and fidgeted. He remained uncomfortable and did not remove his gaze from the earl but said nothing.

The suddenly wasted no time in revealing his apprehension. This was to be unethical but believed he had little choice. "I have seen the girl."

In shock, Richard blinked and swayed his head slightly, but his eyes never left Hanover's as he waited for him to continue.

"I returned to the office and searched through my files. She was brought here about four years ago."

"By whom?" the earl's thoughts were tumbling into one question after another.

"I do not believe the woman to be any more than a servant, but she was genuinely concerned for the girl. Little information was given, but she indeed called her Leslie. I noted it in the file. Without doubt she is correct about her name."

"Why was she brought to you?"

The uncomfortable edginess of the doctor, disturbed Richard but he must have the truth, and the man was aware of it.

"She was much younger, of course, and the older woman was dressed in a housekeeper's uniform. She refused to give me her name other than the one accidently mentioned. I fear, she would have given a false one otherwise."

Hanover hesitated then added, "The girl's face was battered and bruised, and the woman was worried she may have broken bones or teeth."

"And did she?" Hawthorn was trying to check his emotions but felt his hand unconsciously fold into a fist.

"No, only cuts, swelling and bruises. Someone had abused that child. That is why I asked about her face. But there is no way in hell she would have forgotten it unless she chose to."

"So, you think she has used the Sea Horse trauma to forget her past? That is what you are trying to say, is it not?"

"Yes. But she trusts you, Lord Gillford. I understand you wish to unburden yourself of her as quickly as possible, but you are the key to her regaining her memory."

"Me!" He blurted, astonished. "Why me?"

"As I have explained, she trusts you and perhaps your younger sister. I am also persuaded she desires to remember, but she is afraid of where the truth may take her. I wanted you to understand her memory will return, but only when she considers it safe enough to do so."

"Someone in her past has harmed her?" Gillford held his voice steady, but he was seething at the thought of someone purposely striking her.

"I believe so, but there is no way of knowing who it may have been, and that is an issue you must face. I would like to keep seeing her on occasion if you will permit it."

"Admittedly, I had my doubts about you."

"When I recognised the girl, I had my doubts about you, as well. I had to ensure you could be trusted to protect her and would do so."

"I can assure you; no harm will come to her whilst in my care."

"It is a slippery slope, as you well know. If her parent is the abuser and you just hand her over, she will be in grave danger. If they learn you are in possession of their daughter and do not deliver her…"

"Yes, I'm aware, legal proceedings might be brought against me."

"Indeed." the doctor agreed.

"I will handle the situation carefully," Richard assured him. "As far as the other, I have no issue with you seeing her again if you can help her."

"She only needs to trust those around her and believe she will be protected. I do appreciate you coming." Hanover rose and extended a hand.

"Thank you for sharing the information. You did not have to do so." The earl stood and clasped the offered hand.

"If I can offer you any service, please let me know of it." The doctor said assuredly.

"I am obliged to you."

The earl left the place more confused than before. He was to be placed at odds with the war department, who wanted the girl off their hands as quickly as possible. He was also in opposition to his own ethics… never get personally involved.

Richard was reminded of a quote from a recently read novel, Marmion, by Walter Scott. 'Oh, what a tangled web we weave when we practice to deceive.' He should be accustomed to deception. After all, it had been his rule as a spy, but for The Crown, never against it.

How was he to manage Bow Street? Grateful for his discourse with Hanover prior to the magistrate, he now must elicit great care with what he revealed, especially to a runner. He had no issues confiding in Morgan Childs, the girl's safety would be of the utmost concern for him, but a runner seeking a commission was a different matter altogether. To say the least, some of them had questionable credentials.

The closer he came to #3 Bow Street, the more he decided to select several files and give no indication of preference to any of them. Pulling his pocket watch from his waistcoat as he entered, he was pleased to find himself two minutes early, perfect timing.

"Hawthorn! Keep comin' round like this, and I'll be believin' ye' are workin' here."

"Good afternoon, Darby. How do you go on?"

"Can't complain. The magistrate is waiting on ye!" He motioned to the hallway, and Richard made his way to the partially opened door.

As the earl stepped into the office, Sir Childs rose, making his way around his large desk. Extending his hand, he couldn't miss the big, scruffy, muscular man, with the unkept appearance and a two-day growth of facial hair, standing by the window.

After their greeting, both gentlemen pivoted toward the burly man, who was wiping his hand on his long coat and extending it as Sir Childs made introductions.

"Lord Gillford, allow me to introduce Weber… Weber, Lord Gillford."

"A pleasure, my lord." The man nodded.

Richard was intrigued by the intonation. The implication being he was not at all pleasant to meet him.

Reluctantly, he took the offered hand and acknowledged the runner. Weber's grin was caustic and suspicious. He realised immediately this man had no respect for those associated with the aristocracy or most likely anyone else. The earl was an expert in the art of reading people. Throughout his career, he had discovered any form of rank was quite intimidating. But he perceived beyond this man's façade, he held nothing but disdain for any social hierarchy, particularly for the titled members of high society.

It occurred to him if he were to have any success in this investigation, the less people knew of him, the better. Few people would divulge secrets if they learnt he was a member of the beau monde.

His ability to infuse himself into the lives of others, convincing them his worth to be equal to their own, had been crucial to his success in the past. The magistrate had little knowledge of his work for the war department, but his participation on the streets of London was different. The chameleon ability of Richard Hawthorn had been impressive.

Childs directed the two to take the opposing chairs as he sat behind his desk and reached for a stack of folders.

The number of files surprised him. How could there be so many misplaced young girls?

"I am confused by the volume of records. This must be more than one year?" Richard's shock was obvious.

"We eliminated a substantial portion, including some of the other private commissions. Weber has had four in the past year." He stated with concern.

The runner noted Hawthorn's astonishment.

"Mine mostly duh deep pockets of aristocrats and CITs not wishin' to publicise deir wayward chil'ren, who refused to bend to duh power of deir fader's will. But you know how de aristocracy is; avoidin' a scandal, no madder duh cost, and no madder to me, fills me pockets." Weber's voice was filled with venom. "Thinkin' uh buyin' me uh flat in Gretna Green, I made so many trips dere over duh years." Weber grinned at his attempt at humour.

Richard, on the other hand, found nothing amusing about a wayward youth fleeing her home to Gretna Green against her family's will. He remained focused on Leslie but couldn't help, now and again, thinking of his own sister.

He turned to the runner curiously. "Is that what you find, a young female eloping with a beau? Against the family's wishes whose parent sought a better match, I presume."

"Most a duh time, yea. Sadly, duh times are a changin.' These wenches are bein' inerduced to duh romandical notions in deem nasty novels dese days and dey no longer inerested in marryin' fer stadus or wealth. Dey have duh mistaken notion of da 'soulmate' out dere some'ere." The runner's voice filled with vile mockery.

Richard found his depiction of romance and love through a young girl's eyes distasteful. "And you don't agree with marrying for love?"

Unsure why he posed the question or why he cared what the runner thought. But somehow, living in a house with nothing but females gave him a unique perspective on life than most, especially combined with his evenings among his friends and acquaintances at White's. He was beginning to see how a young girl might be easily influenced by a youthful buck who spoke of love when all he truly wanted was to satisfy a male ego and physical desires.

"I don't take wid' marriage at all!" Quipped Weber. "Gots no dee'sire ta be shackled to no needy female. Sides, a runner lief bedder off widout 'em. A bedder runner you makes. Dat's me luv, de adrenaline rush, beatin' de criminals at duh game of cat and mouse. I finds takin' duh Ton's money and havin' a doxy to bed, quite uh easy life. Even shell out fer a high price 'en, now and agin, jist to keep me'self grounded, ya knows."

Good God, Richard thought. He prayed Leslie would not be among his. He would have to consider being deceitful if she were. He would never willingly divulge anything to this callous bastard. But there was something else. He wasn't entirely certain, but the shifty eyes appeared to be assessing him, but why? Did the runner consider him a threat?

The dislike between the two was palpable. Sir Childs, abhorred by the sheer pleasure on his runner's face at offending his lordship, took matters in hand and presented the earl initially with Weber's. Then he would send his runner on his way to attend business elsewhere.

"Well, we are not here to discuss the immorality of the youth. Shall we peruse some of these? Weber let us commence with yours; you have work to be done. Hawthorn and I will manage the remainder."

Sir Childs picked up four files and placed them in front of the earl. Hawthorn inhaled and opened the first. He read the girl's description and recognised immediately it was not Leslie. The girl was fifteen, with blonde hair and brown eyes, but he had no intention of revealing the colour of Leslie's hair or eyes. That would reveal too many details and pique a curiosity he had no wish to. He examined the pages and scanned the comments. The fathers were CITs, one owned a large mercantile business, the other in haberdashery and were both considered to be wealthy, but had no wish to move up in class, no mention of societal concerns or even of an expected unworthy beau. It was more likely the two families did not want to join relations. Richard closed the file and set it aside, not saying a word.

The two onlookers glanced at one another in silence, but appeared to be wondering what assured him this girl didn't suit. Richard ignored their curiosity and opened the next folder. This one had brown hair and green eyes and weighed around ten stones. Ten stones? Goodness, he thought. But then he supposed depending on how tall she was, she might not be heavy at all. He heard Weber snicker and let out a hefty guffaw.

"Didn't figer dat to be yourn chit. Ofden wonder who'd want dat 'en and how in de world dey snuk'er out da house." His laugh was foul.

What a disgusting fool! How could Childs hire anyone so repellent? Richard tried to ignore the repugnant idiot, but damn, it wasn't easy when any one of them might be his ward or his own sister.

The next two were promising, and Richard started a new stack.

Sir Childs observing Hawthorn queried, "Do you have any questions you want to ask about the two you chose?"

"Yes, I noticed these two girls are fairly average, brown hair and non-descript, really. What of miniatures and what of the beau? How did the interview with the parents reveal so little information regarding the alleged captors?"

The runner picked up the first file and read it, trying to recall the specifics. It was obvious even to Weber the two files held few facts.

He recalled no miniatures but a strange situation on one. It was only the father and no siblings. He was a nabob and, since his return to England, had engaged in investing. The daughter was all he had left in the world; his wife had died several years before.

Weber admitted the father was a bit odd, but the man was desperate to find her and added the father was positive she had been taken by a lover; assured she had been compromised but

118

didn't care. Wanted her found and returned to him. But the parent had no idea who it could be, not one name of a beau or even a friend, not one. He named no other relatives, no cousins, nothing. When asked if she might have run away on her own, the father became irate and said absolutely not. He kept ranting she was kidnapped, convinced of it, and the staff had no information.

The other file was not Leslie, but he listened intently as the runner went on with his condescending vulgar description. There was a miniature of the second, but after several months with no sign of the girl, he returned it to the parents, who were none too happy, as the girl had been promised to a baron, who expected his betrothal money returned. The addresses for both girls were in the files.

Hawthorn put aside his dislike for the man only long enough to thank him, hoping to expedite his exit. Sir Childs stood promising to return his property. As he left the office, he closed the door behind him. Morgan sat quietly for a few minutes, then addressed the earl.

"I apologise for Weber. He's offensive and loathsome, but he is the best damn runner I have. He fears nothing and has no issues with descending into the bowels of Fleet Ditch to get his criminal. So, as I regret his manner and disgusting approach to life, I can count on him for the most despicable crimes against humanity. It's also one of the reasons the wealthy will pay him to find something they've lost. He rarely fails. He has succeeded in every assignment I've ever given him, and you hold the only private contracts that have not been fulfilled. And those eat at him.

I am glad you didn't share too much. I didn't realise just how seriously they bothered him until I witnessed his hand balling into a fist at your reaction to them. He would like nothing more than for one of his files to be your girl, not for the money but something far more nefarious... pride. I promise you, if she is one of his, I'll never divulge it. You have my word on it."

"I am most grateful. Where the devil did you find such a person? And how long has he been here? I cannot recall ever seeing him before." Richard could not shake his uneasiness.

"Around two years ago. He had little background to verify. Mentioned he had been travelling frequently. His size and temerity motivated me to give him a chance. I gave him the dirtiest and filthiest cases I had and one month to bring them in. He did and here he is."

The two returned to the remaining files. Richard uncovered six he wished to research further. Sir Childs had the clerk record the numbers and note who borrowed them. Hawthorn thanked him for his time and all he had done.

"I hope one of them precipitates your investigation. If I can assist in anything else you require, call on me. You never said, is the girl with you, or does she remain in Ireland?"

"Sir, I'd rather not share that information, not even with you. We have been acquainted for a long time. I never had a reason to distrust you, nor have I now, but I cannot take chances. She is young, fragile, and frankly, I don't trust some of those around you."

"I understand. I hope to see you soon."

The two said their goodbyes, and Richard left and began searching for his groom and curricle. It was nowhere in sight, so he loitered outside the building lost in his wool-gathering.

Suddenly, he felt a large hand clamp down on his shoulder. Reacting quickly, he turned to discover Weber standing next to him.

"Didn't mean to startle you, your lordship." He said sardonically.

The earl intuitively suspected, he damn well did mean to startle him.

The runner gave him a grin of satisfaction as he clearly enjoyed the surprised look of the earl. "You don't care fer me much, do ya?"

"Let's just say I don't approve of your perception of the human race."

"Fair enuff. But we're from two differnt worlds, you, and me. I'm fit for mine, and you, I dare say, do well enuff in yours."

"I will accept that." Richard eyed him cautiously, still searching for something he was unsure of, but his gut told him to keep his guard up and pistols close.

Weber addressed him as if he were an emasculated, egotistical aristocrat. It was debatable if he was aware his adversary was a decorated special agent for the British Crown. But it was doubtful - very doubtful. If he had, he might have been less pompous and a bit more cautious... or would he? His arrogance had told Hawthorn a lot about the man. Yet, it also left many unanswered questions.

"Good!" Weber turned and took a few steps, then glanced back at the earl, "If 'n I can help ya, let me know."

Richard was appalled at the notion. He was well aware of the type of help he was offering and had no interest. Yet neither did he want him to assume he thought him a threat.

"Thank you. I will bear it in mind." He was seething with anger and disgust.

The man arrogantly strutted down the street. The runner knew he was good at what he did, and he didn't care what anyone thought of him, least of all a highbrowed earl.

If this man had the opportunity, he would undermine every effort to protect Leslie at all costs and would spare no energy to learn of the girl's identity. The bounty played a role, but there was something far more dangerous… pride.

The earl was incensed this guttersnipe had become aware of his investigation. Rather than gain ground, he felt as though he had lost some.

Interrupted by the sound of his groom and horses pulling up behind, he turned away. "Where the bloody hell have you been with my greys!" He snapped.

Shocked by his tone and speech, his Tiger held his tongue as he jumped down from the curricle. He ducked his head and stood silently as his lordship took his seat and ribbons.

"Damnit to hell, don't just stand there. Let's go home."

"Rite' guv'nor." Jonathon shot to his step.

Lord Gillford cracked his whip above the heads of the greys, making a loud snap, and the equine leapt forward. The ride back to Upper Brooks Street was quiet except for the quick-paced, extended trot and rhythmic clip-clops of the horses' hooves.

Richard was in a surly disposition and vented his frustration on anyone who crossed his path.

Above all things, at this moment, he longed to be with his family. He had his fill of the unsavoury aspects of life for one day.

He tossed the ribbons to Jonathon, dashed up the steps and threw open the front door prior to Carson's arrival to the threshold. The butler assisted him from his riding coat and took his hat and gloves. Without a word, Richard barely allowed him time to snatch them before he released his hold and left the butler in the entryway wrestling with the outwear.

Richard ascended the stairs by twos, taking notice of no one. A housemaid hugged the balustrade and considered leaping to the floor below as the earl hurried past. Without breaking stride, he proceeded to the crystal decanter on the sideboard in the blue drawing room, poured two fingers of the dark amber liquid, raised the vessel to his lips, tossed back his head and drained the glass.

"I am going to assume you had rather a stressful day." A soft voice alleged from across the room.

Richard reeled to see his mother holding her embroidery in her lap, staring at him with a concerned countenance. He glanced around, to find the room otherwise empty. He poured another brandy and strode to her side. He took the seat next to her and released a prolonged and loud exhale.

"Quite so!"

His mother set aside her stitching and faced her son. "This has been difficult for you, has it not?"

"What has?" He barked.

His mother recognised the cold expression, unsure if it was Leslie or bearing the burden of two worlds that seemed to be crashing into one another.

"All these new responsibilities, along with your old." She offered gently.

Richard considered her words for a moment, not exactly seeing it the same way. However, he did understand her concern.

"Mother, how am I faring in taking over father's obligations? I mean, regarding you and my sisters. I do not include Clarice so much; she seems to be managing her new situation better than all of us. But in particular, Emily? These last few days, I have wondered – well, not wondered – so much as worried I am not attending to her in the manner which I should. I'm bewildered by her. One moment, she appears like a giddy child; the next she is so mature, that I worry she will run away with some buck, believing me to be an overly strict guardian. I have no idea how to oversee a sixteen-year-old girl."

"And you ought not be required to do so. It is my duty, Richard, and I have been unjust to you and them. I have been nothing but selfish the past year, more concerned with the dead than the living." She sighed remorsefully.

"Ridiculous! You adored Father, and you lost a significant part of yourself when he died. I don't blame you for any of it. He indulged you, which is as it should be – until he left you alone."

"But I'm not alone! I admit I felt as much for an exceedingly long while. I no longer cared what happened to any of you, wallowing in self-pity, wishing I had been taken with him."

Richard swiftly pitched his head toward his mother and clasped her hand in his.

"Do not say such things. My sisters and I would have been devastated had we lost you as well. We were barely able to survive Father, and I'm not certain the girls have done so. Clarice has taken care of you as if she has been accustomed to it all her life. She has managed the estate business in my absence, which I must admit was shocking."

"But you were away; it was not your fault. Your father had no time to teach you, and I do not believe he even realised he had inherited the earldom. He was already so extremely ill. But he never taught you his responsibilities and accounts. Clarice was here, and I am immensely proud of how well she adjusted during his illness."

"I do not begrudge her that! Do not consider for an instant I do; I am proud of her. I cannot imagine the state we might be in had she not done so." Richard was sincerely grateful to his sister.

"I agree and am happy she is bright and intelligent, but I also imagine it to be the reason she is still unmarried. Men do not appreciate a smart wife, who resembles her father and is nearly as tall as yourself, of course. She is pretty enough, but

124

her ways are much too progressive for many of the eligible bachelors."

"It's called intimidation, mother, and yes, she is very much thus. I dare say, many men are frightened of her." Richard laughed. "It's Emily whom I am worried. In the last year, there have been over fourteen girls fleeing their families, and that is in aristocratic homes, not the trades or the impoverished."

"But why?" His mother said shocked.

"From what I gather no one spared the time to understand or care for them. It is as though we are on the brink of some precipice. They are searching for importance in their lives, which the young men have not matured enough to comprehend. They are no longer satisfied with embroidery and fripperies." He paused. "Does that make sense?"

"Yes, Richard, it does, I am afraid." The countess put her stitching in her box and closed the lid. "You see, women already mature much faster than men. We have to be prepared early to bring new life into the world, take care of husbands, children, houses, servants, everything that makes a man's life convenient and worthwhile."

"Doesn't sound quite fair, does it? When all a man must do is bring an income of some sort into the home."

"That is not a simple task either, Richard."

"Doesn't appear so very difficult."

"If it was *not* difficult as you say, why are there so many poor and downtrodden sleeping in the streets of London?"

"Hmmm," Richard mulled that over in his mind a minute. "I suppose I am one of the thoughtless privileged classes."

"It is easy to forget them in our world." His mother whispered.

Prior to being consumed by the grief of her husband's death, the countess had devoted a significant portion of her

125

idle time to the poor, who called the streets of London home. She was beginning to comprehend how much she had lost over the last year.

You are so incredibly wise, mother."

"Nonsense, just old. Age and experience are what makes one wise, nothing more."

"You are far from being old. Look at you; just as lovely as when I was a small child. I once thought you were the most beautiful creature, I had ever laid my eyes upon."

"Once! What happened to alter your mind?" His mother gave him a derisive smile.

Richard laughed, "I grew up and discovered a few other women on my own."

"Yet, you never bring one to seek my approval."

"Someday, mama, someday."

The time with his mother had soothed his ill temper, and he found himself in a far better mood when a little slip of a girl came dashing into the room and sat beside him.

"Oh Richard, there is a new hat shop on Bond Street. I saw it just today. Please may we go? I am sure you may open an account."

The earl looked at his younger sister, rather surprised at her request. Remembering those fourteen files he had only a short time ago found so disturbing, He placed his arm around her squeezing her shoulders. "What do you know of accounts?"

"Well… I know that in all the other shops where we make purchases, they ask Clarice if we have an account, and she says yes. Then she gives them your name, then signs for our items, and we bring all our things home."

Richard burst into laughter, and Emily beamed up at him.

"I was right, was I not?" Her delightful smile begged for acquiescence.

He grabbed her chin with his thumb and forefinger and raised it to peer into her eyes.

"It is fortunate you are a pretty girl, and it would be wise to comport yourself accordingly. You shall require a husband of considerable wealth, my dear sister."

"You really believe so? But why?"

"I have seen your debentures. Your fancy is quite extravagant and believe all you must do is desire it, and it will be yours."

"Well, it does seem so!" She retorted, pouting her lips.

Richard adored her innocence, and unlike many modern young women, she had no interest in learning books, numbers, or even history. As long as she could read her romance novels, speak French, and play the pianoforte, she was content.

"If we could only manage to keep her quiet and less fidgety, we would not have to worry about ridding the house of this one next year. A fine noble wife, I dare say." Richard stood, pulling Emily to her feet and kissed the top of her head.

"You will miss me, you know." She smiled up at her brother cheekily.

"Yes, we will. I am truly not at all anxious to see you leave us anytime soon." Her mother interpolated, her voice cracking a bit.

He turned to see his mother's misty eyes. The thought of any of her children leaving home saddened her, especially after the recent death of her husband.

Clarice and Leslie were chattering as they entered the room but were hushed at the noticeable silence. "Is something wrong?" Clarice came to a halt and glanced at her mother and siblings.

Easily assuming the role as the head of household in her brother's absence, she remained attuned to any shift in demeanour. Emily glanced up at her sister and flashed a wide smile.

"No, mama and Richard were merely contemplating how to rid me from the house next year. Selling me off to a rich duke, you know. I suppose I would not object to that so very much. I believe I would make a fine duchess."

Clarice tittered as she strolled past her sister. "I can see it now, the dubious duchess!"

"Clarice!" Her mother chastised.

"And you will have to curtsy anytime I enter the room and call me your grace."

"God help us all!" Richard scoffed.

The door opened, and Carson announced dinner. The laughter continued as they made their way to the family dining room.

After the meal was completed, the countess stood intent on retreating to the blue saloon. Richard stood to observe their departure but abruptly interrupted, deciding to inform Miss Smith of his findings. He was not ready to disclose his concerns about her past but felt compelled to share enough to reassure her that he was progressing. It appeared the smallest bit of knowledge stimulated her memory, like the locket and the engraving within.

"Mama, I wish to speak with Leslie in private."

"Certainly, dear." She offered her daughters each a hand and proceeded to the blue parlour. The earl motioned her to the seat next to him. Aware of the staff beyond the nearby doors, he chose not to provide further cause for gossip. They were more than capable of ascertaining secrets in the normal process of servicing the household.

Richard pulled out the chair next to him, and she gracefully took her seat. Every move she made convinced him she had been well-schooled. Females were trained to be ladies; it was not instinct. Befriending females around the world, he easily deciphered the station of a woman by the manner in which she conducted herself, and he was not wrong in this case.

She folded her hands in her lap, and her vibrant violet-blue eyes fixed upon Richard as he settled again into his chair. Upon first setting eyes on him in Ireland, she found him quite handsome. But with the passage of time, his kindness and considerations complemented his attractive and refined appearance. He had shown great patience with her from the beginning.

He understood her fear of boarding the ship when they departed for England. Many gentlemen would have been annoyed and bullied her to comply or manhandled her onto the ship. But he had been gentle and considerate. He had become her protector, her memories, her connection to the world and now she was depending on him for safe passage to her past. The past with which she was uncertain she wished to return.

Richard's voice broke into her conceptions. "I have news from Dr Hanover and Bow Street. Some I shall not share. I hope you understand. Unless it is factual, I do not wish to cause hope or despair."

"I understand. Do you have upsetting news?"

"That depends on whether you choose to believe it, as the doctor most certainly does."

"Dr Hanover? But I have never seen him before?"

"Are you certain of it?"

Leslie respired and stared at Richard in disbelief. "Dr Hanover recognised me. He made no indication of it."

"I am aware." Richard placed his elbows on the table, lacing his fingers. "His questions gave me pause on several occasions. But when I returned to his office, he had a file of a young girl, maybe thirteen; he wasn't certain of her age. She was brought to his office by an older woman, dressed in servant's clothing, either a housekeeper or governess, he wasn't sure."

"Did they not provide him a name?" She was hesitant, not knowing if she wanted this knowledge.

"No, only the first name."

"And?"

"The woman called her Leslie. When the doctor asked for her last name, he was told it did not signify."

"What – what had happened to her?" The strain in Leslie's voice caused him to snap his head up to look at her.

"Do you remember? Tell me if you do."

"I do not, not really. It is only a feeling, but it is as though I detect what you are about to say before you do so."

"What am I going to say? Tell me."

Placing her hands to her temples, she began massaging them. She spread her fingers across her face, touching each side of her nose with her smallest, lowered her head and exhaled heavily.

"It is the headache again?" He asked quietly.

"Only a little." Pressing her fingers to her forehead again, trying to force away the pain.

Richard reached for one of her wrists, held it on the table, and began stroking the inside lightly with his thumb. It was a habit started in Ireland; it always seemed to calm her.

Leslie continued. "It is the reason he asked about my face, is it not? Had it been bruised."

She slowly brushed her free hand against her left cheek and circled it with her palm, then looked at Richard with tear-filled eyes. "Somehow, I know it's true. I do not remember it, not exactly, but - but it is like a dream when you awaken, unsure if it is real or not."

A tear rolled down her cheek. She quickly snatched the folded cotton serviette laying on the table and dried her tears.

"I can feel the swollen face, the dark purple colour of it, and it hurt…" she snapped her eyes to his, "Mrs Jenkins, her name is Mrs Jenkins, she was my governess."

Richard released her wrist and sat in silence, watching her as she desperately attempted to remember. Outrage was building at the idea of anyone striking this beautiful child, and why? He was more determined now than ever to find where she belonged. Not to take her back but to safely remove her from it. Taking her wrist, he removed the serviette and placed his hand over hers.

"I will never let anyone hurt you again, Leslie. I promise you, I will not!"

"I am not sure you can prevent it." She said dolefully.

"I have names from Bow Street." He interjected, wanting to turn the subject. Not that this conversation would be any better, but she had to know. "There is a runner, and he has several cases of runaway girls."

She looked up in surprise. "You think I ran away?" She studied his face carefully.

"Possibly! What I do know is that I do not trust Weber."

"The runner?"

"Yes, he is incredibly determined and proud, but he does have a file that may be you. I am afraid he is a danger to us. I will begin contacts tomorrow."

"You do not wish me to go with you, do you?" A sense of alarm swept across her face.

Richard witnessed the dilated pupils and panic. "No. I do not! My first duty is to rid us of this runner as soon as possible. I don't trust him. I cannot fully comprehend why, but my gut tells me he is dangerous."

He raised her hand to his lips and kissed the back of it. "I promise to do everything in my power to keep you safe."

When he released it, she returned them to the safety of her lap, never certain of his actions to console her. She had seen him comfort his little sister in much the same way. Whether he thought of her as a child who was alone and frightened or if there was more to his touch and comfort. She questioned how he perceived her; if he only saw her as a sister, or worse, as a mere child, she could not bear it. She was falling desperately in love with him.

"Thank you."

"I hope to interview them within a sennight and will continue to search for your grandmother."

"My grandmother? You said nothing of searching for her."

"I thought you knew I would attempt to locate her."

"Is she alive?"

"That is what we are to discover. If Leslie Marian Merrick still breathes, I hope to find her and link her children and children's children."

"Do you believe, she may be aware I am missing?"

"One never knows. It is amazing where paths might lead, especially those which are less travelled. It is the reason we dive into rabbit holes and leave no stone unturned." He gave her a grin.

She giggled and turned the subject once again. "Was your work dangerous in the war department?"

"Sometimes, yes!"

"Were all your assignments a success?"

"We weren't talking of me." He raised an eyebrow and grinned.

"I know. It seems all we talk of is me, and it is tiresome."

"Well, you are my assignment, and I must keep at it if I am to solve this mystery."

Leslie lowered her eyes... an assignment. Was that all she was to him? An assignment that was keeping him from his duties as the earl.

What did that mean anyway, duties of an earl? She smirked to herself. She had no idea what a man of noble birth did. It seemed to her all the aristocratic bachelors did was gamble, go to boxing matches, and race curricles and horses. She didn't understand the fascination of any of them.

"What will you do if you find my family? Will you just turn me over to them? There must be a reason I bolted." Her voice trembling, her eyes filled with uncertainty.

"Most certainly, I will not. I hope to learn more about them if I should find them. It is another reason I prefer to keep your whereabouts unknown. If your parents learn you are in London and demand your return, there would be little I can do to prevent it. The possibility of returning you to a dangerous situation is something I refuse to do. I will not ignore the fear you have in this town, and I no longer believe your nightmares are from the trauma of the shipwreck."

"Thank you." She lowered her eyes again. "Many times, I think no one believes me, even though everyone says they do. I wonder how anyone can believe such outrageousness. You cannot imagine how it feels."

Leslie seemed determined to force herself to remember her past. She must remember. Time was running out. Even tomorrow might be too late.

CHAPTER 13

Richard had no appetite to break his fast the following morning. He snatched a sweet biscuit from the sideboard and impatiently waited for his coffee to be poured. He unfolded the freshly ironed daily journal and placed it at his elbow. However, the attempt to read the paper failed. His thoughts consumed with the interviews planned for the day, so he left the periodical unread and fled to his study.

He ambled around his desk considering whether to send introductory letters to the families requesting interviews. It would be the proper thing, but most were not members of the aristocracy, so he reconsidered. Many were Nabobs and CITs, and he was not inclined to afford them the same protocol. He also was aware if they were prepared for his visit, he would lose his advantage.

The ability to manipulate people, especially when they were surprised, had always proven to his benefit. He was damn good at making those in his favour feel comfortable and the opposite for those he suspected of deception. His chameleon approach could be cold and intimidating, or he could charm the truth from others. All too often, he found the most agreeable were harbouring enemies of the Crown, some knowingly, some did not, some willingly, and others not so. Richard was skilled at unmasking a fraud. In many ways, he had grown cold and calculating. Emotion and compassion had no place in his life. Reflecting on many of his past indiscretions sickened him and were regretful. Nevertheless, in the majority of instances, it was his life or his adversary's, leaving him with only one choice.

A housemaid discreetly entered his study and began pulling back the heavy drapes. Richard winced and grunted at the sudden flood of light. Nervously and hastily, she tied the sashes, curtsied, and reeled to exit. The earl aware of the abrupt brightness paid little heed to the young girl, but habitually nodded as she left the room. Lost in his mission, he situated himself behind his mahogany desk retrieved the files tucked in a drawer and absorbed himself into his quest.

Arranged by importance and when they might receive callers, he glanced over them again for the hundredth time. The CITs and Nabobs could be visited early, but the peerage must be put off to the afternoon avoiding dressing gowns, breakfasts, and the lack of interest, along with possible refusals for interviews.

By late afternoon, Richard had withdrawn two girls from his list. There had not been enough information on either file to remove without consideration. However, upon being received amicably by both families, he was certain neither was his ward.

The earl elected to postpone his next visit until the following day. Examining the documents in the carriage, he preferred to interrogate Mr. Jameson early in the morning. The information Weber had gathered was sparse. Yet it had been the only one that was truly favourable.

George Jameson was an extremely wealthy Nabob. He recalled an odd statement Weber had mumbled at Bow Street... "thought I had a donkey." When he inquired its meaning from Jonathon, his Tiger looked shocked. He explained to his master it was a vulgar term used for extracting blunt from a fellow without doing much for it. In his Tiger's opinion, it was as bad as thievery.

After an early dinner, he made his way to White's. His conversational skills were growing weary. He required assistance keeping four females entertained without the evening becoming a dead bore.

His closest companions, Sheffield, and Worthington, both unmarried and adverse to the idea of being leg shackled were always ready and willing to accept invitations which included a meal.

They were rarely seen at balls or other gatherings avoiding the marriage-seeking mamas but if they did attend, it was to establishments renowned for providing nectareous late-night suppers. The Gillford House with its renowned French Chef, Renee' and his lovely sisters, an invitation would not be turned down. Now with three charming young ladies, plus the delectable French cook, they only enquired which evening.

After confirming the engagement, they tossed back a few tankards of ale and reviewed the betting books. Richard retired early, not wanting a case of hot coppers when meeting with the Nabob, who was so willing to throw away a fortune to locate his runaway daughter.

***

The following morning at the ungodly hour of eight o'clock, the hired coach ordered was waiting in front of #6 Upper Brook Street. Richard knew better than to arrive in his coach or curricle. Either mode of transportation would find closed mouths and uncooperative staff.

Twenty minutes later, the earl raised the knocker at the Jameson resident and let it drop. He tugged at his cravat, pulled down his waistcoat and cleared his throat. Just as he rolled his shoulders to stand straight and tall, a grey-haired elderly man opened the door.

"State your business." The crusty old butler grated, showing no sign of affability or refinement.

"I am with the war department; I am here to speak with Mr. Jameson."

The only change in the head servant's countenance was his eyes, as they widened, but only a bit.

"The war department?" He stammered.

"In service to his majesty," Hawthorn added boastfully for effect as he presented his card.

It was apparent the butler had no idea what to make of this and was uncertain how to respond. He stood in silence for a moment, obviously considering his options. Realising he had none, retreated a little and opened the door, ushering Richard into the adjacent parlour before closing it behind him.

"I will inquire if the master is in."

"Inform him it is of the greatest importance... to the Crown."

"Yes, sir." The servant eyed him curiously, turned and sauntered down the hallway.

Richard looked over the room. It didn't appear to have been touched for years. The furnishings were old and outdated. The furniture's fabric was worn, and the dark velvet drapes faded.

His back was to the closed door, but he heard the shuffling of feet and turned as a portly man, rather short with a dishevelled appearance entered. His hair was thin and didn't appear to have been trimmed in some time. His face was clean-shaven, the only sign of neatness or cleanliness for that matter. His lordship stood silently, waiting for an acknowledgement.

"I say, old boy, what's this nonsense about the war department and daring to intrude into a man's home at this hour? Who the devil do you think you are?"

"I am Richard Hawthorn. I am on an assignment for the war department."

"Yes, yes, that is what my man implied. Declare what business you have with me. I've never been in service to the military or had any dealings with it. So, state the matter and be off. I've no time for such foolishness."

Annoyed by the pompous old man and the possibility of who he might be, Richard cleared his throat and ignored the rudeness. "I beg your pardon, sir, but I have reason to believe you may be searching for a young girl." He figured to disarm him immediately.

The old man's shoulders slumped as he drew further into the room. He offered his caller a chair, which Richard almost declined, but he had caught the man off guard and wished to maintain his advantage. Reluctantly, he took a seat.

Jameson took the seat across from him and sat in silence for a moment. He seemed to be gathering his thoughts. "A young girl, you say?"

"Yes. It was my understanding your daughter went missing several months ago."

The man attempted to hide his anxiousness, but it was obvious he wanted more information, much more.

"Have you found her?" He said with a shaky voice.

"That is contingent on various facts. That is why I am here."

"Is she alive?"

Good God, what a question! Although unprepared for such a question, he remained composed and confirmed, "yes, but she is not well."

The old man sat up and leaned forward, eager for more information. "Where is she? I need to see her and surmise if she is mine."

"That is not possible."

"Why not?" Indignant, the man reclined, his voice booming. "If she is my daughter, I want her returned immediately. She belongs to me, no matter her condition. I will have your head for this defiance."

Now, he was getting somewhere. It was the first sign the pieces may be falling into place. He had to choose his words carefully.

"It is difficult, sir. She was in a shipwreck, and we have not established if she is your child."

"A shipwreck?" Jameson straightened. "It can't possibly be my girl. She's never left England in her life. Pardon my outburst and ignore any offence. I am desperate."

"Yes. This girl appears to be some sixteen years of age. She left Ramsgate, England, on the Sea Horse in late January."

"The Sea Horse? The merchant ship carrying the military brigade that sunk off the coast of Ireland?"

"The very same, sir."

"Can't be my daughter. I have no contacts in the military… wait." he paused, "Unless that young man…" He broke off.

"What young man?"

"N-nothing." He waved his arm, then began rubbing his chin.

"Sir, this girl is not well, and we need to find her family. If there is a possibility, she is your daughter, we need to discover it. Do you have a painting or likeness? I have seen her and might recognise it." It was the truth; he had seen her in Waterford, where he intended to imply, she remained.

Jameson appeared to question his motives, but the mention of the military regiment had raised some sort of doubt. The man turned to his steward, who was standing at the door and flicked his wrist. The butler immediately left the room.

"My servant will retrieve it. Now, when can I meet the girl?"

Richard methodically chose his words, wanting to keep the man unsteady but maintain his interest and in no way give him to believe she was in London.

"She was found by Catholic missionaries outside Waterford, Ireland. She was unconscious for weeks after being adrift at sea. It will take some time for her to recover."

"Why was she not returned to England?"

"To be sure, if it was certain this was where she belonged, we would have done so as quickly as possible. You must understand, sir, the knowledge of where she belongs is unclear and until it is confirmed."

"What do you mean, did she not tell you?"

"She is unable to do so." He must tread cautiously with this knowledge. He had an uncomfortable feeling about this man. Cordial enough, he was but there was something about his regard not to be trusted.

"What do you mean? The chit can't talk, struck dumb?"

What an arrogant old man. The earl had taken an instant dislike to Jameson, and the man was doing nothing to redeem himself and did not care to do so.

"As I said before, she remains quite ill, and the trauma of the wreck has left her…not despondent but detached."

"Oh!"

But Richard did not believe the man cared about her health at all. The injuries to this girl did not seem to signify. It was unsettling particularly if she were possibly his daughter. Any difficulties seemed of little interest to him. His only desire was to have his possession returned.

"The war department is responsible, and until there is a confirmation of family, they must take the necessary action to benefit the girl, along with the department."

"Of course, the Crown wouldn't dare spend an extra farthing, with which there was no need, rightly so."

Such arrogance, he displayed. Reminding himself of his position and to appear impartial in the matter. Afterall, he was simply the investigator.

The butler returned with a small item in hand, all the while intently watching Jameson, who gestured toward his visitor.

141

Taking the miniature surreptitiously not checking it straight away, Richard must withhold any change in countenance. This was not a highly intelligent man, but neither was he a fool.

He slowly and deliberately turned the miniature over. He furrowed his brow, it wasn't Leslie, but damn it to hell, the likeness was striking. He studied it, reaching for his quizzing glass, taking his time, contemplating an acceptable response.

"This is not her." He said unwavering. "This is a woman, not a girl."

"Of course, it isn't a girl. Any fool can see that!" Jameson barked, "It's her mother, but she looks remarkably like her."

"Awww!" It was all he could manage. His wheels were turning so quickly he was afraid he would be unable to think clearly.

"The girl is quite ill, drawn, but even with the age difference…." He broke off.

It wasn't Leslie, that much was true, and she had changed drastically from the first time he had seen her. He returned the miniature to Jameson.

The butler reached for it, and the old man snatched it to his side with disdain. The servant immediately stood and returned to the door. The entire exchange between the two was odd.

The earl remained silent, observing Jameson with the miniature. He was staring at it, rubbing his thumb across it, then clutching it with a tight fist.

"How long has she been dead?" Richard broke the silence.

"What makes you think she's dead?" Jameson snapped angrily.

"I beg your pardon. The way you…"

"Nearly ten years." Inhaling deeply, his expression softened a little.

"I am sorry." Richard said, studying the man, and he did not like the instability he saw in the man's eyes.

Jameson's stern grimace returned quickly.

"It doesn't signify. She wasn't the sort of wife anyone would hope for." He snarled.

In those few words, Richard had found what he was seeking and decided he should take his leave before revealing more.

"I regret to have wasted your time, sir, and I do appreciate your patience. I will take my leave now. I have many more families to interview. The war department is anxious to relieve themselves of this child, and I must finish my assignment."

Jameson said nothing nor did he look up, as the earl stood. He only flicked his wrist in annoyance and stared into what Richard could only describe as darkness.

The butler silently escorted him to the door. However, when the servant presented his coat and hat, he slipped a missive inside the headpiece. When the earl lifted his gaze to meet the butler's, he was met with only a blank expression. He donned his hat, secured the note, and took his leave.

Once settled in the carriage, he removed his topper and opened the message.

"Drive to the corner of Wells and Castle Streets. Wait fifteen minutes, and I will come along. Say nothing."

Accustomed to clandestine rendezvous, Gillford thought little of it and its request. He instructed the driver to make his way to the intersection and pull up the horses. After ten minutes of shuffling through papers, Richard examined the pedestrians. Most were housekeepers, maids, and other servants proceeding to the costermongers lined up on the nearby street.

An elderly woman making her way up Wells Street, carried no basket for goods or a reticule. She wore a dark grey coat with a rather large hood, which was pulled over her head for a bonnet. She meticulously surveyed her surroundings, looking one way and then the other. Hawthorn watched with interest; certain this was his messenger. Drawing open the door without pause or hesitation, she climbed inside and quietly closed it behind her. She glanced up at the earl as she pushed back her hood. "I beg your pardon, but I cannot be seen in your presence."

Richard studied her manner of dress, recognising it to be one of a servant, but it gave no indication of station. She was unmoved by the impropriety of leaping into a stranger's equipage and had little problem taking control of the conversation.

"Thank you for waiting. I must speak with you, sir. I am Mrs Jenkins."

An icy chill coursed through his veins. The startling revelation left the Crown's esteemed spy dumbfounded. Yet, his training and skills did not betray him. Outwardly, he exhibited no sign of name recognition, but inside his body convulsed; he willed himself to breathe normally.

"Mr Jameson's housekeeper and the wife of the butler who passed along my missive." She continued.

Richard only nodded. Startled he was unsure what to make of this intercourse. The one person he never imagined locating now sat across from him in the seclusion and privacy of a hackney. He could ask anything he liked but thought better of it. He chose to allow the woman to speak her peace.

"Am I to understand you think you may have found Leslie."

Not wanting to confirm the information, he was fastidious with his words.

"I am not at all certain of it, ma'am."

"Mr. Hawthorn, that is your name, is it not?"

"Yes."

"Mr Jameson is a fool and, if I may speak freely, also quite balmy!"

Richard was taken aback. Why would anyone continue to work for someone they believed to be insane? But he was not well-versed in the customs and choices of household staff. So, he refrained from comment.

"But I assure you, my husband is not. It is his profession to read people without question. He believes you did recognise the miniature and thank the good lord above; you did not say so." She heaved a sigh and appeared to settle.

Hawthorn, also an expert, was beginning to understand the imperturbability of the butler.

Unaware of his attachment to Leslie, the housekeeper continued as if the identity had been confirmed. "It is the reason my husband and I have stayed in the Jameson house. You see, we protected Leslie for years and have grown quite attached to her. It is for her safety we remain. In the horrid event, she is returned to him."

"Is she in danger there?" For the first time in months, he was to learn something of importance regarding his ward.

Mrs. Jenkins had no qualms in divulging her thoughts regarding her master. "Mr Jameson is not in his right mind. Oh, he seems well enough, as long as his wife, God rest her soul, or his daughter is not mentioned. He conducts his business and runs his household with little interference."

"It appears to me you and your husband are responsible for the smooth running of domestic matters." Richard discerned.

"Thank you, we do our best. Most of the time, it is quite easy with only Mr. Jameson to care for. He never has guests or business associates. Other than the house being in disrepair, there is not much to do. But never mind that. I cannot linger, and it is Leslie of which I am most concerned. If this girl is our dear child, you must never advise her father of it. If she does return to England, which God in heaven, I pray she does not, he will find her and bring her back and lock her away again."

"Lock her away?" Hawthorn was struggling to restrain his temper. "What do you mean?"

"He kept her locked in that house and many times in her room. I was the only one allowed to spend time with her. I was to teach her only what a well-bred female needs taught and prepare her for adulthood."

"You did more than that, did you not?"

"Indeed, I did! I taught her everything I could. Knowledge, especially for a young lady, is powerful. She is well-read, fluent in French, exceedingly knowledgeable in history and is excellent with numbers. She is bright and learns quickly. She was taught proper behaviour and can manage under any circumstance." Mrs. Jenkins lowered her eyes. "We were employed in a fine house of the peerage before Mr Jameson offered us a sinful amount of money to come work for him. I was only the governess then. I sometimes wish we had not taken his greedy offer, but then where would our poor Miss be had we not stayed to protect her."

"Mrs. Jenkins, do you know what happened to Leslie?"

"No, not really. She told me someone who had known of her situation promised to take her away. But she would not divulge the name. I have no idea how anyone could have been in contact with her, but it appears someone did. She said it would be safer if I did not have any information and not to worry if one day she was gone. She knew Mr. Jameson's wrath would come down upon my head if he thought I knew anything about her escape. At the time, I did not question it. Now, of course, I regret it."

"Are you the one who took her to Dr Hanover?"

The older woman's eyes shot to his. "You've spoken with Dr Hanover?"

"Yes, I have."

"I am, but I did not give her name nor mine." She said curiously.

"I am aware. He was of little help because of it."

"I am sorry, but you do not understand. Mr. Jameson, he…" she broke off.

"Did he inflict the bruises?"

She looked up at Richard with such sadness there was no need to answer.

"It is all right, Mrs Jenkins. Is there anything else you can tell me that might help Leslie, if indeed this girl, is she?"

He noticed she was sniffling and attempting to hold back tears.

"Do not allow her to return to England, and I beg of you, do not bring her to London. He will find her and drag her back. He had never intended to let her out of that house."

"Why?"

She hesitated, but it was obvious to Hawthorn this woman had been carrying grief and despair in her heart for months.

"You see," she paused, "God forgive me," she looked up to the heavens. "He – he, when the evening comes, he seems to go out of his head. He speaks to his wife as if she is alive. I think he has been unsteadied for some time. But after Mrs Jameson tried to take her and leave, he was completely unhinged. He accused her of cuckolding him, which may have been true. I don't know and couldn't blame her if she did. But he locked her up and called his personal doctor. It wasn't long before she took gravely ill and died. No one ever indicated why or how. Things seemed fine whilst Leslie was young. But as she grew older, the more she looked like her mother. He went wild with rage and locked her in her room. I fear what he might do to her if she is returned now. Mr. Hawthorn," she stopped and with haunting eyes stared into his. "I believe, somewhere in his broken mind, he thinks she is her mother. Truly, I do. You cannot bring her back to London. Please, I beg of you."

Richard reached across the carriage, took her hand, and squeezed it as she wiped away her tears with the other. This woman cared deeply for Leslie, to the extent she and her husband remained in an unbearable situation to protect her. He wanted to assure her the girl was safe and protected, however, he did not dare risk it. He could only hope the questions and his answers had been enough for her to decipher she was safe and protected.

"I promise, if my ward is Leslie, I will not allow her in London."

"Thank you." She leaned forward to exit but fell back again. "I nearly neglected to mention, he still pays people to search for her. They roam the streets, and the Bow Street runner is still in his employ. He came again yesterday. So please do not trust anyone."

Interesting, but not at all shocking information, but he gave no response. He raised his head to step out of the carriage, and Mrs Jenkins stopped him.

"You mustn't! I cannot be seen with you. If I am recognised, no one can confirm with whom I was conversing. Thank you again." The housekeeper alighted from the carriage and swiftly headed down the street.

Richard banged on the side of the yellow post chaise, and the horses moved out. His mind was reeling from the information he had just received. He had to remove Leslie from London. He wasn't as concerned about the ruffians in search of her, but this runner was going to be a problem. Childs had said he was one of his best, a seasoned hunter. He feared he would soon come under his watchful eye, believing wherever the earl was to be found, Leslie would not be far. Damn ruffians and damn the runner… Jameson must be using all his money to try to find his daughter.

CHAPTER 14

As soon as Richard reached #6 Brook Street, he thrust the ribbons at Jonathon, bolted up the steps and nearly bowled over Carson upon entering the foyer.

"Pardon me, my lord." The butler scrambled out of his way, rather shaken.

The earl tossed off his coat and hat and hurled them at Carson.

"Mother in the blue?"

"Yes, sir." The muffled sound came from under the riding coat.

Richard flew up the stairs and flung open the doors to find his mother alone on the far side of the drawing room. He straightened his waistcoat and ran his hands through his hair.

"Mother!" Drawing her attention as he hurried across the floor.

"Oh!" she glanced up a little startled. "Yes, dear?" Overwhelmed by his anxious and swift strides, she put aside her needlework.

"I must make some arrangements. I need to remove Leslie from London immediately. I hate to ask Clarice to cut her season short, but the season will be over in a few short weeks."

"Richard, I don't believe I have ever seen you so agitated. Whatever has happened?"

"I have some information, and I should have shared it with you before. I should have told you about Leslie's grandmother."

"You found her grandmother?" She moved to the edge of the chair but did not stand.

"No, but I have her name, Merrick?"

As soon as he said the name, the countess clasped her hand to her mouth nearly losing her breath. "Mary Merrick!" she gasped as her past flooded back to her.

"No, Leslie Merrick." He looked at his mother curiously.

"No, no dear, Leslie's mother was Mary. Oh, dear Lord, Richard, she's Marian Merrick's daughter." She was misty-eyed. "She looks exactly like her. Exactly!"

"You knew her mother?" He poured himself a brandy and downed it swiftly, then returned to his mother.

"When we were young." His mother began, "Surely, you remember the Merricks. They are from Kent. Well, maybe you do not. We lived most of your young life in London, then you were off. But your father and I were both from Kent. We still have a cottage in Sevenoaks with a couple who tend it for us. You ought to remember, we took summers there on occasion. The Merricks were dear friends. You must know her husband Admiral Merrick."

"Admiral Merrick was her grandfather?"

"Yes. Mary was their only daughter, and we spent much of our childhood together."

"What do you know of her husband?" Richard asked.

"Not much of anything. You see, Mary ran away with him." She glanced down and then back up to her son's face and frowned. "One of those girls you spoke of the other evening.

"Oh, I see!" The earl leered at his empty glass, but moved closer to the countess, needing information more than a drink.

"He took her off to India, you see, where he made a ridiculous amount of money, doing whatever it is those Nabobs do to make their fortune."

"What was the cause of her death?" He interrupted.

"I'm afraid, I don't know. You see, when she returned to England, she was shunned by the peerage. I tried to send her messages, but none were ever acknowledged. Before your grandmother passed, she saw Lady Merrick, and she was devastated by her death and said little about it. She told Mama she had tired of her husband and had planned to leave. She was to come to her parents, and she intended to bring her children. That's all she told mama."

"Children?" Richard looked disconcerted.

"Those were your grandmother's words." She assured him.

"How many and what were their ages?"

"I'm sorry, but I only knew Mary and nothing of her children. Our poor Leslie is Mary's daughter. I knew I recognised that child!" She clasped her hands in her lap, gazing up melancholic.

"So, Leslie may have siblings?" Richard was staring at his mother in disbelief. If so, what happened to them and where were they? This made no sense; Jameson mention no other children. He only had the daughter, or at least it seemed so.

This morning, he had very few details and in less than a few hours, he had pieced together a sizable amount of information. But what it meant for everyone's future was still in question.

"Perhaps. As I say, those were your grandmother words, if my recollection is correct. I would think you would be obliged to speak with Lady Merrick to be certain."

"She's still alive!" Richard looked at his mother, surprised.

"Oh, my goodness, yes. She still lives in Kent. At least, I assume she still does."

Moving to the sideboard, he poured another glass of brandy, only because it was the strongest thing in the cabinet. He was in desperate need of something powerful.

"Be so kind as to pour your mother some sherry, or ring for some hartshorn, but I am not certain there is any to be found in the house." The countess extended her arm, obviously unsettled.

Richard handed his mother a cordial of sherry. She stared at the minuscule amount of liquid in the delicate vessel, and raised an eyebrow, believing her son had grossly underestimated her need for something stronger.

The earl tossed back his head and drained his. Soothing as it was, his mind was still working out the details of his next course of action and could not have sworn on his life to its contents. Should he take Leslie to her grandmother, would it be safe?

With that sleazy Weber slithering about, it must be done without delay. Richard had no doubt he would be pursuing her relentlessly and would no doubt return her immediately to her father, no matter the danger. People meant nothing to the reprobate.

"Are the girls in their rooms?" He returned his thoughts to the matter at hand.

"No, dear, they went to the new hat shop. You know the one, Emily had to have that bonnet. Clarice took them with your missive."

God, he had forgotten about the new shop and the letter he had sent with Clarice for an account.

"How long have they been gone?" Richard did not like the idea of Leslie out of the house without him, not now.

"Most of the afternoon, I would say. They should be returning soon." His mother assured him.

The earl walked to the front window, his legs apart, hands clasped behind his back. He surveyed the pedestrians up and down Upper Brooks Street in search of the familiar gaiety of three bright, cheerful girls.

He downed another snifter of the amber liquor, then turned back to his mother, placing the glass on the cabinet. "I shall try to find them." He ambled toward the door.

"Richard, what is wrong?" His mother was aware he was more than concerned, he was troubled.

"Nothing." With Leslie beyond his reach his anxiety was at its peak. "I don't believe."

"That expression is familiar to me. Pray, tell me." She demanded.

He faced his mother. She had eased to the edge of her chair once more and waited for the explanation he was contemplating how to convey.

"There is a Bow Street runner searching for her." Halfway across the room, he avoided his mother's judgmental eyes.

"What? Oh, dear Lord. Why?"

"Her father hired him."

"Her father?" she respired. "Oh, Richard, it is imperative we find her and remove her to safety. If everything they've said of him is true... oh dear. I had not considered it. I only think of the Merricks, and I suppose he has every right to her. But unless he has changed."

"He has not! From what I've been told of him, he is worse. I saw him today and I believe it to be true."

"Oh, dear God!" She placed one hand on her bosom and the other swishing at him. "Go, go, in search of them."

As he hurried across the parlour, a commotion was coming from the front entry. The countess and Richard recognised the hysterical cries of his older sister.

His mother sprang from her chair and rushed toward the door. Clarice was shouting as she ran up the stairs. Upon reaching the landing, she was wild-eyed, breathless, and shrieking uncontrollably.

"Oh, Richard, something dreadful has happened." She screeched and fell into her brother's arms.

"Where are Leslie and Emily?" Richard took her by the shoulders, pulling her away from his chest. As much to comfort her as to keep her focused.

"I don't know." She cried, panting and wheezing.

"What do you mean you don't know." Richard's voice had raised an octave, giving her shoulders a shake.

"Exactly as I have said. I cannot find them."

Clarice's eyes welled up with tears. She trembled and struggled to speak as Richard's grip unconsciously tightened around her shoulders.

Lady Gillford realised she must assert herself over the rapidly deteriorating situation before it spiralled into chaos. She snapped at both of her older children and gestured them further into the room. They had to regain a sense of calm if they were to understand any of the details that had placed her daughter and Leslie apparently into danger.

"Richard, pour your sister some brandy, and you might as well fill three glasses."

The countess guided her daughter to the settee, as the earl hastily filled and delivered the glasses. Clarice sipped hers as her mother encouraged her to take deep breaths. Richard downed his, then knelt in front of his sister, his stomach in knots.

"What happened, Clarice?" Somewhat in control, he took his sister's hand. He must obtain the needed information without upsetting her further.

"We were walking down Bond Street, and this man approached us. He introduced himself, but of course, none of us acknowledged him, as it was improper behaviour. Then he said he was a Bow Street runner."

155

"Oh no!" The countess gasped.

Richard's breath caught and his grip tightened around Clarice's hand as she continued. "Leslie squeezed my arm tightly, clearly afraid. Emily was holding her other hand, and I only assume she did the same. He said he needed to speak with whichever one of us was Leslie."

"Oh, dear God!" their mother cried, taking another sip of the amber liquid.

"Well, you know Emily," his sister glanced at her mother exasperated, "she does not have an ounce of common sense and immediately pipes up, confessing she was Leslie. She began castigating him, saying he had no right to address her directly as they had not been properly introduced. Then he reached to grab her by the arm, and when he did, Leslie jerked her backwards. That is when I stepped in between them. I told them to run, and I stomped on his foot and hit him in the stomach with my reticule. He tried to manoeuvre past me, and I – I," she hesitated glancing down at the clenched fists in her lap, splayed them, stretching her fingers. "I am sorry, mama, but I threw myself at him, hat, skirt, and all and knocked us both to the ground.

Two burly men nearby assumed he was accosting me. They rushed to help, and as you can imagine, it took him a while to explain himself to the other gentlemen. But it was long enough for the girls to get away. But then I could not find them, nor which direction they fled. I was hoping they would have come home. But I see they have not. Oh, Richard, I am sorry."

"No, no, at least you are safe." The very idea of his tall, disproportioned sister blocking a Bow Street runner to the ground was impressive. "It's the one-time, your inordinate height served you well."

Clarice tried to smile at the acknowledgement of at least providing the escape. "Oh, Richard, we must find them."

The earl nodded, but his thoughts were racing and was wearing a path in the rug in front of his sister. "Does Emily have friends whom she might seek for safety?"

"You know how she has become. The less she shares, the less we can interfere. She has many friends, but I have only met a few of them." Still visibly shaken, Clarice took another sip of brandy at her brother's direction.

Lady Gillford returned to a nearby chair. "Richard, do you think it was the same runner you spoke of?" Her face pale and worried.

"I am afraid so, mother. As I told you, I did not like Weber from the moment I met him…"

"Dear God, that was his name!" Clarice responded nearly screeching again but was ignored, as she clutched the amber coloured liquid and sipped again.

"He is the reason I decided to remove Leslie from London. But how did he find her? I shared with no one she had returned from Ireland, not even Sir Childs. He warned me this runner was the best he had, even if he was despicable."

It suddenly occurred to him; that the man must have decided to watch the house. It did not take a Bow Street Runner to locate the Gillford House.

"Damn it, for the first time in my life, I have allowed personal feelings to interfere with an investigation. It has made me slip and now I've placed Leslie in more danger."

Richard reeled around and threw his half-empty glass into the fireplace. It shattered against the stone back of the firebox, and when the flames licked the brandy, the fire flared, sparked, and crackled.

The sudden sound of exploding glass and the flash of fire startled his mother and sister and they both jumped in their seat.

As soon as the countess collected herself, she stood and met her son, enveloping his arm with her own. "Richard, it is not your fault. You cannot help the way you feel, and the girls had no idea they would be in danger, especially during daylight hours on Bond Street."

"I ought to have, I was careless. I told myself I was becoming too involved, and I allowed it anyway." Richard covered his face, then massaged his forehead with a thumb and middle finger.

"At least they are together. Emily knows Mayfair and everyone in it. She has saved herself from many scrapes over the last few years as much as it has brought me much frustration. I am sure she has found safety with someone."

"I am going to send messages to Sheffield and Worthington; they will help in the search. I wish I knew where to begin. Why did they not come home? God help me if I run across Weber, I will kill him with my bare hands."

"Richard, I will go with you. Maybe I will think of where she might have gone."

"Mother, if the girls return before we return, direct Jonathon for us. I will leave him the curricle; he will find me."

His mother nodded and suggested Clarice might want to change her dress. She was dirty and unkempt after her wrestling match with the runner. She brushed her hands down her skirts and assured her brother, that she only wished to wash her face and obtain a new pair of gloves and bonnet. Richard agreed, and she dashed upstairs.

The earl rang for Carson, and upon his swift arrival, he presented Richard with quill, inkwell, and parchment. Hawthorn raised his eyes to his butler. Did this man, overhear every word? It appeared, even out of sight, the butler's ears remained nearby. Even in his distress, he chuckled at the ever-attentive servant. He quickly scribbled two quick notes to his friends.

The earl was in the foyer being helped into his coat and slipping on his gloves when Clarice descended the staircase. She was pulling on a fresh pair, as Carson stood with her cloak at the ready.

They made their way down Upper Brook Street, past Grosvenor Square and continued on, checking the nooks and corners, questioning each acquaintance they passed. When Richard and Clarice approached Hanover Square, he halted.

"Thank God!" He whispered.

"What?" His sister looked at him curiously.

"It's Sheffield and Worthington."

CHAPTER 15

Emily now leading the escape, flew around the corner, dragging Leslie in her wake. Recognising a familiar shop from earlier in the day, she dashed inside and quickly moved to the back of the establishment. Out of breath, both girls stooped behind a table stacked with linens.

"Oh, Emily! Why did you do such a thing?" Leslie scolded.

"What?" The younger sister looked at her, a bit vexed, and still winded.

"Why did you tell that awful man you were me? He could have taken you."

"Oh no, he would not." She boasted, then paused. "Well, if he had, he would have soon let me go. I was hoping you would run away, but I did not think of you dragging me with you. But thank you! At least now I will not worry about you. I can get us to safety."

"We must go home. Richard will be worried, and if Clarice returns without us, everyone will be distressed."

"No! We can't go home." Emily was shocked at the very idea. "Use your head, Leslie. If that man is searching for you. He more than likely knows where we live, and he will go there first thing. We can't go back there."

"Emily! How are we to do otherwise? We have little choice." Impatiently, Leslie stared at the young girl wondering where her head must be.

"Do not be silly." Emily had regained her breath and was contemplating. "I have plenty of friends that will help us. All I need do is think of who we can trust to do such a thing."

The girls remained in the shop behind the pile of linens for some time. The shopkeeper, a kindly old gentleman, observed their dash into his store. Now their peculiar behaviour was worrisome, so he decided to approach them.

He recognised the girls from their earlier visit. "Is there some way I may assist you ladies?" The short and stocky man had a friendly face and a genuine smile.

Emily stood and brushed off her skirt, turned to the man severely, as if she had aged into maturity in the past ten minutes and was now an adult in charge and would act the part.

"Maybe you can." She decided. "An odious man was bothering us, and we rushed into your shop for safety."

"He did not follow you inside, did he?" The man asked, suddenly alarmed.

"Oh no, you know how street ogres and beggars are. Once we reached a place of safety, he ran away." She flicked her wrist and was as calm as the morning breeze.

"Thank goodness. Did you not have another lady with you earlier? A rather tall girl?" He questioned.

"Yes, that was my sister, and I am afraid we have lost her in the commotion." She said, still holding her shoulders erect and attempting a look of well-bred sophistication. Leslie thought she looked a bit silly but said nothing.

The man looked sincerely concerned and anxious about these two young girls being left quite alone.

"What can I do?"

"Do you have a messenger in your employ?" Emily suddenly knew who she must summon.

"Yes, yes, I do."

"If you would be so kind to have him, send a missive. I shall have someone come for us in a carriage." She declared exuding an air of unwavering confidence.

"A wise choice. Follow me and I will take you to my wife in the apartment at the rear of the store, she will prepare some tea whilst you wait."

"Oh, that would be lovely." Emily chortled.

The runner had terrified Leslie and was astonished at how Emily took control of the outrageous circumstances. She could only shudder in disbelief. She listened in awe to the effortlessly crafted tale, in which the young girl successfully and easily convinced the shopkeeper. She appeared completely unfazed by the situation in which they had found themselves.

They followed the merchant, who made quick introductions to his wife and told their disturbing story. The kind-hearted elderly woman gathered the girls around the table, brushed the chairs of with her apron and placed the teapot to boil.

With quill, inkwell and parchment at hand, Emily quickly scribbled the missive, and the milliner called the delivery boy, as she dusted it with a sprinkle of sand. She provided the address, along with specific instructions.

"Now when the butler indicates he will pass the missive along to his master, which he will. You make it clear you will wait for an answer. Tell him it is of the most importance; we must be assured the viscount receives it immediately."

Leslie was astonished by how readily the young girl devised such a plan. Then so easily summoned a viscount. A viscount? Goodness! Apparently, Emily was accustomed to weaving tales to achieve her wishes. Leslie's only concern was Richard's reaction, he had been confident that no one was aware of her returning to London. But evidently, this runner had discovered it. She had already determined her need to leave London, even if alone. Upon reflection, if Emily indeed had a plan, she might as well go along.

Recalling the stories the earl had shared of Emily's scrapes in recent years, Leslie was beginning to understand how they occurred. The young lady's mind seemed to make snap decisions, and then it was like a puzzle for her to unravel. Leslie was confident that Emily had never considered she might actually be in peril.

This was no jest, and she was well aware of it, even if Emily did not. The young girl appeared to be completely oblivious to any type of danger. Life was one devilish adventure after another. "God help me," Leslie pondered, "I have to regain my memory." She possessed pieces, but at present they were alone and in danger. It was no crucial to put them together. She had placed someone else in jeopardy.

It was imperative they get word to Richard, but how? He was the only person she truly trusted, and they desperately needed him. He alone understood the reality of her danger.

The wife of the milliner sat with the young ladies, enjoying their second serving of tea and cakes, when the delivery boy burst through the door, gasping for breath. He bound to have run the entire way.

"Aye, I deliwered' da' missive mum and' you wuz right 'bout dat butler, cagy one 'e wuz. But 'e deliwered it to da viscount and 'e said to tell de youn' lady, de viscount 'ould be 'ere directly, 'e would."

"Oh, I knew he would come." Emily clasped her hands together in delight. "Everything will be quiet right and tight shortly. As soon as George arrives, he will take us to safety."

The sixteen-year-old produced a huge, childlike grin, feeling quite pleased with herself. She sat back in the chair, took another bite of her cake, and giggled.

Leslie rolled her eyes, sighed, and inhaled a deep breath. Oh Lord, where was Richard? She was placing her safety in the hands of a precocious child. God help them! She hadn't been able to eat a bite and was still very uncertain about her future. The only dependable person she knew was unavailable to her and now she was forced to rely on his wayward sister. It was

163

apparent Emily would either lead them out of this adversity or they would be in far deeper than she dared her imagination to wander.

Within the hour, the tinkle of the front doorbell was heard, and the milliner left the back to greet his latest customer. "Good afternoon, can I be of service to ye' me lord."

"Well, I suppose maybe you can, and then again maybe you can't. You see, I was told to bring myself to this address and make it quick. I have a young friend who seems to find herself in scrapes quite often, and I fear she has gone and done it again. Brunette, about this short." The viscount raised his arm, extending his hand just about his shoulder height.

"Well, sir, I just might be the one to help ya. I am not quite sure about it. If you will wait just a moment."

The milliner was headed to the back when he saw the younger girl peeping over one of his display cases. He wasn't exactly sure what to do, so he halted. She waved her hand to the side, motioning to him. He stared at her strangely, and she made the motion again. He realised he was between her and the gentleman and needed him to step aside where she could make out if it was her friend.

As the customer came into Emily's view, she stood quickly and called out, "Oh George, it is you. I am so happy you are here. Come quickly! Oh, do hurry, George."

The young nobleman was perplexed as ever and gave her a disgruntled look but headed her way just the same. He was a tall, a bit on the thin side, typical of being caught somewhere between a boy and a man. His dress easily gave him away as a distinguished dandy of the Ton. Tan knee breeches, gleaming top boots, ruffled cuffs with a white muslin shirt, collar stiffly pressed, an impeccable waterfall tied cravat, brightly coloured waistcoat, deep brown tailcoat, and a taller-than-normal beaver top hat. "Emily?"

164

She snatched his hand, practically pulling him off his feet and ushered him to the back, where Leslie and the milliner's wife were waiting. Emily quickly made introductions, then turned her attention to George.

"Oh George, you must help us." She chortled.

"What the devil sort of fix have you gotten yourself into this time, Emilia?" the viscount removing his hat and holding it under his arm.

"Oh, George, don't be cross with me. It was simply unavoidable." She pouted her lips.

"It always is, Emily." He appeared doubtful and shrugged his lightly padded shoulders.

"Please, George, I do hope you can be of assistance."

"What the deuce have you done now?"

The viscount, barely twenty years old, had inherited his title five years before. His father had taken a spill from a horse and broken his neck. He had been forced to grow up quickly. But with the guidance of dependable and honest estate managers, along with his indulgent uncle as a trustee, he was set. He was not seduced by vices that enticed so many of the young nobles his age and was extremely interested in the estate running. Yet he maintained his youthfulness when it came to his friends. Emily had been one of those companions since childhood. Due to his access to somewhat unlimited funds from his trustee, he had become her saviour on many occasions.

"Oh George, I do think I have stepped in it, but good this time. I am being pursued by…" she stopped and glanced around. She pushed the viscount backwards across the room before she continued, remembering that she had told the milliner she was running from a beggar. She pulled George's cuff to have him lean toward her.

"I am trying to elude a Bow Street Runner." She whispered.

"What?" Astonished, he quickly straightened. "Good God, my dear girl, what will you do next?"

"Shush! I told the milliner we were running from a beggar."

"Well, if you don't beat all Emilia Hawthorn. What the devil did you do to get a Runner after you?" The viscount placed his fists on his hips, attempting a pose of righteous indignation.

"I didn't do anything, honest I did not." She lowered her head and pushed out her bottom lip into the pout, which normally won over the viscount. But a Bow Street Runner was going to take a little more than a pout to convince him.

"Let me see if I understand this. A runner is pursuing you, yet you have done nothing to provoke it. Damme, if I can swallow that one."

"I did not, George. You see, I told him I was someone else."

"Well, that's an odd thing to do, even for you. But that can be easily rectified." He lowered his fists from his hips somewhat relieved.

"No, no, George, I wished him to believe I was this other person, you see."

The viscount shook his head somewhat awed because no he did not see. "What? Why on earth would you take such a notion, you silly little chit?"

"I had to do it, George. It was the first idea that popped into my head when I realised, he meant to take her, and she is not capable of protecting herself like I am."

"Her? Who is her?" He quizzed with an irritated tone.

Emily cut her eyes away toward Leslie, then cocked her head in that direction.

The viscount gave her a curious look, bent to her ear, and whispered softly.

"What is the matter? Is she simple-minded or dim-witted?"

166

"Of course not!" She bellowed and he jerked his head away.

"You ain't makin' a blasted bit of sense, Emily. I am beginning to think this is all a hum. Now, what's the real reason you call me down here?" He said audaciously.

"Oh, do be quiet, George and listen to me. That runner grabbed me. Which means he had planned on grabbing Leslie, and I could not let it happen. So, I was right to do it."

"Grabbed you? The devil you say. We need to go immediately to the magistrate."

"No, no, I said I was the girl he was looking for, and now I must get Leslie to safety."

"Oh, Emily, do not tell me you have gone and involved someone else in your mischief this time around?"

"Well, not exactly."

"You're enough to drive a man right out of his senses, you know."

"Please, please, George, you must listen to me."

"Come along, Emily. I will take you and your friend home and put an end to this. I rightly say your brother is not going to be happy about it. But he can get you out…"

Emily stomped her foot, crossed her arms, and leered at the viscount.

"George, I am telling you we cannot go home. If you continue to interrupt me, we will be here all night, and we need to go to Kent."

"Kent! Good Lord, girl, I am not about to take you to Kent." The viscount looked frightened to death thinking about taking two single young ladies away from London. "That would be most improper. I don't suppose you have so much as a lady's maid with you, do you?"

"Of course not, we were with Clarice."

"Clarice? Then what the devil do you need me for? And where is she?"

"We don't have her anymore. Please remain silent for only a moment, and I will explain it to you."

"Fine, you have two minutes." The young man crossed his arms, took an arrogant stance, and stared down at her with expectations of the tale to come.

"You see, Richard is trying to help Leslie regain her memory and find where she belongs. He is responsible for her... "

"She doesn't have her memory?" He dropped his arms to his side and leaned toward her.

"George. Silence."

"Sorry."

"She is staying with us, and we only meant to go shopping for bonnets, and this runner came up to us unexpectedly and inquired if one of us was Leslie. I told him I was Leslie."

"What did you do a fool thing like that for?"

"I told you Richard is trying to protect her."

"From what?"

"Well, we aren't precisely sure, but he believes she is in danger."

"Well, wouldn't the runner be the proper person?"

"No, Richard believes he is hired by whoever wishes to harm her. Oh, George, please, it is too complicated, and we only need to leave London as quickly as possible. I figured that out all by myself, and Leslie is in agreement. So, you simply need to escort us to our estate in Kent, and we shall be safe."

"Well, if what you say is true, you have surely landed yourself in a fix this time, my girl."

"It is true, George; I would not tell a hum regarding someone else's safety. But we must hurry. It is growing late."

"Well, I must say, you have never found yourself in a scrape before that involved anyone but yourself.

He stared at her in silence, attempting to make sense of the latest information. He paced a few steps one way and then the other, then drew to a halt in front of her.

"By Jove, I'll do it! But we must make one stop first."

"Oh, George, I knew I could count on you."

Emily instinctively embraced his arm, causing the young man to blush despite his tanned complexion.

"All right, all right, stop that!" he said, brushing her arm away. "If you do not mind your manners, we will be forced into a special license, and one of us will surely kill the other within a fortnight."

George considered the most clandestine manner with which to manage the operation. Something of which he had little knowledge. Aware Emily excelled at such things, sought her advice. It seemed she had taken after her brother, and she quickly explained her covert plan.

"Now, first of all, we need to get the two of you out of here without being seen."

Emily twirled to the shopkeeper and his wife, who were still sitting at the table with Leslie. There was an exit into the alley, and it was decided George, and his driver would bring the carriage around to the secluded entry. The ladies would be handed quickly inside and draw the curtains.

Emily thanked the shopkeeper and his wife and obtained a promise never to speak of the girl's coming into the shop, even if a Bow Street Runner should come nosing about. The viscount passed the couple a guinea and thanked them for their kindness to the girls. Of course, he was also aware it would ensure their silence.

The mission was accomplished, and the threesome were on their way. The well-sprung, shiny black carriage quickly made its way down the streets toward the viscount's residence.

"What stop must you make George?" Emily asked straightening her skirt.

"My house!"

"Whatever for? You shan't be long, I hope. It is essential we make it to Whitton Park tonight."

"Oh, believe me, my dear girl, we shall indeed make it tonight, but not without my housekeeper for a chaperone."

"Goodness gracious, George, we do not have time to worry about such trivialities. We are obliged to consider Leslie's safety."

"I am thinking of her… and you! But mostly, I am thinking of my own safety!"

"Oh, you would! I have no notion of compromising you, George!"

"You may say that now, Emilia. But…" the viscount gave her a sardonic grin.

Leslie had remained silent after exchanging pleasantries. She had been observing the two engage in lively conversation and perceived the rather odd relationship between them. Initially, their interactions appeared all most sibling like, but as the bickering continued, she realised, even if the two conducting the tete-a-tete hadn't discovered it yet, it was their unique way of flirting with one another. She determined it was time she interjected.

"The viscount is correct, Emily. We indeed do need a chaperone for such a long journey. It would be quite improper to place Lord… oh… it has just occurred to me; I have no idea how I am to address you, my lord."

"My Lord?" Emily scoffed, then chuckled "Just call him George."

"I shall not!" Leslie was appalled at the very thought.

"It is perfectly acceptable, Lady Leslie. Emily has no sense of propriety; I fear she has made it her ambition to thwart it all. I am Wyndham. But under the circumstances and the fact we shall be sharing a carriage into the evening hours; you may call me by my Christian name. I will not be offended. Or you may just call me Wyndam."

"Thank you, my lord. First of all, I am not Lady Leslie…"

"You cannot be certain of that! You could be." Emily interrupted.

"Very doubtful. Nevertheless, I prefer Lord Wyndham, and I will feel much obliged if we have a proper chaperone along." She arched an eyebrow at the pair. "Considering my situation, I must offer my apologies to both of you for placing you in this inappropriate position. It is entirely my doing, and I am gravely sorry."

The odd situation, now more apparent to the viscount, was becoming a bit more uncomfortable. Unlike most of Emily's scrapes, this might be far more serious than her ordinary childish ones. This was not a young girl attempting to free herself from society's shackles; this could be dangerous if the story were true. Of which, by now, he had little doubt.

When they arrived at Wyndham's residence, he had the driver take them straight to the mew, requesting the young ladies remain inside the carriage. He promised to be no longer than one half-hour.

Emily was exceedingly displeased with the idea of spending five minutes in a building that house animals, but for a full half-hour, she crossed her arms, curled in the corner of the carriage, and pouted. Leslie observed her with amusement. She assumed this spoilt child had never been tethered to a trunk adrift at sea. But then again, she had no recollection of it, so she decided she might have been a bit too critical of her new friend and saviour. After all, Emily had demonstrated on several occasions her loyalty to a stranger, who had been cast upon her family with little warning.

Within twenty minutes, Windham was assisting a fifty-ish older woman into the carriage. Once everyone was seated and he had instructed the driver to Whitton Park, introductions were made.

The housekeeper was not at all surprised to learn Lady Emily was embroiled in yet another caper. But once the story unravelled, she was shocked by Emily's courage and quick thinking. She had thought all young ladies of the Ton were helpless and gentle in nature.

By the time, the story had been completed, they all settled back for the lengthy journey. Chatting and riding along in one of the viscount's newly sprung carriages on one of the new roads to Kent, they were soon out of Town.

CHAPTER 16

It was close to eleven when Richard and Clarice returned to Upper Brook Street. They had spent the entire afternoon and evening going from one place to another, calling on everyone she remembered being friends or acquaintances of her sister. No one had seen or heard from Emily in days.

When they entered the blue drawing room, they found their mother asleep on the sofa, her head wedged in the corner, propped by a small pillow. Her cashmere shawl was draped around her shoulders and clutched tightly in her hands.

Clarice slipped quietly into the hall asking Carson to bring a fresh pot of tea and whatever René might have left in the kitchen. They had not eaten since leaving in the early afternoon. As she turned back toward the drawing room, the thwack of the knocker was heard from the front entry.

Despair filled her when the footman revealed the empty-handed Sheffield and Worthington. Neither had located the wayward daughter and Hawthorn's ward. Waiting at the landing she quietly informed them of the tea and light repast being prepared.

Richard pulled three glasses from the cabinet, only to see Clarice's countenance and set another. The deafening quiet of the sombre group was only disturbed by the splashing sound of the amber liquid striking the bottom of each glass. "We would retire to another parlour, but if Mother stirs, she will worry if we aren't here."

"Oh, Richard, what shall we tell her?" Clarice tearfully whispered.

"The truth! I am learning she possesses more strength than she appears. And she is fully ready to champion Leslie's cause."

"Really?" Clarice looked at him puzzled. She had no doubt of her mother's compassion for others, but she was only recently out of mourning from her dearly departed husband and hadn't seemed to be interested in anything or anyone in the past year.

"I have not had the opportunity to share with you. She was friends with Leslie's mother."

"What?" just catching her loud outburst. "'Pon my soul, she is not!"

"Yes, another reason I must manage this carefully. Now it is personal."

There was a noticeable catch in Richard's voice. The others glanced at one another, but no one dared mention it. Clarice reached across the table, placing her hand over her brother's.

"Oh, Richard. It was already personal... for you!"

Her soft gaze met her brother's as he raised his palpable eyes to meet hers. He despised being out of control, and now, not only had he lost someone he was beginning to care for, but also his younger sister. He, along with Clarice and two of his closest friends, had scoured the whole of Mayfair and discovered nothing. It was as though they had vanished.

"Was there anyone who was not at home we should perhaps consider?" Hawthorn, who never wavered when his assignments led to dead ends, displayed signs of anxiety.

Sheffield and Worthington assured him everyone they contacted had been home. His sister hesitated and her brother noticed arching an eyebrow.

"There is one person," she said apprehensively, "who wasn't. The butler refused to give me any information, but I..." she paused.

"Clarice, please, if you've something to say, do so."

174

Hawthorn's voice was somewhat cross. She inhaled deeply before continuing, afraid to mention the name.

Richard had eventually learnt of Emily's escapades and based on the conjectural circumstances; the earl decided her association with Viscount Wyndham was to blame. Clarice had attested ineffectually on his behalf. However, to the elder, out-of-touch brother, his observation was that Wyndham was always at the centre of her scrapes.

"It is… it is," she looked straight at her brother, knowing he was going to be angry. "George, Viscount Wyndham." She recoiled, waiting for his explosion.

"Why, of course!" Richard boomed, "I should have known!"

His mother bolted straight up from the settee. He had forgotten she was sleeping across the room. Although, at the mention of George Thynne, it probably would not have signified in the least.

"What on earth is the matter, Richard?" The countess tossed the shawl to the side, exhaling and frowning. "You have not found them."

It was a statement which four reluctant faces confirmed, as she drew closer to them.

"Did I hear you mention George? I was certain he would know of Emily's whereabouts if anyone would. What did he say?"

"He didn't say anything; he wasn't home, and the cranky old butler wouldn't give me any information, even when I told him I was Emily's sister."

The countess looked at her oldest daughter with inquisitive eyes. "Have you ever met the butler?"

"No, but what does that signify?" She asked with annoyance.

175

"If you told Carson not to breathe a word of your whereabouts and a stranger showed his face at this door and said he was your uncle, do you think Carson would give you up so easily?"

"I hadn't thought of that." Clarice lowered her eyes.

"I am sure Emily has embellished the tale, and Lord, help what poor George thinks about it, but he always rushes to her aid no matter, and now is just as deep in this mess as she is." The countess consoled.

"Do you mean to say he doesn't instigate all her escapades?" Richard glanced at his mother."

"Lord no, Richard. The only thought that comes to mind is somewhere unexplored and unconfessed, he cares for your sister. He always manages to rescue her from these scrapes, no matter the cost."

"I would imagine he does save her just so he can get her alone and take advantage," he growled.

"Oh no, Richard, I have spoken with his mother on many occasions. She lost her husband long before I did, and she has been such a comfort to me. But she is of the mind George genuinely cares for Emily and is trying to keep her... um, how can I phrase this where you will not frighten us all to death again with your bellows."

"What are you saying, Mother? He wishes to keep her from scandal so he can marry her one day?" The earl said mockingly.

"Yes, that is what she believes. We suppose he will be the first at your door asking for her hand once she is presented at court next year."

"Well, he will be the first I will send on their way." He groaned.

"Now Richard, you have no idea what all George has done to protect your sister's reputation."

"Or soil it!"

"You must cease such talk." She turned to her older daughter, "What precisely did the butler say to you, Clarice?"

"He had no idea where the viscount had gone. When I asked him when he might return, he said he did not know. I asked if it would be later this evening, and he said, I would be wasting my time if I returned before tomorrow."

"Hmmm," Lady Gillford looked at the four faces staring back at her. "Which one of you gentlemen would care to escort me to Viscount Wyndham's residence?"

All three immediately stood at the ready, awaiting her command.

"It is quite delightful how swiftly the old lady can attract such handsome young gentlemen." With a smile, she linked her arm through her son's and subtly hinted to her daughter to remain at home.

***

The countess made long strides up the viscount's entry steps with three dashing Corinthians on her heels. Hawthorn reached around his mother, raised the knocker, and followed its decent to a heavy thud. She gave him a look of indignation. Hawthorn took a step back to the lower step but smiled at the petite but daunting lady, still dressed in black, standing alone on the landing.

When the butler opened the door and saw the gentlemen serving as a backdrop for the shorter elderly woman, his eyes lowered to her face. At once, his countenance changed, but before he uttered a word, she took command.

"Jeffrey!" she barked as she waltzed past, brushing him aside, her guards in her wake. Once inside the entry, she swished her skirt and turned on the older man, who remained near the door in stunned silence.

"Countess, uh, Lady Gillford," He stammered.

177

"I understand you refused to tell my daughter where George can be found. Well, as I am sure and you have no doubt, he is with my daughter, and I demand to know their whereabouts."

The usually docile, quiet woman stood stern and unyielding, cocked her head to one side, waiting for her expected answer. The butler ushered the four into the downstairs parlour and closed the door behind him.

"My lady, please, I beg your pardon, but I do not know exactly where they have gone." He pleaded.

"Pray, then enlighten me with what knowledge you do own. He is only attempting to help her. However, I fear this time it is more than a simple scrape she has found herself in and am doubtful the viscount can resolve this for her."

"Yes, my lady. I feared that might be the case. But you know the viscount, where she's concerned. He cannot refuse her, and he assures me he will return by the morning. He brought our housekeeper along to ensure the young ladies would have a proper chaperone."

"Well, I am pleased, as usual, he has not forgotten his head." she proclaimed.

Richard stepped to his mother's side to say his peace but was abruptly silenced by the swift lift of the countess' arm and the backward pitch of her hand. It halted just short of his nose. Unaccustomed to his mother's command of a room, it took him by surprise, and he snapped his mouth shut. Whatever he wished to express was quickly forgotten.

"Jeffrey, did you see the ladies?"

"No, my lady, they did not enter the house. His lordship was only inside long enough to secure the housekeeper and notified me of his intentions to aid Lady Emily and her companion. He firmly stated that if anyone, anyone at all, unfamiliar to me came around with inquiries to deny any

178

knowledge. I am sorry for declining your daughter, but I am not acquainted with her."

"It is perfectly fine, Jeffery. If anyone else inquires regarding his lordship or the young ladies, do as the viscount has instructed you."

"Yes, mum." The butler showed the first sign of stress. He was quite accustomed to Emily's mischievousness and the viscount's involvement. But something told him, this time, it wasn't just childish pranks.

Unable to hold his tongue any longer, Richard stepped forward. "It is quite possible now that we have come, you will have another caller. So, it is of the utmost importance that you tell anyone else the same tale as you told my sister. And if they should ask why we were here, you may share we were in search of my younger sister, but you knew nothing of her."

"Yes, my lord!" The butler was having uneasy feelings about this entire situation.

"Jeffrey, please tell Lord Wyndham I will be awaiting his visit upon his return." The countess commanded as she approached the front entry.

"Yes, mum, I will."

The four quickly took their leave, leaving the butler bewildered.

Lady Gillford motioned for the groom to tether Richard's chestnut to the coach, as he peered at his mother curiously.

"I wish for you to join me in the carriage. I must speak with you."

Hawthorn gave Worthington and Sheffield a dubious look.

Immediately, Sheffield adjusted their plans. "My driver will see you home. Worth and I will walk. The night air will do us wonders."

Worthington was looking around at the pedestrians walking up and down the street. "We will hang about in search of stragglers who may wish to pay the butler a visit."

"Good idea, Worth." Hawthorn handed his mother into the coach and took the seat across from her.

The groom closed the door, and Sheffield motioned for his driver to be off. The two friends made their way slowly down the street, keeping an eye peeled for any conspicuous loiterers.

Inside the coach, the countess adjusted her gloves and her bonnet and placed her reticule in her lap. She was relieved by the latest information, eased back against the velvet cushion, and shut her eyes.

Richard, however, was not. The damn runner was obviously watching him, so how was he going to protect Leslie. It was apparent, the further away he stayed, the safer she might be.

However, in the hands of some infantile viscount and his precocious sister, going God knows where, there was no way in hell he could rest until he discovered them.

Inconsolable, it was beyond his belief he must place his trust in a wet behind-the-ears young buck. One he could only remember as a rough-housing twelve-year-old jackanape. Yet this infantile boy must be depended upon to find safety for his runaways. God help him!

"When I get my hands on Wyndham!" Richard couldn't help but mutter as he stared out the window into the darkness.

"That is why I wished for you to ride with me. It is no reflection on you, but George has been a Godsend for your sister."

"I rather doubt that mother." Giving her an incredulous glance.

"Richard! He has spent a great deal of time and money extracting your sister from some embarrassing situations over the past three years."

"He has no reason to do so." The earl moved uncomfortably in his seat, waiting for the set down he was certain was forthcoming.

"Yes, he has. I agree with his mother. I have watched Emily, and she shares the same sentiments towards George. She holds the viscount in the highest regard."

"She is far too young to own her feelings." He snapped defensively.

"Richard, you cannot just appear one day and become such an interfering brother after being away so long."

"The hell I can't!" Richard barked. "I am their legal guardian."

"Your sisters love and respect you. But they hardly know you nor you them, especially Emily. She has turned to George for the entire of your father's illness and the past year in your absence. And now, you have Leslie to worry about. Your sisters are still not your priority. Not that I blame you; I do not! Leslie needs you more than your sisters, but you must face facts. If Lord Wyndham chooses to ask for Emily, and she cares for him and wants to accept, you will not deny them."

"*Lord* Wyndham, indeed!"

He jerked his head from the window to face his mother, attempting to understand this newfound woman. In a few short weeks, she had evolved from a grieving, helpless widow into a steadfast, and formidable lady of consequence.

"You believe he has turned into a decent young man?"

"I do. I've witnessed his transformation since his father's accident. Yes, he was a spoilt, indulged child. But after his father's death, he devoted all his time from school to Lady Wyndham."

"You must admit, he was a wild and unruly youth," Richard argued.

"I dare say you all were. If the reports from Eaton and, more especially, Cambridge are true."

He gave his mother a droll look and wondered how many stories his father had passed along to her during his years at school. Perhaps, he should reassess his opinion of the viscount, particularly since it seemed he was outnumbered in his grievance against the matter of his sister and George.

He let the subject drop and turned back to the window. He began to speculate where Wyndham may have taken them. Of course, from what he was hearing, it would be wherever his sister wished him to.

Also concerning was the return of Leslie's memory. The last thing he wanted was her memory to return without him. He didn't trust her response to be sensible and it could be dangerous.

As the carriage drew up to the Gillford house, he noticed someone in a dark coat slip into the alley out of sight. He wasn't certain but guessed it to be Weber or at the very least one of his hired cronies. His mother had enough with which to worry without him leaping from the coach and running down the street like a raving lunatic. Furthermore, he had no doubt what Weber was up to, and he would have his day.

CHAPTER 17

The following morning at half-past the hour of ten, Lady Gillford and the earl were having breakfast when Carson entered, announcing a caller.

"My Lord, The Viscount Wyndham."

The countess tossed her serviette aside and anxiously stood in anticipation.

Richard swiftly pushed his chair back, wiped his lips, stood, and threw his serviette onto his plate. "Show him in immediately."

Carson stepped aside, allowing the young buck to pass into the chambre. He nodded to the earl and bowed to the countess, who returned to her chair, and found the viscount quickly at her side, taking the hand she presented. "Oh, George! We are relieved you are here."

"Lady Gillford, I apologise for taking so long to come to you. I know you must be very distressed."

Richard cared nothing for excuses and only wanted knowledge of his sister and ward. "Never mind that, Wyndham; sit down and out with it." Richard barked as he retook his own.

"Yes, my lord." The young viscount took the seat nearest the countess and at the opposite end of the table from his lordship, which appeared somewhat safer.

Gillford was impressed with the young man, and to his relief, he no longer appeared to be the twelve-year-old jackanape of his youth. The immediate desire to rip the boy's head off and place it on a serving plate was slowly dissolving.

"So, where is my sister and my ward?" The earl cut right to the matter.

"Yes, yes, of course." George acknowledged, nervously watching the footman fill his cup with coffee. "You see, I was completely unaware of the circumstances when Em… Lady Emily summoned me. Had I understood, I would have certainly consulted you before agreeing to her request. But you know how your sister can be, she has a way of influencing others to do her bidding. But having heard the complete tale, I am not at all certain she doesn't have the right of it."

The countess smiled patiently at George. He was disturbed by the situation and was relieved to be relinquishing his responsibility of it.

However, Richard had no patience and was only interested in their whereabouts. He was confident, regardless of their actions, his management of the matter would be far superior and effective than the young viscount's. He had no forbearance for explanations or excuses.

"George, if you please, where are they?" The earl flared indignantly.

"Yes, sir, my lord. I have taken them to Whitton Park. I am sure they will be fine for a day or so, but if what they have shared about this Bow Street runner is true, they shan't be for long."

Immediately Richard relaxed somewhat, his mind began to recalculate his plans. "No, I dare say they will not. But at least they are in a well-staffed house, and it is remote enough with limited access. What the deuce prompted Emily to think of going there? I admit, it was not a bad notion. I was bloody well thinking of it myself."

"That's another blasted thing." The viscount interjected, "Emily has told this runner, she is Leslie. Unless someone tells him otherwise, he is searching for her. I fear she may be in more danger now than her companion. Does this runner wish to hurt this young lady? The runners are supposed to be on the right side of the law and all, but some of the rumours makes one wonder." He had turned his full attention to Lord Gillford.

"Rightly so, but no, he will not harm them. His pride and pocketbook will ensure their safety. But knowing Leslie, she will set him straight if he attempts to kidnap Emily," then snickered, "Doubtful, he will keep my sister long, she'd prattle him to death. It is her best weapon."

The countess gave him a reproachful glance. However, George seemed to agree with the earl.

After a swift light-hearted moment, the three hastily returned to the seriousness of the predicament.

"So, it is true?" Wyndham had hoped the tale he had been exaggerated.

"I'm afraid it is," Richard said. Deep in consideration, he sipped his coffee and surveyed the young nobleman.

The viscount was more frustrated than before. "Good Lord! Emily seems to attract trouble, does she not." He raked his hand through his hair and then begged everyone's pardon for acting in a way he considered ungentlemanly.

"Yes, she does." Interjected Lady Gillford, "but this time it is truly not her fault."

"Well, I ain't convinced of that yet!" The youth learning early the power of the raised eyebrow.

"She can certainly make it worse." retorted the earl.

"She means well. But things just seem to happen when she's around." George shook his head, clearly exhausted from Emily's latest shenanigans.

The countess looked kindly at him, leaned forward, and clasped his hand that lay on the table. "Well, at least she has you."

"Thank you, mum. I will always do my best to protect her. She's just not used to being a proper lady yet and her actions are so impulsive. But she is coming around, at least I hope she is."

"You would like that, wouldn't you, George?" She said softly.

He gazed into the caring, gentle, and kind eyes of the countess.

"Yes, ma'am, I would." He admitted almost in a whisper.

She patted his hand and sat back in her chair. She cast her eyes to the far end of the table. Her son was in deep thought, and he had been quiet too long.

"What are you going to do, Richard?" She interrupted his ponderings.

"I am attempting to decide. I can't leave from here to go to Whitton Park; Weber has spies posted on the house. I saw them last night, or at least one of them. I must think of another way." He twisted his mouth to one side.

"I was reasoning the whole thing out on my way back to Town," the viscount said, interrupting. "If you send your chestnut with my groom, I will board him at my mew until you are ready to go. Then drive your carriage to my address, or one of my grooms can meet you somewhere else. If you leave here in a closed carriage, the runner will be waiting for it to take flight, which it will, but long after you have departed."

"You know, George, that is not a half-witted idea. I would rather you not be involved to the extent of departing from your residence. However," Richard paused, rubbing his chin, cogitating. "I can meet him at Tattersalls on sale day. In the abundance of activity - people and horses - one will be easily lost in the crowd." He squinted as the ploy came together.

"Carriages, too. If he is fool enough to hang around and wait for your next move." The viscount added enthusiastically.

"He might imagine I wish to buy a new pair and maybe even a new coach to elude him."

"Indeed!" The youthful male interpolated with excitement.

Lord Gillford couldn't help but chuckle at the boy, who was excited about the clandestine plan to eluding one of Bow Street's finest to protect his fair maid. He didn't like it, but he was beginning to see what his mother might. Sitting across the table might very well be his future brother-in-law, it could be far worse. After all, she was sure to be carried off next season by someone. It might as well be a viscount.

"Let's do it, George. Is your groom with you now, or must you send him around?"

"He is here; I told him to take my phaeton to the mews. Didn't want it to stand out front. After confronting the girls in the middle of Bond Street, it makes me think he probably has spies watching everyone, and if he believes me to be involved, my place too."

"I hope he hasn't figured that out yet," Richard said.

"I am afraid that is wishfulness. Jeffery said he had a visitor this morning before I returned. Around the ungodly hour of half past eight o'clock, dressed like a servant, he came to the back entry, I suppose hoping to elude my butler and find an unaware maid. But he had given orders to the staff, if anyone came to any door, to leave it to him to answer."

"What did he want?" Richard said, realising the craftiness of his nemesis.

"Wanted to speak to the master if he was at home or when he would be. Jeffrey said he seemed nervous, probably suspecting if he were seeking a job, a butler would know full well he would not ask for the master, and a maid might not."

"Followed us last night. Damnit!" The earl said.

"That is what I suspect." The viscount agreed.

His mother gave her son an apologetic glimpse. "I am sorry."

"No, Mother, we had no choice but to go to Wyndham."

"But had we not gone..." Her voice trailed off.

"Do not fret. I believe we have it sorted out. I will travel to Whitton Park and ensure everything is nice and tight and contemplate what to do next. We should have a day or two before the runner discovers us. One thing is for certain; Wyndham cannot return there, not yet anyway. But he can go to Sheffield and Worthington and let them in on our plan. You can do that, can't you, George?"

"I will do whatever you ask of me, sir. I have as much to lose..." he stopped short, "I mean..."

The countess and earl glanced at the viscount's change of colour from his neckcloth to his cheeks, and he swiftly turned his direction to inspect his nails, hoping his last remark had gone unnoticed or at the very least ignored.

Lady Gillford smiled at him again. "It is all right, George. We all know how you feel about Emily?"

"Sorry, ma'am. I have no right to feel that way, but I just plain can't help myself. My mother says I must keep my affections hidden until after she is out in society. Says it ain't right for a gentleman to steal that from a young lady."

Even Richard had to grin at that. The thought of anyone thinking of his wayward sister as a lady, either must genuinely care for her or certainly be dicked in the nob. He hadn't decided which category the young viscount fit into just yet. But George was proving to have a quick wit and was making a good impression on him, for now.

"Did you come in an equipage with one or a pair?"

"Only one, just in case." George grinned at his forethought.

188

"Nice work. We will switch your horse for my gelding. Thank God, he is solid and good-minded."

"Has he been hitched before?" The viscount inquired.

"A backband and belly billet has been strapped on him. My Tiger believes in putting a horse through all sorts of mischievous training. Says it makes a better partner if they experience a bit of everything. But he has a good mind, and I believe he will do fine."

Sure enough, the chestnut did well and paid no mind to the harness. Richard entrusted them to go easy with the ribbons.

It was settled they would meet in two days at Tattersall's next sale. The meeting was set for 10:00 in the morning. That would allow him time to reach Whitton Park before midnight. His lordship said he would enlist his chaise and four, and maybe Weber would think he was going to leave straight away.

It was a sound plan. The earl and viscount agreed it would be best if they avoided further contact, ensuring the runner's men remained spread a bit thin. George sent a missive to Sheffield and Worthington to join him at White's. It was the one place plans could be designed without fear of their nemesis or his cronies lingering about.

George and his groom depart the mews in the viscount's phaeton, while Richard prayed, they did not push his chestnut too hard.

His mind quickly returned to Leslie and Emily being alone at the estate in Whitton Park. There were plenty of loyal staff there, but they were still unprotected should Weber discover it.

Hawthorn considered notifying Sir Childs but decided otherwise. He was skirting the edge of authority and his assignment. He understood her family; the law and the war department were no longer on his side. But he would be damned if he would turn her over to a madman. He was still

189

uncertain of exactly what had gone on in that house, but whatever it was, it had been enough to traumatise Leslie into losing her memory.

Richard had to admit his own truth. He had fallen for the damsel. Even though he knew nothing of her past, his feelings had already interfered with his investigation. It didn't matter to him if she had married the bloke who stole her away to Ireland. He was dead. The earl wanted her, and by God, he would find a means to have her. He refused to entertain the idea of anyone forcing her back to that house.

For the subsequent two days, the earl was like a caged lion. When he was at home, he paced the floor and stopped only to fill his brandy glass, which seemed to have grown to his hand. He slept in his library and where he also took his meals. He made a point of going out at least twice daily if only to wander up the streets, through the park, and then return. If it were paid cronies following him, the agitation of aimlessness might be enough for a misstep. And if it was Weber, he would play a fine game of cat and mouse, irritating the devil out of the cretin and possibly forcing his hand.

Two days crawled by like weeks, but the day of the sale finally arrived. Hawthorn met with his tiger to discuss the meeting at Tattersall's. Jonathon was to drive the chaise and four rather than the usual coachman, ensuring there was no hesitation when George's man entered the carriage. He was to return post haste to the Upper Brooks Street mews.

The next morning, he was to hitch the coach with his pair of greys and bring his mother to Whitton Park and bring Emily back to London.

"But guv'ner, oo's to look af'er Miss Clarice? She'd be lef' 'ere all alone she 'ould."

"No, she won't. Going to have my mother's sister come and stay with her." The earl quipped.

"De devil yu sez'" The Tiger uttered horrified.

"Jonathon!" He snapped irritably.

"Can't 'elp it guv'nor, you'd know'd 'ow she is."

"I do, but you just make sure neither of my sisters go about alone. I will tell them both, and I trust you to keep an eye on them until we return once we get this mess straightened out."

"An iffin' dat runner cum's about, do I 'ave yur purmiss..."

"No!" Richard cut him off. "Stay out of his way. He is a legal runner, and we must deal with him carefully. Only if my sisters are in trouble are you to interfere."

"If'n he duz, then duz I 'ave...?"

"He won't! But if they do get into trouble, you get them into the carriage and drive it hell-bent for leather to Whitton Park. Do you understand? I mean every word, Jonathon."

His lordship gave his tiger a warning look, and Jonathon knew he was to mind his manners and would only do what was necessary. Even though he didn't care for it above half.

When the earl entered the house, he found his mother in the drawing room. She was pacing the floor and wringing her hands.

"Oh Richard, I'm glad you're here, come sit with me. I have been reflecting on this plan. It is risky business you attempting to reach them. I worry that Bow Street runner might be trouble."

"Yes, mother, I am afraid he is. The worst part is that he's within his rights and the law. I'm on the edge of it, including with the war department."

His mother stopped and stared at her son. "You are not suggesting you will turn Leslie over to him, are you?" She was very nearly panicked at the thought.

Richard put his arm around her shoulders. "No, Mama," He assured her. "I will do no such thing. I have no doubt her father is out of his mind, but I have no right to keep her from him. I am hopeful if I can reach her grandmother, she will have enough influence to keep her out of his hands."

His mother brushed back a lock of hair that had dropped across his brow, "You are worried, but there is more to it, isn't there?"

Richard tried to hide his concern and growing affection for Leslie, but this was his mother. She knew him far better than anyone.

"I have denied all manner of improprieties, but not knowing her situation has nearly driven me mad. This runner is exceptional but has no scruples. He will persevere until he locates her. From what the housekeeper told me, Jameson has more than just the Runner searching for her. She is in danger, Mother, and since she is not of age, I have no legal rights to keep her from them."

"You love her." It was a statement, not a question. When he glanced up at her, she needed no answer, a mother knows her child's heart.

"I did not want to... truly I did not."

"When it comes to the heart, it matters not what we want." She patted his hand and turned the subject. "When will it be safe for me to come to Whitton Park?"

"I left instructions with Sheffield. Unless there is an issue, Jonathon will escort you tomorrow. You must have Aunt Joan come and stay with Clarice."

"Oh Richard, Clarice will have a pet! Joan! Oh, must we?"

"Yes, mother. I intend to send Emily home. George, Sheffield, and Worthington will ensure their safety. They will continue the season immediately, and they will need Aunt Joan to chaperone."

"I suppose so. But dear God, Joan? She will not approve of any of this."

"You would not have little more than a year ago." He grinned at his mother.

"I suppose not." She smiled and squeezed his hand.

"It is the quickest way to clear Emily. We mustn't forget Weber thinks she is Leslie. The sooner she is out in public, the sooner that much will be behind us."

"Rightly so. And James and Thomas do not mind watching out for them?" The countess questioned but knew the answer.

"No. They will do whatever is necessary."

"You do have such dear friends." She said fondly.

"And you must trust Sheffield's decisions regarding the journey to Whitton Park." He advised.

"I am obliged to conceive a way to ensure Leslie's safety." Lady Gillford said.

She did not intend to play an idle role in this. "When I arrive in Kent, I shall visit her grandmother. I am confident she will know more than you expect. She was always a rather cunning old woman and has lived through quite a lot."

Richard furrowed his brows. His mother was forming a plan of her own without explanation and was certain he would not approve. She had surprised him on more than one occasion in the past few days and was beginning to frighten him.

"Mother!" He glared at her. Suspicious of whatever she was concocting.

"Never you mind. We must first ascertain the circumstances. Then I shall share it." She smiled and turned the subject, "Is Bixby on his way to Whitton Park? I presume no one will pay him any attention. I question whether these ruffians know he is your valet."

"He has already and no, it is doubtful he was given any notice. But rest assured, by the day's end, Weber will be vexed and furious over the deception." Richard leaned down and kissed his mother on the cheek. "I am sorry to trouble you with this. I had no notion bringing a sick girl home to find her parents would turn into such chaos."

"You have given me life. It was precisely what I needed to put my mind straight and return to the living. Furthermore, I am quite fond of Leslie. Whatever you decide to do, you have my blessings." She said, with a glean in her eye.

What the devil did she mean by that? Giving him her blessing? He shook his head slightly.

His mother touched his sleeve. "Richard." Turning back to her, she said in a quiet voice with soft eyes. "We love her too!"

His chest suddenly felt heavy. Why must mothers always know their child's every thought? He smiled, kissed her forehead, and quietly left the room.

CHAPTER 18

The swap at Tattersall's was critical. George's groom arrived early. It was a heavy sale day, with gentlemen milling about the large courtyard. The sale area was already crowded, enabling the viscount's man to easily make his way to the back of the buildings undetected. He walked the chestnut gelding toward Piccadilly and found a place to safely secure the stepper, then eased his way back to the building, where he casually leaned against the wall.

At precisely ten o'clock, Jonathon drew the chaise and four to a halt just outside the Tattersall gateposts. He sat casually in the driver's seat and paid no mind to the gentleman, who stepped from the coach in his blue-grey driving coat, top boots, and beaver hat pulled low over his brow. That same gentleman confidently entered the gates, then soon lost himself in the crowd. There was a set of four matched bloods being promenaded in front of a group of spectators, and Richard nonchalantly slipped between them; weaving his way through the sea of men, then, without notice, turned down a narrow alley. He emerged on the backside and saw the stable hand propped against the wall and his big chestnut calmly tied nearby.

The hosteler was stationed near an alcove, barely visible unless one was actively seeking him. Upon catching sight of the earl, he swiftly removed his black multi-capped riding cloak. As Richard approached, the groom observed him deftly slip from the blue-grey coat without breaking stride.

Only a nod passed between the two as they effortlessly exchanged attire. As soon as the equerry had secured the new outerwear, he touched the brim of his hat and disappeared into the sale area, blending with the crowd.

The earl approached his gelding and facilely mounted the saddle as the final large silver button was fastened. With a gentle nudge, the chestnut veered towards Park Lane, then towards Piccadilly, and settled into a trot. Richard would be across the Thames and gone from London by the time the groom departed Tattersalls hours later.

***

Embarking on the lengthy ride, he held Browne to an easy, gentle pace. He hoped Bixby was making a steady drive of it as well. Leaving early that morning, the valet ought to reach Whitton Park several hours ahead of him, even in a chaise. That should provide the stablemaster ample time to prepare for his late-night arrival and for Bixby to have a warm bath ready.

The shadows grew long, and as the sun set, the air began to chill. This summer had missed its calendar debut and seemed reluctant to show itself at all. The temperatures were dropping, and the wind bit into the skin. Richard raised the collar of his riding coat and fastened the throat latch.

The road to Whitton Park was not heavily travelled. The last thing he desired, although prepared, was to encounter a highwayman. He hadn't carried much on his person other than pistols, which might be enough to insult a hungry thief seeking a larger bounty.

Richard's mind wandered to the comfortable bed awaiting him. After ensuring both girls were safe, he intended to retire to his chamber and sleep until well past noon. The last few days had been challenging. He had discovered many things about Leslie, confirming his suspicions that she was indeed in danger.

Weber had thwarted his own intentions to remove Leslie from London and of all the little scamps, his sister had managed, somehow to remove her from harm. The worst of it had been the uncertainty of their whereabouts. Having to rely on a spirited youth, who by all appearances had matured into a respectable gentleman had almost been more than the earl could tolerate!

Richard Hawthorn depended on no one. He never asked for help, did not require it, and did not want it. Clandestine operations were always dangerous. Add a capricious sixteen-year-old, a gallant white night, a girl with no memory and a Bow Street runner; the entire chaotic episode had been exhausting.

The hours passed slowly on the lonely road. Richard made effective use of his stops, providing Browne with water, feed, and ample rest.

At least he was confident he hadn't been followed. He had seen few travellers after leaving London. Now, his mind had turned to the girl's safety. He had to clear Emily's identity, which he had no doubt Weber had already discovered that ruse, but he had to be certain. However, keeping Leslie secure was going to prove more difficult. He wasn't at all satisfied with how the grandmother might fit into the plan. If she was, as his mother had remembered, a cunning old bird, she might be his only hope of protecting her.

Solitude always evoked recollections of Mrs. Jennings' words. She had known nothing of how Leslie left the house or with whom. The idea of her being held prisoner by her own father disturbed him. My God, how was he expected to return her to that? It was not a good idea to dwell on the abuse. It merely incited his ire. Deciphering the unknown facts disturbed him nearly as much. He was convinced a male had rescued her. Although marriage may not have been the original plan, by the time of the Sea Horse disaster, she may have fallen in love with whoever it was.

Richard relished tormenting himself by his attempts to piece things together. Leslie would find it incredibly difficult to recover from the loss, despite the man's identity. She trusted the individual to safely rescue her and whether a husband or at the very least, a lover it would be devastating.

Why the bloody hell had he agreed to bring her back from Ireland? Why had he gone to Ireland in the first damn place? He was a damned earl. For God's sake, he had not been forced to go. He also might have declined to escort her to London. He should have dropped her at the London office and let them find another damned pigeon to find where she belonged. It was a damn desolate road to Whitton Park in the dark with only your thoughts for company. He believed he might be a bit touched in the head. Bloody Hell!

Oh, good Lord, where was he? Richard glanced around the dark route and the trees that bordered the road. Adjusting himself in the saddle, chastising himself to cease contemplation. What was the hour? It was too dim to read his timepiece, and why was there no damn moonlight? Perhaps there would be a tavern or a village soon. Browne was managing the slower trot easily, occasionally very nearly lulling Richard to sleep.

An hour later, the moon had fully risen, and he recognised the imposing stone wall as it came into view. The glistening of the familiar stones lining the road was a welcoming site. The massive iron gate loomed just ahead. Guiding Browne through the entry, he was relieved to see the long-pebbled road up to the estate. He was tired and weary, but the delectation of the journey's end motivated him up the winding drive. Once around the final bend, there was the wide stone bridge, on its far side stood the large gothic rock, four-story estate. The expansive open front lawn at the foot of the bridge, allowed the late evening breeze to catch his face. Startled, he was certain he had drifted off several times.

The lanterns were illuminated and the stablemaster was waiting to unsaddle and rub down Browne. Bixby had indeed made it. Upon reaching the grand crossbuck doorway, it swung open as Richard slid from the gelding's back.

"Evenin' me lord." The stablemaster nodded taking the reins without saying another word. It was obvious the earl was exhausted. The head hosteler glanced over his shoulder watching his weary lordship slowly making his way to the rear of the manor.

Too fatigued to make his way up the path to the garden, Richard opted for the servant's entrance which was a closer and led through a spacious pantry. The storage area was faintly lit by the moonlight shining across the gleaming counters in the kitchen which provided enough light to make his way through.

He had removed his hat soon after dismounting and considered placing it on the long wooden table he brushed by on his way to the back stairs. The weight of it was almost too much for his six-foot-plus sturdy frame. Every one of his muscles ached and seemed to have collapsed beneath him upon arrival. As he raised his left Hessian to the first step, he was convinced it had gained two stones, only to surmise the right had done the same, as it followed.

Footsteps hastening down the narrow stairwell, but he was too drained to lift his head. He prayed it was not a thief and if it were, he might take whatever he liked without a word if he would only drag him up the steps before searching his pockets.

"Lord Gillford!" A male voice exclaimed.

Then a female gasp. The next action he determined was four hands and arms removing his hat from his grip, his heavy riding coat from his arm and all other items he had hanging from his tired body and exhausted mind.

He sensed a strong hold under his left shoulder and a much lighter one to his right.

"Come, my lord, we will take you into the library. You are plumb knocked up." The woman avowed.

They were conversing in some foreign language he identified only as murmurs and mutterings. Lord, even his ears were knackered.

Once inside the grand library the earl sank into his expansive leather chair and lifted his head to gaze up at the mahogany-filled bookshelves that towered at least sixteen feet on three walls. He lacked the strength to turn his head but felt the coolness emanating from the floor-to-ceiling glass wall behind him. The garden lay beyond those windows, where he ought to have entered. He imagined the roses, carnations, azaleas, and geraniums in full splendour, but that must be left for another day. His bloodshot eyes were packed with grit and dirt from the dusty London Road.

The next voice was one of deliverance… Bixby.

"Good God!" His valet was taken aback by the unrecognisable figure slouched in the plush Louis XV bergère chair. "My Lord, you are spent!"

"Noticeable, eh?" Gillford slowly raised his eyes to his attendant and smiled. "A glass of brandy might help."

"Let's get you upstairs. There is a fresh decanter on your writing table, and your tub is being filled." Bixby turned to the butler. "I shall require your assistance, Dillard."

The two men compelled his lordship to his feet, and he willingly embraced each about their shoulders. Richard chuckled as he allowed his weight to be supported by his loyal servants.

"If I didn't know better, I would swear I was eighteen again and properly shot in the neck!"

"If only!" whispered the valet under his breath.

"I heard that!" he quipped, slightly cocking his head.

.

When the earl broke the surface of the warm bath of the large copper tub, Bixby stood nearby with a glass of amber liquid.

"Oh God, you are a top swell!" Richard sighed as he reached for the golden nectar, slinging water across the floor. His muscular arms once again recovered enough to bring the refreshing liquid to his lips. The lids of the hazel eyes closed slowly in raptured delight as the slight burn of the liquor trickled down his parched throat.

"That should rid me of the layers of dust coating my gullet." Richard sank back into the tub, resting his neck on the edge.

He downed the remainder of the spirits, handing the empty vessel to Bixby, who placed it on a side table, returning to his lordship.

"Another! To be sure it is filled to the top. I believe some of the dirt is now mud."

"Yes, sir." The valet snatched it and then turned back to his master. "Mrs. Dillard fetched a plate from the kitchen, along with a tankard of ale."

"Just bring the brandy presently. Pray, what is the hour?"

He glanced at the clock above the mantelpiece. "Half past two o'clock, sir."

"Took me longer than it should have." The earl pondered. "Poor Browne, he is likely in need of a stiff drink."

"As tired as you were, it is a wonder you did not end up at the white cliffs of Dover."

"If I had nodded off, once more, it is most assuredly to be where we would have been."

Bixby promptly left the room, only to return swiftly with a glass filled to the brim and handed it to his lordship. Richard drank nearly half in one swig and handed the remainder to his valet before dunking his head underwater. Emerging again from its warmth, tossing his head back; his long, wet chestnut locks scattering droplets about the room, narrowly missing his man servant, who quickly dodged the spray avoiding the disaster.

Soaking for another quarter hour, Richard was somewhat rejuvenated. Amidst the glow of the candlelight, the tall and imposing Corinthian shimmered as tiny beads of water trickled down the magnificent arms and legs. Bixby tossed a small cloth over his damp hair as the earl wrapped a large drying towel around himself. He slipped into a thick robe, securing it tightly against his body, and slid into a pair of soft slippers, unable to recall the last time he had felt so physically exhausted.

He returned to his bedchamber, catching sight of the delectable tray of cold meat, cheeses, and bread, which only minutes ago sounded repulsive. He devoured it as if it were his last meal and drained the tankard of ale. It was amazing what a few glasses of brandy, fresh meats, and a clean body could do to restore a man to mere exhaustion rather than the inability to function properly.

Removing the cotton robe, Richard shuddered as a chill rushed down his exposed spine and quickly donned a dressing gown, along with a thick brocade robe.

Warming his hands by the fireplace, he glanced at the Gaudron clock on the mantel… three o'clock. Emily and Leslie should be fast asleep, but he needed to confirm they were there. He had ventured too far not to ensure they were indeed safe and wouldn't rest unless he laid eyes on them peacefully sleeping. Then he would return to his bedchamber with peace of mind and pass out until the afternoon!

CHAPTER 19

The earl interrupted a chambermaid, who was removing the dirty linens and his riding attire, to inquire as to which apartments each of the girls occupied. Grabbing the comb from his dressing table, he ran it through his wet hair. He dried his freshly shaven face, stopped, and stared at the exhausted man in the mirror. Heaving a rather vocal sigh at the drooping eyelids and bloodshot eyes with the weighted bags underneath, he had been endured a stressful day. Another sideways glance at the glass revealed the turned-back covers of the bed where he longed to collapse. Shortly, he thought, a quick check down the hall first.

Stepping into the hallway, he padded down the family wing, the soft slippers barely audible. His sister's bedchamber was next to their mother's new set of rooms. Her ladyship had not wanted to return to the countess' apartments and chose another with a small sitting area.

He lumbered past the double mahogany doors and paused at the adjacent one, slowly turning the knob, easing the heavy door ajar. His sister was resting peacefully, breathing steady and gentle, like a purring kitten. He stood watching for a few minutes. What a mystery she was. He was certain there was nothing that kept her from a tranquil slumber. How nice it must be to live in the world of a sixteen-year-old who pictured life with wide-eyed wonder. He closed the door and looked toward the normally unused suits further down the hallway, with only the moonlight casting its shadows along the corridor.

The family wing had been constructed by the first earl to accommodate a large number of children or at the very least, a considerable amount anticipated. Now they were rarely used and only opened and aired when a close relative or dear friend was to occupy them. He was not surprised that Leslie had been placed there.

It was inappropriate for him to peek in on her, but he simply did not care. There were numerous reasons for him not to do so, yet only one important enough to cast them off… he was in love with her. It was time he admitted the truth, at least to himself.

Regardless of the outcome, his affection had grown into much more. He wanted to ensure she was safe, resting and not having one of those troubled, terror-filled, sleepless nightmares.

The heavy door creaked as he eased it open; he thought to shush it but doubted it would pay any heed to his authority. The bed was near one of the windows and the moonlight cast a shadow across the tester. The drapery had been fastened at each corner to allow the cool summer breeze to pass through. He quietly stepped inside.

Leslie's copper-brown hair was flowing across her shoulders. The counterpane tucked just above her waist. The light sleeveless chemise was her only defence against the night air blowing softly through the opening.

Richard walked over to the casement closing the glass until it was only slightly agape. He turned and was arrested by the sight of her resting peacefully. He should go, but he'd had just enough drink to ignore propriety. A chair sat between the window and where she slept, it wouldn't hurt to sit for a moment, his muddled mind argued. A wisp of hair trailed across Leslie's forehead, and the gentle breeze made it dance in the moonlight. He was mesmerised by the way it lifted and gently fell back to her brow.

She was beautiful. He couldn't see those violet-blue eyes, but he imagined her opening them and watching him sit in silence nearby. Lingering too long, he rose to take his leave, but something compelled him to her side. He lightly clasped the wisp of hair and tucked it behind her ear. Unsure if it was exhaustion or inebriation, he was unable to resist tracing the back of his fingers gently down her cheek past her earlobe. When he touched the tender skin of her neck, a jolt shot through him, causing him to retract his finger as if he had been stung. How did she evoke emotions and responses like no other woman he'd ever known?

As he withdrew, a small hand grabbed his wrist stiffening in alarm. Startled, his eyes flashed to hers and watched in dread, as her lips parted to release a scream. In one motion and with lightning speed he covered over her mouth and whispered her name.

Those violet-blue eyes he had longed to see were wide with terror. Recognising her intruder, they softened, and her body relaxed. She sat upright in bed paying no heed to her attire and flung her arms around his neck.

"Richard!" she whispered and nestled into his arms as he embraced her small frame.

"Yes, I am here. You are safe."

"Oh Richard, how I have missed you so." She murmured, her gentle exhale sending shivers down his spine. Before recovering from that uncontrolled sensation, she began kissing his neck, under his chin, his cheek, his forehead… Good God, he quickly pulled her away.

"I did not intend to wake you. I only wished to ensure you were resting and were truly here. I have been going mad with worry."

"I was afraid of that," she peered up at him, but not withdrawing, "and I am sorry. I attempted to explain to Emily we must go home, but she would not hear of it. Then Lord Wyndham agreed with her, and they whisked me away from London."

"And they were correct in doing so. I was returning to escort you here but thankfully Emily's swift action was sound. I fear I have placed you in danger."

Richard adjusted his posture, attempting to free himself from her hold. This was uncomfortable and quite improper. He was in no condition to make rational decisions and she remained steadfast. He removed her arms from around his neck and she lowered them to the counterpane. He caressed her face delicately cradling it, savouring her presence and the relief of holding her again.

"Dear God, had anything happened to you." he murmured holding her steady.

Leslie's eyelashes fluttered open meeting his which revealed more than words conveyed. Her countenance changed to concern, he was weary, with bloodshot eyes and drooping lids.

"You are knackered to death." Brushing away a lock of hair from his brow.

He shuddered from her touch, "I need to go. I should not be here, and I am too..."

"No!" she cried, "I beg you... please do not go."

She tried to throw her arms around him again, but he snatched them both.

The days without him had been emotionally arduous for Leslie as well. She had not been parted from him since they left Ireland. Their separation had been frightening and gruelling.

"No, Leslie. I cannot." He made the move to stand, swallowing hard before admitting. "I do not trust myself tonight. I've had too much drink; I am depleted and have little willpower."

"I don't care, Richard. You are exhausted, and you haven't slept. Please just stay with me awhile."

"But I do care. Until we learn..."

"I do not need to have all my memory to know there is no one else. There is only you."

"You do not know, how many times must I…"

"Yes, I do!" Leslie said firmly pulling her arms free of his hold.

"How?" Richard, regained a firm hold on her arm, staring down at her. His heart was pounding unsure if it was fear or relief, and God, he was so tired. The smell of fresh linens, the aroma of the summer breeze, the fragrance from the summer flowers, then there was her scent. He could easily slip under the cover without thought or concern. Oh God help him.

"Earlier today, in the garden. I remembered my grandmother. I saw her face, heard her voice, and then the ache pierced my head until I dropped to the ground."

"Were you alone?" Panic struck him.

"Yes." A slight whimper in her voice, lowering her head.

"Oh, the devil Leslie, I am so sorry. I never… I wanted…" He drew her close and sheltered her in his arms.

"I'm fine, Richard, really I am." But she clung to him. He was her only place of solace, and now that he had returned, she was determined not to release him. He was her refuge and wanted him to stay, she needed him to stay.

"Richard." She buried her face into his chest, her voice muffled by his robe. "My, mother… she is… dead… I"

"I know." He said, then quieted her.

"Oh, Richard! My father? I… I… believe… but I can't… why can't I remember more?"

"I believe you do not wish to."

"My memory is returning, but… there are pieces, confused thoughts…" She stopped and tried to wrap her arms tighter, but he pulled her away from him, holding her still.

"We will talk tomorrow." He pleaded with her to let him go, "Leslie, I must rest."

"My fears are real, and… it's my father, is it not?" Ignoring his pleas she continued.

"Yes, they are." He replied, "I met your Mrs. Jenkins or rather she found me."

"You did?" She peered up at him, "It is crucial to remember Richard; I cannot hide from what I do not know. I have to protect myself, but I am not even certain from what." She was becoming agitated.

"I will protect you, Leslie, if I must take you to the far ends of the earth, I will. Your father will never take you back to that house, nor will those ruffians he has after you."

She clutched the shawl collar of his robe and tugged on the soft material to dry her tears, without noticing it was a dressing gown, until she brushed against the tanned skin and detected the tickling touch of the coarse brown hair on his chest. She pulled back and stared at him. "Richard, what are you wearing?"

He had forgotten he was only in an open-collared sleeping shirt.

"Good God!" He jerked the robe across his body and tightened the sash. He tried to rise from the bed again, but Leslie grabbed his arm, keeping him in his place.

"I must go. I am not dressed properly, and…" staring down at her dishevelled chemise that revealed more of her breast than he was able to bear in his current condition, remarked, "neither are you."

"Please, don't leave me." She assured him, then met his eyes, "I… I want you to stay with me. I must tell you…"

"It can wait until morning."

Leslie reached for his face and held it firmly.

"No," she whispered, half certain, half unsure.

He had little strength to defend himself, much less to resist her compelling cries. She had something to say, and she would not rest until she did so.

"God help me!" He sat down again and took her hands in his.

"Richard, please…" She hesitated and raised her violet blue eyes to his, and he could see the tears forming in them. "Lay with me… if only… for a little while."

"You don't know what you're asking."

"Yes… yes, I do. I… I want you to stay." she closed her eyes and inhaled deeply, her breasts rising and falling was nearly his undoing. She slipped her hands from his and held on to his arms, then slowly raised her gaze to his begging him to remain with her. There was something in them he had never seen before… desperation. "Please, do not leave me."

Richard latched onto a handful of her red sable locks and tenderly brushed them away from her face. She offered her lips, and he lowered his mouth, taking them in. With heat and desire, which she couldn't understand or control, she pulled him down into the feathered mattress with her. He could not and did not defy her.

The weight of him plummeted them into the dishevelled linens as he lost himself in the passions he had been withholding. She threw her arms around his neck for balance, then once found him lying beside her, slipped beneath his robe and inside the silken sleeping shirt. Her hands eased across the taut muscles of his shoulders, then to the sleek, slender strength of his back. The sensations of heat like the coals in a fire slid down her body and she dug her nails into him as though she were hanging on to something she didn't understand.

209

The touch of her talons scraping across his bare skin sent him over the edge and any power remaining vanished and his honour was lost in the thunder of urges that rumbled to the depths of his soul. His heart throbbed, and the unbridled heat that he had smothered and checked for weeks was unleashed in a flurry of fervour too much to ignore or dominate.

He released her, slowly sliding to the crook of her neck and shoulders, suckling the smooth ivory skin and his tongue swirling against the sensitive flesh. His arms reached for the thin chemise and lowered the sleeve down to release the breasts beneath it. Kissing down the décolleté until he felt the rise of her bosom. Moving over her, tremors shot through him as she raked her nails up and down his spine.

Closing his eyes and thrusting his head back, he growled. "Oh God." His voice low and uncontrolled. He made one last effort to stop what he knew neither wanted to end. "No, Leslie, I should…"

His one weak attempt to pull away, thwarted by the delicate arms that latched tighter around his neck as she rose with him. God forgive him; he was too tired and just inebriated enough not to care about the consequences. His body was overcome with uncontrollable yearnings and too weak to fight.

He ripped the thin chemise open, tiny buttons scattering, exposing the opening he wasted no time exploring. He returned to the delicious mound that rose to meet the gentle touch of his tongue. He twirled, sucked, and kissed his way to the hard, pink nipple, placing his hands to support the arch in her back, which grew higher with intensity. He grasped the nipple softly between his teeth, and Leslie let out a moan that drove him to insanity.

His control lost; he was now driven by pure lust. He directed his yearning to the concaved area of her abdomen, tossing the counterpane aside and sliding downward until he reached the small navel, then further slowly and methodically.

Leslie's fingers, wrapped in the damp chestnut locks, pushed him into her naïve and innocent form. Driven by urges, which she had no understanding but could not withstand, her breath was short and haggard, and parts of her ached for him. She was begging for his touch in places she had hesitated to explore. She couldn't understand why, but she longed for his cosset. She could not have stopped the cravings that were washing over her, even if she had known how. Every light stroke of his finger and flick of his tongue satisfied her, as he revelled in her body.

Richard's exhaustion was overtaken by animal instinct and the hunger that had been building for her. He had dreamt of worshipping the parts of her that were now pleading for his attention. He flicked, fondled, and kissed his way further, his eyes drifting from closed to lazily gazing up at the dark-haired beauty who was arching beneath him. He felt as if he were in a trance, but his uncontrollable proclivity drove him to perform.

Her moans and gasps with each newfound sensation suggested satisfaction of those desires seeking comfort. He was well experienced in providing such relief and, if not exhausted, could have been more masterful and punctilious. However, her silky, taut skin was luring him to continue. Her slender legs encircled him as she hoisted her knees, completely consuming any remaining strength he had with that one sensual gyration. His chin brushed against the soft, springy curls of the one place he had fantasised about incessantly. Good God, could she possibly know what she was doing, or was it purely a response to desire, uncertainty, and passion? Either way, she was destroying him, and he did not have the willpower to stop.

As he pressed further into the thickness of the covering and his lower lip touched the velvet layer of skin, his tongue blazing the trail to the small delicate flesh that would bring the liberation she did not yet understand she sought. He flicked the fragile pearl. Leslie gasped, and uncontrollably heaved her hips to meet the sensation.

211

Male cravings since the dawn of time overpowered and propelled him forward as he swirled and excited the fragile skin, causing the writhing of the sable-haired beauty's hips. Sensations so intense she was uncertain of wanting more or seeking refuge from the ferocity of them. He slipped his hands beneath her, burying himself, the taste of her driving him mad. Whimpering in confusion with desires, she was certain she was unable to withstand any longer but did not want it to end.

Richard's fatigue was demanding consideration, but he had begun a process he could not abandon until he had extinguished the fire inside her. She was unaware of it, but he knew her yearnings were nearly satiated, and he pressed on. With the rigidity overtaking her and the sound of torment crossing her lips, her entire body shattered and collapsed with the fervid vibrations, which turned to throbs, engulfing the sensitive flesh. He moved his body towards her, peering at the eyelashes that fluttered over the glazed, unfocused violet-blue eyes. Panting, heated breaths were the only sounds passing from the swollen, slightly parted lips.

He pulled her frail form to his and held her until she calmed from the tremors. Her face pressed to the curve in his neck, she drew back slightly.

"Richard… I…?" Leslie's voice was weak, barely audible.

"Leslie, I… I am sorry, I should not have." He whispered into her hair, holding her in a tender embrace.

"Don't." She placed two fingers on his lips. "I have never…" Her voice trailed off; she didn't know how to express her mysterious but sybaritic feelings.

Richard tightened his hold, and they both lay still for a brief moment. When she attempted to pull away, the heaviness held her still. She lifted her head from his neck, peering up to his face. His eyes were closed, his heavy limbs motionless.

"Richard!" she whispered, but no response. He had fallen asleep, "Oh Lord," she realised, he had passed out from his exhaustion. She smiled and returned to the recess between his neck and chest, wiggled her satiated body to his, pulled the covers over them, shut her eyes and slept.

CHAPTER 20

Ting, ting, ting… "Six, no, seven." Richard was roused from his slumber by the soft chimes of the French Boulle/Delaunay mantle clock. With his eyes still shut, he murmured, "seven… it can't be." He had intended to sleep until noon. So why did he have this urgency to wake? Struggling, he attempted to open at least one of his heavy lids. The one eye that yielded, acknowledged the early morning light, slowly dancing through the paned window glass. Ugh, the sunshine was so bothersome in the morning hours.

Wait, the window was on the wrong side of the room. Both eyes flew open, and he glanced upward… ponderous green velvet graced the canopy of the four-posters. With little movement of the rest of his body, he flung his arm above his head. Richard's heart stopped as his hand found the intricately detailed carvings of the mahogany headboard; his fingers easily slipped through to the gilt-embellished silk wallcovering.

Where the hell was he? Afraid to move, he turned his head, lifting it slightly from the pillow where it lay.

"Jesus Christ! Leslie!" His breath caught at the sight of the red-sable hair draped across the alabaster skin of the unclothed form next to him. With an unsteady head, he attempted to recall the night before. He lifted the covers to discover his own state of undress, "Oh my God, what have I done?"

He lowered his head back to the pillow but bolted upright. He must get out of this room without being discovered, most likely by her maid. Damn it to hell that would be the same maid that attended his sister.

He peered over the side of the mattress, discovering his brocade robe crumpled on the floor. He swung his legs slowly from beneath the linens and reached for the heavy garment. At

214

least he still had on his dressing gown, whatever the hell that nonsensical consideration was supposed to signify.

Placing his arms through the cumbersome sleeves, he gazed at the sleeping figure. He had vowed not to do this, yet here he was… guilty! He had compromised her. Adding insult to injury, he had little recollection of it.

He quickly tied the sash, donned his soft shoes, and crept to the door. He eased it open finding the hallway empty, discreetly made his way back to his own chamber and softly closed the mahogany slab behind him.

"Thank God!" he muttered as he leaned against the massive double doors. Later, he would confront the reality of what happened in the early morning hours, but first, he had to rest. His body longed for sleep. He strolled to his grand tester draped in burgundy velvet, threw back the counterpane and collapsed between the linens. Sunlight streaming through the transparent glass panes, now on the proper side of the room, the thought fleeting through his mind for a brief moment before he was lost again in slumber.

Richard rolled over to peer at his familiar, Antoine Gaudron Louis XIV clock… "Awe, two o'clock… much better." He turned onto his back and sighed as he stretched out his arm to the empty side of his bed. The memory of waking next to the umber-haired goddess had been pleasant, but now he must confront the consequences of his actions.

He pushed himself up to a seated position and leaned against the headboard adorned with rich mahogany panels. Suddenly mindful of the aching in his groin and the rise of the sheet below his waist. As he reached beneath the linens, the recollection of the night before slowly returned. He had pleasured her… pleasured hell; he had shattered her senses and she had savoured every second of it.

A lock of his chestnut hair fell over his brow. He brushed it into place and tried to remember the unexpected rendezvous in the morning hours. She had begged him to stay and refusing her was insurmountable. Even if he had not been prostrated, he doubted he could have resisted her. He raked his hand through his hair again.

 He could use all the excuses he chose, but it was bound to happen. He only wished he had not been so damned tired. The saving grace of that, was he had been incapable of ruining her. But compromise her, he did!

He recalled her every movement, the shape, her moans, and whimpers. As he sat in his bed and stroked his own needs, he relished in her release. He had brought her to the edge and held her through the splintering bliss and recovery of her first time. He wanted her and not for only one night. He closed his eyes as his own body fractured, aroused by the memories.

After the convulsions of his own body's indulgence ceased, he opened his eyes and tried to think of what to do next. He hadn't ruined her; he hadn't sought his own pleasure; however, he had dishonoured her when she was vulnerable and afraid of a past, she still could not remember. The erased recollections of a father who was demanding her return to the house where she had been imprisoned and abused. Having been restored and loathing his actions, he chastised himself. How could he have taken advantage? For the first time since he had met her, he found himself embodying the debauched persona of his past.

He called for Bixby, and he quickly entered from a small side door. "I need a bath and fresh clothes."

"Hessians or top boots? Waistcoat? Cravat?"

His valet, always professional and discreet, offered no sign he was aware of the late return of his employer. But Richard assumed he had. There was nothing but a paper-thin wall between them.

"Top boots, no and no! Not this morning. I plan to spend time in the gardens."

"Yes, sir!"

"Bixby!"

"Yes, my lord?"

"It is no one's business how late I came to my chamber."

"Never, my lord." Dipped his head and left the room.

Completing his toilette, he headed downstairs. Hearing loud voices, which included the shrieks of his sister, he hastened his steps. As he drew closer to the small drawing room, the language was urgent and panicked. When he flung opened the parlour, he was met with a hysterical sibling, a frantic housekeeper, a distressed butler, the troubled stablemaster and an anxious groom.

The four servants turned swiftly to his lordship in silence. Emily bolted to her brother. "Oh, Richard, something terrible has happened." She clutched Richard around his waist, sobbing.

He removed her arms, gently separating from her hold, and knelt to meet her gaze. Before he could speak, Emily unravelled.

"I am so sorry, I-I am at a loss as to what might have happened... I don't know... where to... to have anyone even begin to look... Oh, Richard." She screeched.

Gripping her shoulders, he lightly shook her, hoping to halt the hysteria.

"Emilia, you must compose yourself and be sensible." His voice was stern, yet bewildered. What the devil was happening?

"Had we known you were coming; I am confident she would have remained."

A chill ran down Richard's spine. He looked to his staff. "Mrs. Dillard, tell me immediately, what has happened?"

With tear-filled eyes and wringing her hands, she replied, "Oh, your lordship, if we only knew."

He led his sister to the nearest settee. She was still weeping into his muslin shirt.

"Someone say something for God's sake," Richard demanded.

It was as though his entire staff had been struck dumb, or worse, no one was willing to be the bearer, which terrified him.

"I cannot fix what I do not know, anyone!" He was not shouting, but his unyielding tone remained steadfast.

"She has gone!" Emily cried, "and her belongings with her."

In an instant, gasping for breath, nauseated and with a pale complexion, the earl was convinced that he was to blame.

"Since no one witnessed her departure. It must have been in the middle of the night." His sister whimpered.

He swallowed hard and glanced at his loyal staff. None in this room would dare utter a word of what he was about to confess. "No, she did not go until this morning."

In confusion, his sister confronted him. "Pray tell… how… how do you know?"

"I know." He released her.

Richard stared at the case clock… half-past three. Good God, he last saw her at seven, but she was asleep, or he assumed she had been. He rose and paced as he calculated the hours It would have taken her at least an hour if she had woken immediately after he exited from the room. She would need to dress and pack, ensuring to conceal the presence of another in her room. The desperate faces surrounded him, and they were all seeking answers from him.

"When did you first become aware of her absence?"

"My maid knocked on her door at two o'clock," Emily muttered.

"Two o'clock! And no one thought it necessary to rouse me before three?" Richard roared at the notion one and a half hours had passed.

"We all are accustomed to Leslie dressing herself and going to breakfast without need of assistance. When I entered, I inquired if she was in the garden. Only then did we become aware she was gone. After querying the stablemaster and returning here, you were dressing. We were waiting for you to come down."

"For God's sake, I was in no rush with my toilette. We have wasted half an hour with me unaware."

He grabbed his head rubbing his temples and eyebrows to ease the throbbing pain behind his eyes. He turned to the stablemaster and groomsman. "Pray, is there a horse missing?"

"No, my lord." They answered regretfully.

"Mrs. Dillard, did she take time to eat anything?"

"No, it does not appear so, my lord"?

Richard reclined in the large wingback, fingers stroking his forehead as he leaned it against the high back. She had affected all his sensibilities. He found himself unable to think clearly, and his usual clandestine skills and covert thoughts had vanished.

He commanded everyone to search all areas of the estate, including every building, old and new, whole, or dilapidated. He told the stablemaster to have the other stablehands assist. He had to consider she may have been abducted.

He turned to Emily, "search her room for a note."

That frightened him above of all else. If there was not one… but who would dare to intrude upon such a large estate in the light of day with servants about. Then again, how did a grown woman manage to slip out without notice? The housekeeper interviewed the maids, the butler every footman, and each groom and stable hand. Perhaps someone might have seen her and thought little of it.

"Where are you going, Richard?" Emily asked warily.

"I'm going to Westerham."

"Westerham? Why?"

"Her grandmother lives there."

Bewildered, Emily watched her brother take his leave.

CHAPTER 21

Richard reined in his chestnut in front of a charming cottage on the outskirts of Westerham. The residence was meticulously maintained, featuring an iron and stone fence, as well as an enchanting garden that extended from one side to the rear. He handed Bixby the reins to his gelding, lifted the latch of the iron gate, and casually strolled to the door, straightening his waistcoat as he raised the knocker.

The sound of shuffling footsteps was drawing closer. A stooped postured elderly domestic presented himself and gazed up at the tall gentleman.

"May I be of service?" the butler's kind eyes brought a smile to Richard's face.

"Might I inquire if Mrs Merrick will be receiving callers this morning?" He passed him his card.

Taking the small stiff paper, he asked the visitor to wait in the foyer whilst he checked with his ladyship. He complied, as the grey-haired butler plodded away.

Lord Gillford inspected the paintings on the walls, the elegant case clock standing proudly and the candelabra with twelve tapered beeswax candles on an oak demilune. The cottage was not excessively large, yet it was well constructed, and the interior and contents were obviously of quality.

Hearing the familiar sound of footsteps, he glanced up to find the butler approaching, his expression suggesting his request for an audience had been granted.

"Her ladyship will receive you. If you would care to accompany me, milord?" The butler turned and tottered back down the hall.

Richard stepped into the room and was instantly taken aback by the violet-blue eyes smiling from across the room. The elderly lady standing, balanced by an ebony walking stick, both hands gripping its ivory knob, steadily and gracefully curtsied and bowed her head.

"Welcome Lord Gillford." The soft and weak voice held an air of strength and a life lived with authority and grace.

"Lady Merrick, it is a pleasure."

"Please, my lord, I have not been addressed as such in many years."

"It does not make it any less so."

"I suppose not. Please let us sit. I tire easily from standing these days."

Richard waited for Leslie's grandmother to take her seat, and she nodded to the earl to accept the chair across from her. Those familiar violet-blue eyes focused on Richard's countenance.

"Would you care for tea? I would assume you have travelled a good distance."

"No, thank you, ma'am. Not so far this morning. I passed last evening at the Crown Inn in Maidstone."

"Yes, clean and aired sheets, I understand." She said. "I have ordered a tray prepared with refreshments if you change your mind."

"Thank you," He replied.

"I have something a little stronger if you would like." She said, "Although it is a bit early for it."

"Yes, ma'am, it is a little early."

Richard fidgeted in his chair hoping to conceal his anxiety.

"I suppose you will be relieved to learn your journey to Westerham was not wasted, are you not?"

Richard exhaled the air so rapidly that his hostess nearly laughed.

"Had I been aware you were holding your breath; I would have been more forthcoming." She smiled with genuine appreciation.

A small laugh slipped through his lips. "Is it that obvious?"

"I am afraid it is." She smiled eyes twinkling with approval.

"Did she arrive safely? Is she well?" He felt a profound sense of relief, yet he could not dismiss the danger she faced.

"She did, late last night. I must tell you it was quite a shock when I was aroused from my bed in the middle of the night to find a dead granddaughter at my door."

His head snapped toward the lady and met her gaze. "You knew!"

"Indeed, I had a hand in the planning of it."

"I ought to have come to you immediately. I mean, I should have hastened my search for you. I was not certain at all if you were alive until my mother assured me you were."

"It is questionable on some days." She smiled in jest, then inquired. "Your mother?"

"Yes, Elizabeth Hawthorn, she is now the countess of Gillford. You may know her as Campbell, I suppose."

"Lizzie Campbell Hawthorn, is your mother?" She almost looked shocked, but then her eyes softened, "These changes everything. I remember you as a child, Richard."

Her reference to his Christian name startled him. Then recalled his mother saying they were family friends when he was young.

"I had forgotten. I am sorry; I have been so worried about Leslie for days" he said. "I am embarrassed to admit, my head is a bit rattled."

"It is understandable. However, it is also fortunate you are not on one of your old assignments with the war department." The older woman's eyes twinkled again.

Richard's eyes shot up to meet hers.

"The Earl of Gillford was unfamiliar to me. Richard Hawthorn, on the contrary, is a dear friend's child. My late husband, the admiral told me of your successes in the war efforts. You protected many lives with your dedication, including some of his own men."

"Your husband was a well-decorated subject of the king as well. I am terribly sorry for your loss."

"Thank you! But you did not come all this way to discuss your own and my husband's escapades in the war, did you?"

"No." he said quietly, "Can you tell me what happened and your part in Leslie's flight? I have been tormented by so many questions; unable to find answers without jeopardising her recovery."

"I can share my part. But Marcus' and Leslie's difficulties were their own," her voice fading slightly, "and only theirs to share."

Marcus, the name abruptly drawing his attention. It was the one he wished to know yet didn't want to hear. There was another man involved. His heart ached as he gathered the courage to listen to the story he dreaded.

Perceiving the woman's visage, her blue eyes glistened with newly formed tears and appeared fragile. A profound bond existed between these three. Lady Merrick swallowed and cleared her throat, holding back her emotion with the strength of a well-seasoned military wife.

"As you know, Marcus was lost in the wreckage of the Sea Horse. I regret the inability to speak of him without sentiment. It is too soon, even with the joy of finding my granddaughter alive. At my age, the loss of your children is exceedingly difficult.

As I am certain you have discovered, my only daughter was unexpectedly taken from me, add to that the effect of continual wars on an already weakened heart took my only love far too soon. Then the Sea Horse tragedy claimed the remainder of my family. It has been difficult."

Richard's entire life was being held captive by the soft and slow murmurings of an elderly lady's wish to absolve her conscience. The reminiscence of a plan which seemed in all appearances to have been partially her idea had ended in disaster. This woman had lost her entire world to tragedies. He remained calm and suppressed his own desire to press her faster as she continued.

"You see, Marcus knew the house, including the hidden passages where Leslie sought refuge from her father's mad rampages. After my daughter's death, his wrath was directed toward Leslie. Marcus tried to confront him on several occasions. The arguments escalated into physical altercations. If one has ever visited Bedlam, the insane can become extraordinarily strong when agitated. He had endeavoured to defend Leslie, but that decisive battle proved to be the ultimate conflict between the two. He fought for her until he no longer could do so, and he finally had enough, and came to us for consolation and protection. Her likeness to her mother was her transgression."

The woman was immersed in her tale, and it was almost as if he wasn't in the room.

"The admiral accomplished a change to his name and purchased a commission for him. We had visitors come in search of him. He was to be taken back to London to face the audacity of what he had attempted to do, which was remove Leslie. He hated leaving her behind, but we had little choice.

After Waterloo, Marcus was to be reassigned to Ireland, and together we executed the plan. You know the remainder of it."

Richard believed he did, except for one crucial element. It appeared there was so much familiarity, Marcus needed no explanation. She was distressed and had nothing left to be revealed of her story. Or maybe she believed it to be Leslie's to disclose. She had remarked it was she and Marcus' story to tell. He would not question her further.

"Lady Merrick, do you think she will want to see me?"

"I am not certain. When she regained her memory the morning you arrived…"

"All of it? Fully?" Another burden for him to bear. Her past had returned, and she had been alone.

"Why yes. It is the reason she departed from Whitton Park. She indicated she left a message."

"I received no message. But why did she think she must leave? I am sorry; I would have escorted her."

"I suppose she will supply those answers to you. Maybe it would be better if you went into the garden unannounced." she paused, "Do you mind if I call you Richard? I can see you did not remember me, but I certainly remember you."

"Of course," He smiled, taking her hand giving it a tender squeeze.

"You see, she has been confined in that house for so many years with no social exposure or normal discourse of any age, much less her own. Mrs Jenkins did her best, but it was not the same. It is difficult when your sole source of contact is a madman." She retorted gravely. "Jacob will show you the way."

"Thank you." Richard rose to go, but the elderly lady lifted the ebony stick and blocked his path. He gazed down upon her.

"If you love her, be patient. She lost her entire world on that dreadful ship and is only now feeling the weight of that loss."

Following the slow-moving butler, his eyes drifted toward the heavens. His greatest fear was that her lover had perished on that ship, perhaps he was her husband. If not, someone she hoped to marry. God, how was he to help her through this?

His eyes scanned the greenery, an open space filled with roses and assorted other flowering plants. It was well kept with walking paths of cobbled stones meandering in a myriad of directions. His breath caught as the first sight of her sitting in a pale-yellow muslin day dress.

She was facing away from him, deep in the garden, oblivious to his exit from the cottage. His gaze remained fixed on the bright sable locks, elegantly styled in a loose chignon, with delicate curls framing her face and dangling at her nape. As he drew closer, he slowly closed his eyes and prayed for guidance and strength.

Leslie listened to the approaching footsteps for a moment, slowly glancing over her shoulder, anticipating her grandmother's arrival. At the sight of the earl, she leapt to her feet and whirled around, initially looking surprised which quickly dissolved into a doleful smile. There were shiny streaks down her cheeks from the tears she had been shedding. She brushed them aside and gave a slight curtsy, striving to regain her composure.

"My lord." She said softly, casting her eyelashes downward.

He longed to embrace her and never let her go but hesitated beyond her reach. "I was so worried for you." He said, attempting to maintain an emotionless tone, but his heart was pounding.

"Might we take a seat?" she whispered as she settled at the iron table and chair.

"Of course." She was tired and suffering. The memory recovery, the arduous journey, and his compromise of her would have debilitated a lesser female.

"Leslie, what can I do, how can I help." choosing his words carefully. "I care for you exorbitantly."

"I am aware, but you cannot."

"Why not?" sounding more indignant than he meant.

"You don't understand."

"I can attempt it. I beg you to allow me to." He extended his hand across the tabletop, laying his palm open flat within her reach. She placed her hand in his without hesitation. So warm, so soft, so filled with pain, his heart shattered as teardrops fell from her down cast eyes.

"Oh, Richard," she murmured so softly he had to strain to hear her weakened voice. "It was Marcus. He… he had joined the military with my grandfather's help and changed his name."

She tried to control her sobs but could not. Only discerning half her words, he lightly squeezed her hand. She was devastated; with the ache, only time and tears could heal.

"He… he was going to take me to Ireland… and… he said… grandmama would join us there. It would have… would have been… wonderful." Attempting to hush the uncontrolled weeping.

They sat in silence for some time, he was rubbing her palm and wrist as he had done all the other times, when she was distraught. Discovering it also had its calming effect on him as much as her.

She raised her head and dried her eyes, her lower lip quivering. He moved quickly around the small table and knelt at her side. He wanted to stop the pain and to say he didn't need an explanation. But she was ready and needed to unburden her soul. She faced him and he stiffened his shoulders and braced his heart as she continued.

"It was so dark, the wind was blowing fiercely, and the waves grew so large, they were relentlessly crashing over the sides. The mast had been toppled and ripped away. There were people casting themselves into the sea. Oh, Richard, it was ghastly." Her voice shuddered.

The tears and memories overwhelmed her; she gasped, coughed, and very nearly choked on the pain of it. "There was no way to save yourself. Others were taking shelter below, knowing the ship was tearing apart. It was horrible."

She inhaled a ragged breath; Richard was sure she was back on that ship as it violently tore apart beneath them.

"Marcus wouldn't let me go below. He said it was a death trap. He continued to repeat the trunks would float, seemingly searching for one in particular. He said the military would never cease their search for it. It held strategic maps. I begged him not to separate us, but he kept holding me down, securing me to it. The wind and waves were slashing across us. I don't know how he had the strength, but he did. Then he took my face in his hands and kissed my cheek and told m… me…"

She broke into sobs again, and Richard pulled her from the chair embracing her, just as he had done through her night terrors.

She was still for a moment attempting to control her sobbing. He wished to halt her agony, but she needed to relieve the horror in order to move past it.

"He told me how much he loved me and that he had spent his entire life preparing to come and take me away from that dreadful house."

Large teardrops fell to the yellow dress. His eyes too were moist watching her relive the devastating pain and loss.

"He said he was sorry that he must leave me, but no matter what happened, at least I was away from that awful, abusive man."

Her shoulders were shaking with grief, and she buried her face further into his chest.

"It was the last I saw of him. Oh, Richard," she lamented, "he was the only person in the entire world who I knew loved me, and I him. I had believed when he left me, he didn't care and was selfish for saving only himself. Then to learn too late, it to be the only way to save me. Oh God, he did it for me because he loved me that much."

Richard felt the tears roll down his own cheeks. He had not considered the depth of sorrow Leslie's memories would bring her. It was fresh and raw as if it had only happened yesterday.

CHAPTER 22

"I am so vexed; I cannot abide by it! How am I to be certain of Emily's safety if I'm helpless to go to her. This is the first instance I have not been there for her. What she must think of me."

"Pray, George, do calm yourself. What you mean is this is the first occasion you have been ineffective in her rescue."

The young man cast a glance at the countess. "Indeed, mum."

The countess couldn't resist a chuckle at the young viscount. She was aware he was gathering markers for each opportunity he had rescued her youngest daughter from her own childish escapades. He was a well-behaved lad and had matured into a gentleman, despite the spoiled and indulged only child of a Viscount who had waited years for an heir.

Elizabeth Hawthorn had once loathed the notion of this wayward boy asking for her daughter's hand. Although, it had been obvious from the beginning these two shared a special bond, even as small children. From early on, they had sought one another's company. Of course, in those days his behaviour consisted of teasing her by tugging her pigtails, slipping lizards and frogs into her chair, and pushing her into the nearest puddle. As a parent, it was exasperating to have a young daughter constantly arriving home, wailing, and covered in dirt. However, this same daughter refused to ignore him or refrain from being a constant companion. Gleefully skipping off each morning to meet the little brat.

"Upon our arrival, I shall send a missive. I am confident Richard will have his hands quite occupied with Leslie; she will need you, George. Do not fret you have been supplanted. I dare say that shall never happen." The countess chuckled.

"I appreciate you saying so, ma'am." George dropped his arms to his side and forced a smile.

Clarice hurried down the stairs with her last valise and reticule in hand. Lady Gillford joined Lord Sheffield, who waited patiently in the drawing room. He had been silently observing the procession of portmanteaus and bandboxes passing by the opened door, mindlessly twirling the tassel of the hessian he had propped about his opposing knee.

"We are finally ready, Lord Sheffield. I do apologise for such chaos." She said apologetically.

"I beg of you, say no more. I have two sisters, if you recall. One older, one younger. I am quite accustomed to the mayhem." He replied with full comprehension, "It serves as a reminder as to why I require a townhouse on the other side of the park. In the area where it is most improper for a lady to be seen!" he added.

The countess chuckled as he stood and adjusted his waistcoat. Richard had three of the finest companions anyone could desire. How the four had transformed into respectable young men, she still had no idea. But, indeed, they had! James Sheffield was going to make a distinguished Duke one day.

However, he had proclaimed on numerous occasions, "No need to rush; all in due course." His father, the 5th Duke of Ratcliff, a powerful and wealthy nobleman was healthy and vibrant. Sheffield, his only son, although dependable and kind to his friends and their families, had set his designs on becoming the most notorious rake in the beau monde. He counted on his reputation to discourage the Ton mamas from accosting him with their daughters. However, for those which he cared, there was not a sea too wide or too deep he would not master to bring them to safety. This quest would require three or four days from his usual schedule. Which he declared was not an inconvenience in the least.

The gnarly, wretched Mr Weber and his newly hired extra ruffians had kept Gillford House under surveillance and followed each of them while they were out and about. Weber himself had trailed behind Clarice down Bond Street once more. When he superiorly attempted to accompany her into a shop, she promptly turned and struck him with her reticule. After their initial confrontation, she began carrying a rather large stone in her handbag. She left him with a nasty bruise on his smug cheek.

It appeared, Mr Jameson had doubled his efforts and was determined to locate his daughter and drag her back to his house or go to debtor's prison making the effort.

Therefore, some crafty changes in plans had to be made to outwit the recreants.

"George, we are ready to depart. Is your carriage still in the mews? The countess announced.

"Yes, mum." George moved across the hallway and joined those gathering to leave.

"Then do lead the way." Lady Gillford turned and lay her hand on his arm.

Sheffield offered his to Clarice as her maid took the small valise.

"Mind where you aim that reticule, Lady Clarice; I understand it is quite lethal," James said as he watched it drop heavily to her side.

"Fear not. I am mastering the art of directing its aim. I assure you; my mark was precise on the previous occasion. It makes for a fine lady's weapon." Clarice chuckled as she took Sheffield's arm.

They both laughed as they exited to the Ratcliff carriage. The countess followed George out the back entry, across the alleyway to the mews. The footman let down the step of the viscount's black lacquered coach and handed her inside. The staff escorting the group drew up in one of the Gillford coaches. The procession of equipages rolled away from Gillford house with much fanfare. As the large wheels clattered down the cobblestone road, George's keen eyes made a note of all the curious little men, who scurried like cockroaches in their path as they caught horses tied nearby.

Upon arriving at the small posting inn in Merstham, the entire party descended from their assigned equipage and scattered around the grounds, while Sheffield and Wyndham secured a private parlour for refreshments for the Countess and Clarice.

The servants came and went from the coaches unceremoniously and appeared to be removing and replacing items with every departure and return. The maids entered the transports and seemed to sit for only a moment, adjusting and readjusting their skirts, then descend once again and retreated inside the inn.

Approximately two hours later, the entire party clustered in a small, tight group just beyond the entry of the establishment. The three large carriages had been drawn up close to one another in a staggard fashion. The women all dressed in dark hooded capes pulled the hoods low over their foreheads and mingled among one another. It was impossible for a bystander to distinguish between ladies and servants.

As they reached the coaches, they scattered like ants to quickly enter the conveyances, footmen and coachmen handing each female inside. One of the equipages immediately headed off to Brighton, one the road to Oxted and the other the route to Ashtead.

Alone in his black lacquered carriage, George made his way back toward London. Through the rear glass, he viewed four confused riders gathering in the crossroad, engaging in a lively conversation attempting to quiet their horses, while determining their next course of action. He pivoted forward in his seat with the satisfaction that their plan had been successful. Suddenly a sense of melancholy overwhelmed him, as he pondered Lady Emilia. The days would pass slowly and anxiously until he received word, she was safe.

The two coaches traveling on the road to Brighton and Oxted, soon turned back toward Westerham at the first crossroad. The countess had remained diligent in her insistence upon stopping at Lady Merrick's home. She had told Lord Sheffield and Clarice she had a plot, but it would require Leslie's grandmother to ensure its success.

As they settled in for the journey to Westerham, Clarice cast her mother an inquisitive look. She had cared for this woman for more than a year. Rescued her from certain death countless times following their father's passing. Now, it appeared she did not know her at all. She was full of vigour, determined upon saving the world. Well, at least set on saving Leslie Jameson. She had never known this aspect of her mother but suspected this may have been who she was prior to their father managing all her heart's desires. She smiled and closed her eyes, swaying with the rhythm of the chaise, envisioning her mother restored to life once more.

Clarice felt the coach wheels slowing and opened her eyes to their arrival at a post house outside Westerham. Surprisingly, she had drifted off and awoke to the fading light and the disappearance of the sun. She also learnt they would stay the night at the inn. Then tomorrow her mother would call on her old friend.

It was early afternoon when the Gillford conveyance rolled to a halt in front of the Merrick cottage. A footman let down the step for the countess to alight. After brushing the wrinkles from her skirts, she turned to her daughter and Sheffield.

"The two of you may walk about if you like. I will be about half an hour." She strolled away, not waiting for a response.

Clarice looked across at James. "I am not at all certain what has come over Mama. I have never seen her so... so..."

"Formidable?" Sheffield interjected with a grin.

"Yes, that is a good term for it. I do believe I am a little frightened of her."

"I cannot say as I blame you. It has been some time since I have been ordered about. She is certainly more wilful than I have ever seen her."

"I dare say I agree." She laughed.

The knocker dropped on the heavy door; Jacob once again slowly came to attention.

"Mrs. H... I mean, Lady Gillford." The butler was taken aback, his words coming out in a fluster.

"Good day, Jacob, is Lady Merrick receiving?"

The butler appearing perplexed as he swung the door open widely, ushering the countess inside.

"Uhm, my lady, I – I." The elderly man stammered in confusion.

"Whatever is wrong with you, Jacob? I've been associated with you for thirty years, and I do not believe I have ever seen you so out of sorts. Are you afflicted with the senility?"

"Uh, no, ma'am, I mean, no, your ladyship, I mean, it is only... Oh lawd!" he stuttered. "I beg your pardon. I shall inquire if my lady is receiving."

The countess shook her head, brows furrowed, watching as the butler made his way down the hallway, muttering to himself.

Jacob meandered along grumbling about the disorder that had disrupted his quiet household. "First, the presumed dead young granddaughter shows up in the middle of the night; next, an earl, who served in the war department, intrudes; and now an old friend marches in after nearly five years demanding to be received. What has become of this tranquil residence? It could give an old man a case of the collywobbles; it could."

Mary Merrick was leaning against her cane, waiting patiently, when the countess entered the parlour. "Oh, Lizzie, it is so good to see you!"

"Mary!" The countess rushed to the elderly woman. "Oh, please, please, do let us sit down. You should not be rising to greet me."

She took her friend by the hand, and they both made their way across the room.

"I have less than twenty years on you, my girl. I am not dead yet! And after the past several hours, I feel like a spring chicken." She announced with alacrity.

"What in heaven's name has happened?"

They seated themselves on the sofa, the countess still holding Lady Merrick's hand.

"Well, to begin, your son is in my garden!"

"What? Richard… is here?" Her voice raised an octave, "but why?"

"I do believe he is attempting to reason with my not-so-dead granddaughter."

"Oh, Mary, I didn't consider. Did you receive word regarding the wreckage?"

"I did. Shortly after it occurred. I was Marcus' sole relation after the admiral passed."

"Oh, I am sorry for so much time passing before coming. But I only made the connection in the past sennight. How long has Richard been here?"

"Only a little while. I informed him of what I knew, and I suppose he is learning the rest of it from Leslie. I gathered she has been under your care until recently."

"Yes, but I had no notion of who she was. But I must tell you, something in the back of my mind recognised those eyes."

"The Merrick eyes are unmistakable, are they not?" Lady Merrick widened her lids, exposing her own. "Shame on you for not remembering, my love."

"Yes, I know, it is quite disgraceful, is it not?" the countess smiled. "Oh Mary, I formed such an attachment. She so looks like your Mary. However, after so many years, and considering the Sea Horse tragedy, her time in Ireland and Richard's involvement with the war department, I simply could not remember. But we have all fallen in love with her. and now this mess with her father, and he continues to search for her."

"Yes, and I fear he will find her. My nerves are in such a way. I tried to explain to Leslie she was far safer with Richard, but when she regained her memory and remembered losing Marcus, she ran straight to me. I must tell you; I almost had an attack of the heart when Jacob told me who was calling in the middle of the night. I was certain I was having a dream."

"Undeniably you did."

The countess and Lady Merrick seemed to forget the rest of the world as they spoke of their child and grandchild and the plan contrived by the countess was thought brilliant by Leslie's grandmother. Both convinced it was the only legal means to prevent her father from returning and imprisoning her in his home. All that remained was convincing their offspring of their plot.

CHAPTER 23

Richard held Leslie quietly for a while before pressing her further. Her grief was so severe, and he regretted his need to understand the relationship between her and Marcus. Lifting her chin with his thumb and forefinger, he stared into the tear-filled, violet-blue eyes. When their eyes caught, to his astonishment, she threw her arms around his neck and found his lips with hers. For a moment he was unable to respond until his consciousness met reality, then deepened the kiss reciprocating the passion. His tongue eased across the seam of hers; they parted, and they explored one another as they had two nights before.

When Richard finally broke the embrace and pushed Leslie away from his chest.

"You know you must marry me." He whispered.

"I cannot!" She said bluntly "And you certainly cannot marry me."

Richard jerked his head back shocked. "Why on earth not?"

"I'm the daughter of a CIT!" she said, "an earl mustn't wed a CIT."

Unexpectedly filled with righteous indignation he mandated. "Indeed, I am an earl and by virtue of that fact, I can be married to whomever I damned well, please!" he said, "And I wish to marry you!"

"You do not know me." She said adamantly, "I have lived a life trapped in a loveless house with a cruel father who held me and my mother prisoner and, if he did not kill her, allowed her to die. What can I possibly know about love, Richard? And nothing of relationships between men and women. You once told me I was confused about what it was, and you were correct.

With a hint of frustration Richard let out a sigh, then gently tipped her chin up, "I have never found a woman more born to love than you, Leslie Jameson. I do not care if you were born in Mayfair, Cheapside, or Fleet Ditch. It would make no difference."

He breathed in deeply, regaining his composure. He searched her eyes, then softly uttered, "what did Marcus mean to you?"

She looked up at him bewildered. She opened her mouth but thought of nothing to say, and snapped it shut, but continued to stare at him.

"I can't live with a ghost Leslie… who was Marcus?"

"Marcus?" She searched his face for understanding. How could she articulate the significance of someone so dear to her; the one person who had meant everything to her? Suddenly, her eyes brightened, as she realised, he had not understood the relationship between them. It also occurred to her, if she had any capacity at all to love, it was because of Marcus. The loss of him and the pain it caused her was proof of some comprehension of it. She gazed up at him, then gently reached out to touch his cheek, "Oh Richard, he was my older brother."

He blinked rapidly, so stunned, astonished, and overcome, he wasn't certain he had grasped her words. At first, a feeling of relief overwhelmed him, followed by a rapid sense of anguish as the reality of the situation hit him, leaving him unable to fathom the depth of her grief. She had lost her only brother and so soon after finding him again.

Damnation at the destruction that surrounded her. He attempted to imagine losing Clarice or Emily, but it was beyond comprehension.

My God, her brother had risked so much to rescue her, only to die in such a dreadful manner. He encircled her within his arms.

He helped Leslie to stand and led her toward the house. "We will speak with your grandmother. We must determine the next course of action and locate a safe place for you. I'm convinced it isn't here. The runner will dispatch his men and possibly come himself. I am surprised they have not harassed Lady Merrick by now. Worst of all, Weber has certainly divulged the information to your father, and if he has not already, Jameson will offer up your grandmother's address."

"Oh Richard, they may hurt her; I cannot leave here."

He was about to argue the implausibility of that course of action when they entered the parlour to find his mother and Lady Merrick holding court.

"Mother!" The earl came to an abrupt halt, staring in disbelief, "You are supposed to be at Whitton Park!"

"Indeed, of that I am aware, but we met with some difficulty, and there was a delay. Nevertheless, we are presently together, and need to mend this situation."

He abruptly lowered his chin in surprise, slightly tilting his head to stare at this woman, who was impersonating his mother.

"We must ensure Leslie's safety and put an end to this?" He argued.

"Yes, and we have a solution. Lady Merrick and I, that is." Commanding the room as if it were her own, she beckoned the young couple to take a seat.

"Mary, might I inquire if you possess any brandy or scotch? I fear my son will require it."

241

"In the cabinet behind you, my dear." The older woman gestured in the direction of a mahogany cupboard with double doors and motioned to the earl.

"Richard, pour yourself a glass." His mother ordered.

Without a word, he did so, tilting his head curiously toward his mother, then raising an eyebrow at Leslie as he returned to take his place next to her.

Directing her comments to Lady Merrick, the countess again presided over the small group. "Shall I commence, or perhaps you might wish to state our argument?"

"You are doing splendidly, my dear; carry on." Mary placed her hands in her lap and offered a smile.

"It has been brought to my attention my dear that in a fortnight you will be twenty years old."

Startled and relieved, Richard swiftly glanced in her direction, pleased with the knowledge, just as he had believed, she was older than the information he had been given.

Noticing the room's silence, he nudged Leslie indicating his mother expected a reply.

"Oh, uh, yes. I have recently discovered that myself." She blurted in acknowledgment, then glanced up at Richard in amazement and confusion.

"Well, still not majority, but close enough. It gives us the fortnight to reach my sister's house in Aberdeenshire."

"Scotland?" He bellowed.

"Yes, and Lady Merrick will accompany us."

"For what purpose?" He demanded.

"In honour of Leslie's birthday and…" she paused and, for the first time, appeared slightly hesitant as she gazed at her son and then back to Leslie.

"And what?" He entreated more sternly.

"Um… your nuptials." She hastily exclaimed and leaned back in her chair.

The Earl rose and drained the last bit of scotch from his glass.

"Well, if that don't beat all!" He said, strolling to the sideboard, poured another drink, turned to the two women who had taken up residency next to one another in solidarity.

"I must say, you are taking this much better than I had anticipated." She gazed at her son with a look of confusion.

"Leslie has refused my hand in the garden! Now you two wish to place pistols to our heads."

Both appeared perplexed, but steadfast in unanimity as they sat beside one another glancing toward Leslie.

Miss Jameson in stunned silence viewed the vigorous session of parliament held between the three. At the very least, what she had been told of the sessions in the supreme legislature. They were all speaking at once and no one being heard. It seemed the offer of marriage, which she had only moments ago spurned, was now being put forth by the two persons she held in high esteem. The speeches and chaos surrounded her, and she did not understand any of it.

All three somewhat loudly, presenting their justifications for and against the journey to Scotland, along with the hasty marriage, to which she had not yet agreed. She was staring at the earl when he glanced at her during one of his rants regarding his views on why she was worthy of more than a runaway bride, as though he was ashamed of her.

He paused and faced her, deciphering her thoughts and cleared his throat, broadened his shoulders, wrapped his long fingers around his quizzing glass. Then half raising it to his eye and inhaled a deep breath as only an English nobleman could do when he decides to take command of a room. The two ladies stopped and gazed at him. He was getting better at this, he thought superciliously before proceeding.

"It appears not one of us has considered Leslie's feelings in the matter." With that, he yielded and all three swivelled towards her.

"I – I truly did not wish to interfere, but as I informed Lord Gillford when he offered for me, I believe it would be imprudent for him to marry a CIT's daughter."

"Nonsense!" the countess exclaimed with raised voice.

"Your grandfather was a knighted admiral; your great-grandfather a baron." Mary Merrick said, striking her cane to the floor dramatically, "Your mother was a granddaughter of an earl, my father!" Lady Merrick explicated with grand dignity. "You are gently born and brought up to be a lady. You are not a CIT!"

Shocked at the lineage, of which she had not been privy to until this moment, she began to gather her composure, recalled the exact words uttered in the garden, being an earl, he could bloody well do as he pleased.

Richard, who was leaning over the sofa was forcefully gripping the back. She noticed the stiffened muscles in his arms and wondered how much longer the little settee might endure the pressure of his powerful form. She glanced back at her grandmother.

"Grandmama, do you really believe my marriage to Lord Gillford would thwart my father? I do not."

Lady Merrick glanced at Richard, then back to Leslie. Her countenance softened as she allowed her silence to command the room before continuing. "No, I do not! However, as the wife of a noble Lord and under his protection, your father would be on his own. Bow Street would refuse any assistance and the runners would not consider accepting a private contract from him. He would be at the mercy of inexperienced ruffians and the law on our side. He cannot continue to bear the cost for anyone who chooses to act outside it. I also firmly believe Richard can offer you security. That is what I believe."

She turned to the woman who had become a mother to her over the recent weeks. Leslie lowered her lashes before meeting the countess's kind eyes.

"Lady Gillford, could you truly consider, a CIT's daughter? There will be a scandal and the Ton will not easily forget or allow it to fade quickly from their tattling tongues. And how might that affect Clarice and Emily? I must consider them."

The countess moved to Leslie's side and gently placed her hand in hers. "Pray, my child, look at me."

She lifted her eyes to meet Lady Gilford's and was struck by the sincerity and genuine affection she saw in them.

"You are your mother's daughter. The child of a dear friend who made choices that ultimately took her life. However, before leaving us, she brought a beautiful little girl into this world, who inherited her grace and gentleness. Your grandfather was a distinguished and highly decorated admiral of his majesty's navy, and your two great-grandfathers included an earl and a respected baron. You need not ask me how I feel about you. Whether you consent to marry my son or not, you will forever hold a place in my heart, and I will love you, no matter."

Tears were streaming down Leslie's face. The countess embraced her, but when she looked around seeking Richard, he was gone. She withdrew from her embrace.

"Where is Lord Gillford?"

"I believe he returned to the garden, my dear." Her grandmother nodded in the direction of the opened doorway.

She excused herself and found the earl standing silently, boots slightly apart, with his hands clasped behind his back, peering over the rows of flowers.

Leslie's tiny frame casting a small shadow at his feet she addressed him. "My lord?"

Richard faced towards the heavens and closed his eyes but did not turn around.

"Do you have any affection for me?" He asked quietly.

"You know I have."

"That was before." He imparted.

"Before what?" she asked surprised.

"Before your life was restored to you."

Leslie whisk around him, reaching for his face, cupping it in her hands. "It alters nothing."

"Then why reject what I am offering you?" His eyes, seeking answers in hers.

"Precisely what do you offer me?" she said bluntly, "Protection, security, a title, all of which hold little significance to me."

"You know it is more than that. You have tempted every fibre of my being until I can no longer resist it." he appealed, "You are the very air I breathe."

"And what of your affection?" Her violet-blue eyes peered into his.

Today, he was not exhausted and exposed. He was in full control of his faculties and realised she had known her father was a CIT when he arrived that night.

"Leslie, why did you ask me to stay with you when I arrived at Whitton Park?"

She was fully aware of his question. She lowered her head and allowed her arms to fall to her sides.

"Why?" Richard seized them.

Her eyes remained cast to the stone path as the tears welled.

"Look at me." He demanded.

She did.

"Pray, why?" He asked again, clutching her shoulders firmly and giving them a slight shake.

She withdrew from him and turned away. She could not say the words facing him. Ashamed as she was of what she had done, she would not change it. In her heart and soul, she already belonged to him and always would.

"Because." She paused, unable to hide her emotions "I had regained enough of my memory to know I wasn't suitable for you. But…" she hesitated and swallowed, "I refused to leave devoid of knowing." She stopped, burying her face in her hands.

Richard waited for her to continue. When she did not, he pressed her. "Knowing what?" He placed his on her shoulders and this time squeezed gently.

She turned to him. "Without the awareness of your touch, what it was like to be in your embrace with nothing but the heat of you between us. Experiencing what I did not understand but longed to discover. The mystery of how effortlessly you caused me to tingle and tremble merely by being in the same room. The intimacy I gained without… without ever having felt your touch, it was an irresistible and intoxicating ardency. It would only be the one time, but I desired it, yearned for it. A timeless memory to keep a part of you with me always."

"You knew you were going to leave the next morning, even then, before I came to you?" He stared at her; he had been so tired that night. He had believed it to be a reaction to his absence.

"Yes, I realised I could no longer stay under your protection. I only waited for you to come to me."

"And you knew I would." This was a part of her he did not recognise. She was stronger and more determined than he had assumed.

"Yes, I was almost certain of it and prayed you would."

"And I was too tired to refuse you?"

"Yes." She lowered her head, "Of which I am ashamed. But I can't help how I feel, and I don't know how to stop it. Richard. I tried; I really did. You told me so many times not to fall in love with you, but I could not prevent it. I tried, I truly did."

He wrapped his arms around her and drew her close, tilting her chin upward, softly tracing his thumb across her lips. He lowered his head and gently kissed her. She attempted to restrain herself yet found she was unable to control the growing passion and intense yearning within. She threw her arms around him and sunk into his embrace, meeting his passion with her own. He released her lips and pressed her head into the crease of his neck.

"Marry me, Leslie. You asked me if I loved you; I am uncertain if I know the meaning of it. Yet, of one thing I am unwavering; I cannot live without you. I – I will never let you go."

"And what of Clarice and Emily? I refuse to ruin them with my scandal."

"You will not. They want you for a sister. In reality, my dearest love, not two years ago, you would be seen as the one to wed beneath you. As the son of a second son, I was invisible. Fate is all that as changed our positions."

"It does not change how the Ton looks upon CITs or the scandal of my mama. They did not forgive her."

"The sins of the mother are rarely bestowed upon a redeemed child. Your mother's only sin was falling in love with

248

someone unworthy of her and you will learn members of the Ton have excessively short memories."

"Might we leave London for a while? Perhaps that might help."

"Anything you desire, Leslie. I will give you the moon but stay with me."

Once more he sought her lips. There in her surrender he found his answer. She was his!

When the couple re-entered the parlour, his sister and Lord Sheffield had joined the two older ladies. It was apparent they had been apprised of the plan. All four eagerly waited in anticipation, searching for the response.

The earl hesitated and addressed them. "It appears, we will be travelling to Scotland."

Clarice rushed to Leslie and embraced her, nearly pulling her off her feet. "Emily and I have prayed for this day. Certainly, she loved you first, but I soon followed. It was easy to love you, dearest Leslie."

The countess looked to Lady Merrick. "How quickly can you make ready for Scotland? We must remove Leslie from England immediately."

Mary patted her hand and met Richard's glance for approval. "I shall be ready day after tomorrow. There are many provisions which must be made for so long a journey."

"Will that suffice?" The countess requested of her son.

"Yes, I believe so. We can leave straight away for Whitton Park, return in two days, and leave straight away. It will be a long journey for you, Lady Merrick, but I believe we can slow our pace once we are north of the London area."

Richard reached for Leslie's hand. "Can you leave within the hour?"

There was no mistaking her countenance or the words which followed.

"I cannot accompany you. I will not abandon my grandmother."

He had foreseen this. His only hope was she might consider the danger of remaining.

"Remaining here is not possible, Leslie." He lifted her face to his. "Your grandmother is in no danger if you are not present. You are who they want."

"No, they want Emily." She replied, "she is the one in danger."

Clarice rose hastily. "Oh my God, I had forgotten. Emily told the runner she was Leslie. She is at Whitton Park… alone! We must go to her."

Gillford did not believe Weber had mistaken Emily for his betrothed. He had seen the miniature, and there was no question in her appearance, even if they did favour a great deal. He also knew he would never convince these women his sister was not at risk.

The decision was made. The earl and his valet would go to Whitton Park alone. Retrieve his sister and be back in two days. Sheffield agreed to stay in Westerham for the ladies' protection. He would take the ladies to a local inn and return to the cottage to assist with final details.

Gillford was feeling weary, wondering how he was to manage five women on the journey to Scotland and questioned his friend for counsel.

"Is this feasible?"

"You are the expert!" The marquess quipped.

"This is beyond me, I assure you." Richard poured them both a brandy.

With purpose, Sheffield deposited his empty glass on the cabinet, "I am confident the remaining stages of the journey will proceed without incident if we manage to reach Belmont Castle safely. Weber will not consider proceeding further."

"Belmont Castle? Would that not be an imposition?"

"Of course not! My parents are in London until the end of the session." Sheffield said confidently. "A chaise and four with fresh horses every twenty miles, Grantham will easily be made in two days. We can put up at The George in Huntingdon one night. I will send a missive to London and a notice of our arrival to staff there and one at the Inn. If Lady Gillford and Lady Merrick, require additional rest, the castle shall be safe enough."

"Our arrival?"

"You don't think I will allow you to take all these women to Scotland alone, do you? What kind of friend do you take me for?" Sheffield gave him a wink.

"One that is too damn good for the likes of me."

"I hardly think so. I have not forgotten what you did only a year ago."

Gillford remembered the previous year. He had made the same journey for completely different reasons, but solely because of the unconditional friendship between these men.

"Well, the situation turned out considerably more in Andovir's favour than yours."

"I do not regret it, in the least. They were born for one another." He gave him a half-hearted grin.

"I shall not forget this, Sheffield." He shook his friend's hand, then glanced up at him. "What has become of all of us?"

"I don't rightly know about you and Andovir; I only hope it is not contagious. Worth and I might need to travel to the continent and quarantine ourselves against the spread of it."

Sheffield gave his friend a hearty pat on the back, and they drank to the earl's impending nuptials and any other reason which might be plausible before Gillford took his leave for Whitton Park.

CHAPTER 24

Emily witnessed Richard's arrival at Whitton Park, from the parlour window and was devastated at the sight of her brother alone. She hurried down the stairs and threw herself tearfully into his arms.

However, her mood instantly shifted to excitement when he informed her of the trip to Scotland. Her tears transformed into a plethora of questions with no pause for answers, as was typical with his sister.

Richard was growing accustomed to her exuberant enthusiasm for life and overwhelming personality. He eventually interrupted the onslaught of enquiries to redirect her attention towards preparing for the quest ahead.

Realising the imminent danger facing Leslie, particularly at her grandmother's, Emily swiftly ascended to her bedchamber to ready herself for travel. Trunks, bandboxes, and portmanteaux were tossed around the room as she and her maid packed both her and Leslie's gowns and fripperies. With expediency, the party departed within two hours. His plans had been well orchestrated, and it appeared they would depart for Scotland without delay.

***

On the second morning, Lady Merrick had slept in later than usual. The previous day's activities had been overwhelming, being more accustomed to stationary and quiet days. Her companion was completing her simple chignon when the butler announced the arrival of her guests.

"Assist me to the parlour, Beth and then ensure Leslie has no need of you. I am certain she wishes to appear her finest today with the return of her beau. She may require assistance with her hair. It is lovely, but there is so very much of it. How

I remember those youthful years of an abundance of curls. Age does not treat us kindly, you know. We acquire wisdom but forfeit all our physical attributes." she sighed as she glanced at her own thinning locks.

She rose and took up her ebony walking stick, her maid assisting her to the hallway. The noise and activity coming from the small drawing room ceased when the hostess made her entry. Greetings were made, and a light breakfast offered while they waited on the arrival of the earl and Lady Gillford's youngest daughter.

Clarice was the first to inquire of her granddaughter. "Ma'am, where is Leslie?"

She sat her stick to the side, craning her neck to the young miss. Only then, realising her exceptional height. She had always found Lizzie beautiful, even as a child and this girl was decidedly pretty. It was apparent her children were blessed with her beauty. But the older daughter had undoubtedly inherited her father's stature, which she was certain had caused her some dispirit.

"My dear, I had not realised how very tall you are. But you are quite lovely." Mary said genuinely.

Clarice simply smiled. She understood it was the way of elderly ladies. She was beginning to notice her own mother was speaking whatever thoughts popped into her head. However, the remarks regarding her exceptional stature no longer troubled her, lately it had become an advantage.

"It has been challenging at times, ma'am, but it has also provided me benefits as well. You were to share with me where I might find Leslie?"

"Oh, yes, I do apologise. My thoughts occasionally wander, you know. Completing her morning toilette, I have no doubt. We retired rather late last evening and took advantage this morning. Why don't you accompany her dear; she is certainly almost finished. She was eagerly anticipating Lord Gillford's return today." She gestured for a footman to escort her guest.

***

The glossy black lacquered town coach with its four matched greys pulled past the others lined up in front and came to a stop. The door swung open, and the earl's imposing figure clad in striking buckskin breeches, a dark waist and tailcoat ensemble emerged and promptly put down the steps for the tiny, impeccably dressed young lady stepping out.

"Oh, what a cute little cottage!" Emily exclaimed, glancing around at the limewashed building trimmed by the multi-coloured flora.

It was by no means small, but after living at Whitton Park and Gillford House in London, it appeared so to the sixteen-year-old.

"It is a lovely residence and immaculately tended." Her brother wasted no time in his response. "The flower gardens are charming."

"I am sure that has nothing at all to do with the story of Leslie's acceptance in that same garden." She mused and took her brother's arm.

"Hmph!" Richard replied.

"Oh, I cannot wait to see my new sister. You know Richard, I had already thought of her as such. I just love her so very dearly, and you see, I was right all along. You did have feelings for her; I knew you did. I knew it from the start. I am so incredibly happy for you and for Leslie. Especially now that she has her memory restored and is whole again. I am only saddened that it was her brother she is having to mourn all over again. That part is so exceedingly..."

"Emilia Grace!" Richard abruptly stopped and reeled on his sister. He was exhausted from the incessant loquaciousness since the early morning hours. "I beg of you, to restrain your prattle when you encounter Lady Merrick; she is older than mother and is not accustomed to such fervour. She has already had far too much of it for you to contribute to the chaos. I do not wish to criticise; however, everyone is rather unsettled until we can remove Leslie from those who wish to do her harm. Do you understand?"

"Yes, I am sorry. I… oh, forget it." She declared, "I shall mind my words and strive to remain quiet."

"Thank you!" Wrapping his arm around her shoulders and hugging her to his side, sincerely hoping she understood his impatience.

Richard's attention towards her was abruptly interrupted by Jacob's frantic yelps, wild waving, and anxious countenance, "My lord, please come quickly… to the parlour!"

The butler was out of breath and distressed. Richard released his sister and hurried to reach the panting man.

"Jacob, pray, what has happened?"

"Please, sir, Lord Sheffield is in the parlour. Oh, do hurry, sir!" The butler gasped for breath gesturing towards the inside.

Upon entry into the room, Richard discovered the settee and chairs filled with crying females. His mother, Lady Merrick, Clarice, two ladies' maids and the housekeeper.

Sheffield carefully lowered his glass of brandy and rested it on the mahogany cabinet, while locking eyes with Gillford. He hastened across the room to his friend, who stood frozen in the aperture.

"Where is she?" He roared, leading to more disruption and wails of distress from the already hysterical ladies.

Richard's heart stopped; his lungs struggled to inhale, each breath short and rapid. The ache in his chest felt as if a heavy weight had been dropped upon him, and his head was pounding furiously.

256

"Hawthorn." He heard Sheffield's stern voice break the confusion.

His breath caught. Oh God! Sheffield had not called him that in over a year. His eyes met his friend's as he drew closer before he began to speak.

"Lady Merrick and the countess have been given hartshorn, and the doctor is on his way with laudanum. They are barely holding it together." He gave Richard a ducal authoritarian look. "The local magistrate is in the garden searching the grounds and questioning everyone who was about."

Richard abruptly reeled on his heels, James matching his steps. Nothing more was said between the two as the earl burst through the back egress, the heavy door swinging on its hinges and slamming against the exterior wall of the cottage.

Sheffield gestured towards several men huddled outside the modest stable and scattered across the rear lawn and what appeared to be a gate into some sort of alleyway.

The magistrate, a portly fellow, was dressed in a lengthy black coat, billowy dark trousers and black boots caked with mud. Knowing his friend all too well, Sheffield promptly made contact with the arm of the local law and identified his friend as they approached. "Richard Hawthorn, the Earl of Gillford, Lord Gillford, Mr. Godart, the local Justice of the Peace."

Mr. Godart started to extend his hand to Richard but quickly understood it was not the appropriate time and rather lightly tugged his forelock. A caged lion was approaching him, and he knew without a doubt no matter what he said or offered, it would not suffice. He could only stand his ground in anticipation.

"Where is she?" Again, the only words Gillford appeared capable of uttering. His consternation was beyond comfort.

The calm of the magistrate, usually soothing, held nothing but contempt for Richard. "That is what we are attempting to determine, my lord. We are meticulously inspecting every corner of the back garden, as it is undoubtedly how they approached."

"Have you discovered any sign or indication of how or who may have taken her?" The earl snapped.

"It has not been determined if indeed there has been a," … the man paused and stammered, "an… involuntary abduction."

Sheffield, a bit taller but of similar physique, seized Gillford as he lunged for the magistrate. Stopping just in front of the peacekeeper, who was shorter than both approaching men.

"I dare you suggest she left this house wilfully!" He thundered as James restrained him.

Richard tried to jerk his sleeve from his friend, "Let me go, damn it!"

The justice stepped back and glanced up at the marquess, whose hold was slight and only enough to allow Richard time to regain his equanimity.

"These are unusual circumstances." Sheffield quickly interjected and released his grip.

The earl, habitually tugging at his sleeve and waistcoat, a slight reassurance that he was regaining his composure.

"You mentioned it." The magistrate acknowledged, then addressed Gillford.

"I beg your pardon for the presumption," he remarked, "but you must understand my position."

"I understand nothing, except my betrothed is in grave danger, and I alone am tasked with ensuring her safety not only for my personal involvement" he hissed, "but by the war department."

Hawthorn had no patience for debate or the impertinence of an overzealous magistrate looking to press his importance.

"If your people have found no significant information, I do know where to start, and I must be off quickly. Pray, what if anything have your men discovered." The earl said with disdain, standing confidently composed with an air of superiority that had become second nature.

It appeared in the morning hours before dawn; someone had entered the back gate and a window on the backside of the cottage, where footprints were discovered.

"It was difficult to ascertain much information from them," the magistrate explained. "As it appeared they had also exited the same casement and retraced the same tracks making it impossible to know how many or if the girl left on foot."

The highly skilled military manhunter walked to the exterior egress and quickly determined the prints leading to the opening were not as deep as the ones leading away, suggesting added weight. Although they were vigilant in attempting to retrace their steps, one of the abductors was larger than the other. Two abductors, and they had carried her away. Outside the gate, he discovered evidence of a small two-wheeled wagon, which was pulled by only one horse. Either they transferred her to another gig, or it would take a while for them to return to the city.

"I need to inspect her chamber." Richard motioned to his friend. "Leslie possesses great fortitude. They must have rendered her unconscious."

Upon entering her room, he directed his attention to her bed and lifted the pillow to his face, instantly jerking his head back and tossing the offensive cushion across the room.

"Eather! That bastard will regret the day when I lay hands on him." he raged at the incompetence of the local law, turned, and headed to the parlour.

Sheffield at his side, reminding him not to excite the ladies further, making it clear that he alone, would require them to have sound minds and not hysteria if he was to arrive safely in London with them.

"What do you mean, you alone?" Richard's eye twitched and faced the marquess.

"You need to make haste to London, travelling swiftly and that will be as a lone rider."

"Thank you." Gillford rubbed his face and ran his fingers through his hair, pressing his thumbs into his temples. "The coaches are set and ready to depart. You only need to alter their direction."

"Precisely! Now, let us reassure your mother and Leslie's grandmother you will be leaving straight away."

The countess and Lady Merrick were holding on to the other as if to prevent the other from fracturing. The two sisters were embraced on the opposing settee, the elder rocking the tearful younger sibling.

"The carriages are prepared, and once you have gathered yourselves, the coachmen will be ready to depart. Sheffield will see you safely to London."

His older sister nodded assuredly to her brother, as she rocked and stroked the weeping youngest.

Sheffield returning from the carriages and his groom, interrupted the earl to advise him of mount. "Gillford, Clarence will have your horse ready in five minutes."

Richard turned to his friend nodded and assured him, "you can depend on Clarice for assistance. She has been holding this family together for a year."

The marquess glanced toward the eldest sibling who returned his smile.

"Where will you go first?" he asked.

"Bow Street. I cannot go to Jameson's alone. I am certain Weber has his lager louts posted there. We have outwitted him on numerous occasions, and now that he has her, he will arrange whatever is needed to keep me out."

A feeble voice emanated from the sofa. "I do not believe he will harm her." Lady Merrick glanced up as Richard approached her.

She offered her frail hand to him; he gently enveloped it in his. "How can you be certain? He has done so in the past, and what of her mother?"

"I did not mean he will not eventually, even though it would be accidental. In his depraved mind, he desires to win her affections once more. He is a man of extraordinary pride. He desires to demonstrate to society he can keep his wife without coercion. He shall grant Leslie an opportunity to redeem herself. He provided Mary multiple chances before he, he…"

Everyone remained silent as the elderly woman wiped her tears. "…before he took my Mary from us. I believe he will afford Leslie the same. You have the chance to rescue her, I believe."

Gillford knelt beside Leslie's grandmother meeting her eye to eye. "God as my witness, I will return your granddaughter to you, unharmed."

He squeezed her hand and released it. Through tear-filled eyes, she placed her palm to his cheek and gave him a confident smile. Richard stood and addressed the remainder of the room.

"I must take my leave. Sheffield will escort you to Gillford House without fail. I shall return there as I am able, but I will not do so until I have Leslie." He extended his hand to his friend. "Once more, I am in your debt."

The marquess shook his hand and grabbed his forearm with his other. "Your mount is my pure-bred Arabian; you need not worry about the distance. He will make it easily and can be pushed hard. Neck-or-nothing and Godspeed, my friend!" Sheffield gave his arm one last shake!

"Thank you!" With the final word, Richard Hawthorn, Earl of Gillford, left for London.

CHAPTER 25

"I beg you, let me go!"

Leslie was pounding on the heavy wooden door as she heard the key rotate in the lock. The shuffling footsteps of her deranged father grew fainter, as she hushed her cries. She turned away from the mahogany slab and sank to the floor, her soft shuddering sobs turning to wails. "Oh God, please help me, please!"

Drawing her legs to her body, she wrapped her arms around her knees and rested her head upon them. She pondered the events of the last few weeks and months. With the amnesia completely gone, she was overwhelmed with heartache, fear, and despair.

She had escaped her prison with the assistance of her brother. Who had managed to flee this dreadful place after their mother's death? She had always believed, even before recollection, her father's accusation of a lover had been untrue. But the memories of Marcus, who had saved her, only to lose his life on the Sea Horse was unbearable.

As the wails transformed into sobs, then to hushed tears, she thought of him risking his life to rescue her and the promises he had made for their future. All those stolen meetings and plans at the window leading up to her escape had all been lost in the dark waters off the coast of Ireland.

She remembered the day he informed her their grandfather had purchased him an officer's commission. How he had bravely fought and survived the Peninsula Wars and endured the dreadful days and significant losses at Waterloo. She was so proud of her brother and his career as a soldier.

She recalled their final moments together. He begged her to muster the strength to endure, to keep her head up and never to give up fighting for breath. He assured her the military would never stop searching for the trunk to which he had bound her, and someone would discover her. Just stay alive… for him.

There was his final kiss, urging her never to forget how much he loved her, to live life for both of them, before he gently slid the container into the tempestuous waters. She wept then, as she did now. She recalled him standing on the crumbling deck of the sinking vessel, watching her drift away in the turbulent waters until he vanished from view.

She was certain that his life would have remained unchanged whether she had accompanied him or stayed behind. Yet somehow, as she sat in the darkness of the room which had again become her prison, she blamed herself. He might be alive had he not come to her rescue. It was of no significance, she realised, but the sorrow of finally having her brother returned to her, only to lose him, was traumatic, and the grief of his loss was still fresh in her heart. Just as if it had only happened yesterday.

Dragging herself to her feet, she walked around the room she knew too well. She wiped her tears on the long muslin sleeves of her dressing gown. Good God, they hadn't allowed her time to change her clothes. They had covered her mouth with… something and it was the last she remembered.

She opened the bureau which still held a few of her dresses, older ones she had left behind. She pulled out the yellow, one of her favourites and slipped it on. There was no need for stays, even if she had them. She would never again set eyes on the world beyond these walls.

The dressing table contained none of her hairbrushes or pins. Those lay at the bottom of the Irish Sea. She doubted her father would notice that she had no brush for her hair. He was so delusional he wouldn't care if her locks were in tangles. She ran her fingers through them and shuddered at the pitiful sight in the mirror.

The counterpane on her four poster was the same pink flowered one, worn over the years. The bed appeared untouched from the day she had carefully made it to flee with her brother. She had dared to dream after being a prisoner in this horrid place for four years.

She hadn't always been locked away in this room. In the beginning, her father only refused to let her out of the house, then never downstairs. There were only two maids allowed to speak with her, believing those who had helped raise her would most likely assist in her escape. The remaining servants were told of her insanity and that she must be bolted away for her protection. She had overheard him tell a new domestic he hadn't the heart to send his only daughter to Bedlam. Many days passed when she honestly believed she would eventually go insane as his control tightened. She was now quite convinced that it was her destiny or worse.

The last year, he had barred her in this specific room containing only one window, with a three-story drop to the ground. There were no trees or shrubs and no access to the street to seek assistance. The only reason her brother managed to rescue her was due to his knowledge of the hidden doors and passageways that connected each floor and each room, where they had played as children. No one else was aware of those concealed rooms and accesses they had discovered.

This chamber was so secluded that it was unlikely anyone would ever stumble upon it. Her screams would go unheard, and the thick, heavy door was impregnable. It was the same room he had moved her mother into when she became sick.

She pondered her mother's illness. She had been quite young when her mother died, all she remembered was what her father had told her. Mary Jameson had only been ailing a week or two before she died. Her father had insisted on taking care of her. She had believed it to have been admirable of him to love someone so deeply.

There had been little time to discuss anything other than her loss of memory and a few stories prior to being torn from her grandmother's home so violently. The elderly woman helped her recall some memories and confirmed some of those Marcus had shared.

He had recounted his departure and how he tried to take her with him. She had little doubt she had protested leaving. She was a little girl and had no knowledge or understanding of the instability of her father.

She shivered with fear and consternation reflecting on the confinement of her mother in this room. What if she had not been sick at all? What if her father had treated her mother in an analogous manner? Her mother's death had never been descried. Her father simply saying she had gone to sleep and never awaken.

Leslie walked to the foot of the bed and stared up at the pillows. The same place she had stood the last time she had seen her mother alive.

Suddenly, she was transported back to her childhood. The little girl focused on the faded rose-coloured counterpane and envisioned her mother lying there, so very still. Her eyes closed and the cries of a tiny daughter never perceived, at least that is what her papa said.

Her childish cries calling out to her mama resounded in her ears, as if it were yesterday. She was entranced as she watched her mother's head gently sway to the sound of her child's voice, her eyes fluttering as if wishing to open them. Had she heard her daughter's voice summoning? She would never know. Her eyes blinked and she returned to the present. She wasn't allowed to see her mother again after excitedly informing her papa of her movements.

Leslie walked to the side of the bed and flung herself across it, taking one of the pillows and embracing it. "Oh, mama, what really happened to you? What is to become of me? Am I to be a prisoner here forever." She whispered. "Or for as long as he permits me to live, as I am certain he did you." As her tears began to flow once more, she drifted off to sleep crying softly.

***

Richard was on his friend's pure-bred, riding neck or nothing, allowing the steed to find its own stride and rhythm. He kept his eyes peeled to the road to ensure a smooth path.

In ancient days, the Arabian was bred for war. Its endurance and speed made it the choice that carried Alexander the Great on his conquests. These magnificent and swift animals caught the attention of English breeders when they sought to add speed and endurance to their own horses. The thoroughbred was the result and through its blood and spirit, the Sport of Kings was born.

Sheffield's prized Arabian also bore the legendary blood mark across its shoulder. His friend had versed his noble stallion would deliver him swiftly to his destination without fail or falter.

The earl could feel the proud steed responding willingly to his every ask. He was determined to locate Leslie before nightfall and this magnificent animal was readily fulfilling his duty.

It was six o'clock when Richard drew close to his intended location. There was always a young lad hanging around #3 Bow Street seeking to make a farthing or two for holding a horse. His target in sight as he approached the building, he whistled and threw the youth his reins as he leapt from the saddle.

"Walk him a bit, he has come a long way, and he is tired." Gillford said, "so do not let him stiffen."

"Fetch 'im a bit of water, guv'nor?" the boy said eagerly.

"Not too much, but I will pay you extra for it." The earl called as he reached the steps and dashed inside.

"Where is Childs?" He wasted no time as he approached the front desk.

"In his office, melord!" The clerk looked up, recognising Hawthorn, and motioned down the hall.

Richard never broke stride knocked on the door but not wait for a reply.

Sir Childs raised his head abruptly, irritated by the intrusion, until he identified the visitor, along with the look on the earl's face. "Hawthorn!" The magistrate stood swiftly.

"I hate to intrude, but it is a matter of urgency."

"I surmised as much by your manner. It's the girl?"

"Jameson dispatched two ruffians for the abduction from her grandmother's this morning. Lady Merrick suspects he has gaoled her in a third-floor bedroom, where she was previously imprisoned, before her brother aided in her escape and removal to the safety of Ireland."

"Her brother?" Childs's shock was evident.

"Yes, it appears George Jameson is completely mad. Lady Merrick sincerely believes he regards his daughter as his wife and intends to treat her as such."

"Hawthorn, can you honestly believe that? It sounds impossible." The magistrate had listened to numerous extravagant stories, but this was an especially outlandish accusation. If proven false, the consequences would be severe for his department.

"All the signs were present, Childs. I disregarded them as well. I found it quite incredulous someone might be so delusional. The grandmother shared her story, and once I understood that Captain Merrick had rescued, not kidnapped, his sister, many things began to make sense. Leslie recalled fragments she hesitated to share, but her fear was palpable."

He ran his fingers through his brown hair in frustration. "From the moment we arrived at Ramsgate she was anxious, and it only worsened when we reached London. Although she remembered nothing, she sensed her life was in danger here. She described the room where he held her prisoner.

My mind was filled with a million thoughts when I was convinced a suitor had whisked her away. However, discovering it was her brother, and the grandmother aware of the plan, I am convinced of its veracity. I also..." The earl paused, regretting his decision to withhold information from the magistrate, "I also spoke with the Jameson housekeeper. She met me in secret and shared more distressing events. She had brought Leslie to receive treatment for bruises the man had inflicted upon his own daughter. I fear it is all true, no matter how preposterous it appears, sir."

Lord Gillford was a respected member of the war department, the Ton, and a highly reliable special agent of the Crown. He would never panic or issue a false warning if he were not certain of it. He had suspected the earl's affection of the girl clouded his judgment. Yet, he was convinced of the truth in his words. There was little doubt Leslie Jameson was in danger.

Childs promptly rose, swiftly grabbed his coat and hat, and followed him out the door.

"I'm on horseback, sir. I will meet you there."

Richard proceeded towards the door, only to be halted by the magistrate. "Hawthorn do not approach the house without my presence. This must be official. The girl is not yet of age, and George Jameson now holds the legal cards as she is under his roof." He grimaced, "wait for me?" He allowed no room for defiance.

"Yes!" The earl paused. "I will, but I shan't wait long, Childs. We were travelling to Scotland to be married, in hopes of thwarting the plans of this lunatic. Once Leslie is safe, I shall do everything in my power to commit him to Bedlam."

"If only you had made it there. You know, at this juncture, you have no lawful rights. We must strictly adhere to the law. I am sorry, Hawthorn, but we will rectify this." He declared. "I am close behind you. There are two runners in the back room, and the carriage is hitched in the rear. I will join you shortly, but I insist, do not approach that front door without me."

The earl nodded and promptly departed through the entrance. The young lad was at the Arabian's head bearing a small pail of water and the steed appeared a bit rested.

"You're a good man." Richard tossed the boy a half-crown, and his eyes widened.

"Anytime, guv'nor, anytime!" he grinned, removing his cap, and bowing to his lordship.

Richard seized the reins and urged the horse into a brisk trot. He directed him away from Oxford onto Duke and slowed to a walk. He continually glanced backward searching for Childs as he passed Somerset, then Gray Street, uncertain of the magistrate's route. As he approached Seymour, he drew to a halt.

He dared not risk George Jameson accusing him of harassing his daughter. The father knew nothing of his and Leslie's relationship, but any single man would cause him alarm. If he was as unstable, as Richard was entirely convinced, the man might completely unravel.

At the corner of Seymour and Duke, a youth was loitering about, so Richard decided to dismount. The boy was eager to mind his mount and the earl slipped him a farthing with a promise of more upon his return.

Richard had frequently been in these same situations. He was aware of the importance of approaching silently on foot, rather than riding up on a high-spirited horse and attracting attention. As he turned the reins over, the Bow Street carriage came to a halt behind him.

Two burly males alighted from the coach. Their sheer size was intimidating, paired with the multi-caped coats and shiny top boots, they created a malevolent sight. A groom leaped to the heads of the bay geldings, as Morgan Childs exited to join them. The four men, all towering over six feet, with robust and sturdy builds, presented a powerful and impressive site.

All the runners were of a grand stature, it was expected. It was also why Richard Hawthorn had excelled in his position with the war department. He never hesitated to enter a dubious situation; convince it would require several blokes to render him vulnerable.

Side by side, they marched down Seymour. Their mannerisms and obvious determination were an overwhelming vision of power and strength.

Reaching #20, Sir Childs proceeded to take the lead and stepped up to the front door, gesturing the three to remain at the foot of the steps. He took the brass knocker into his hand and gave one last glance at Richard, praying his actions as a war department spy would not be subjugated by his affections for Leslie.

"Remember Hawthorn, professional." His tone was firm, but it was all the magistrate had time to offer.

The old butler opened the door and inquired his name and business. He attempted to maintain eye contact with Sir Childs, but the three men standing behind him cast an imposing sight.

"I am Sir Morgan Childs, magistrate, here to see Mr George Jameson."

The manservant appeared quite anxious and stuttered his reply, "I-I will in-inquire if the m-master is receiving."

Childs splayed his hand against the door and took one step forward, knowingly unsettling the domestic.

"You misunderstand me. I am here to see Mr. Jameson... immediately."

The old man nodded and stepped back, granting the arm of the law entry. Although he showed no indication of attempting to stop any of them, the other three hastened inside. The diminutive man peered up at the four and swallowed nervously.

"I will inform the master." He motioned them into the parlour and drifted off down the hallway, obviously bewildered.

The four men lingered by the door, and the commotion and demanding voice from the hallway was immediate. The owner challenging who the magistrate thought he was, forcing his way into his home at this time of the evening.

Richard observed the older man approaching down the corridor, adjusting his waistcoat. As he had remembered, the man was short in stature, with a balding head and a portly midsection, characteristic of indulgence in excess food and liquor. He had little doubt that Leslie had inherited all her beauty and charm from her mother.

To avoid being recognised immediately, he positioned himself behind one of the runners. Yet, he had an unobstructed view of the elderly man as he retrieved his topcoat detected its rather odd weight. With the butler's assistance, he monitored the difficult in which the man slipped into it, confirming one pocket clearly hung lower than the other. A small detail which in the past had proven useful.

Jameson was taken aback by the imposing group that awaited him in the parlour but lost no time in asserting the authority he believed to carry in his own house.

"I dare you intrude into my home demanding to see me like I was a common criminal. I have nothing to say to you, sir. I care nothing for your position, and you may carry yourself off and bring your charlatans along with you."

The older man realised he had overstepped his bounds, as the justice step toward him and loom over him.

"Mr. Jameson," the magistrate's voiced boomed, "I care nothing for your tone, and I have every authority to come into your house uninvited and unannounced when I believe there is cause."

George Jameson glared defiantly at him refusing to yield.

"Then state your business," he barked. "Then I trust you have the decency to leave."

"Once I obtain what I seek, I shall be happy to do so." He replied unmoved.

"And what is it you seek? Declare your purpose." The man demanded again undeterred.

"You have a thief in your midst, and I am here to apprehend them."

Richard displayed a calm demeanour despite the immediate shock by the accusation. As he glanced around at the other runners, who appeared completely unsurprised. Apparently, this plan had been devised in route.

"I beg your pardon; I have no thief under my roof," George Jameson said with appalling indignation.

"That, sir, is where you are wrong. The arrest was scheduled for this morning at another location. We discovered the footpads had absconded to this address. If you are unaware of their presence, we will search your home thoroughly. It is the purpose for my men, to conduct a proper search, every floor."

"You are mistaken!" However, Jameson's resoluteness was weakening. "What gives you the impression they fled here. No one enters this house unbeknownst to me."

"Then you admit you're a part of the theft ring?"

A swift response from Sir Childs was one of the reasons Richard respected the man.

"I dare you accuse me of such a thing!" The man was obviously flustered, which was the intent.

"The thief was brought into this house by two accomplices."

"What?" Jameson was beginning to change his demeanour, becoming fidgety and increasingly nervous, with perspiration forming at his brow.

Richard had no idea what the old man might attempt. However, he was certain there was a weapon in his jacket pocket and had no doubt the man would use it. Surely, to God, he would have enough sanity left to know he could not overpower all four of them. At least he hoped he was still that sane.

The magistrate continued. "We have been observing this gang of footpads for some time. The two men have been protecting the thief and ensuring their safety. We have had the house under surveillance for days. Today, the two left, but the thief did not."

Jameson was showing signs of clear agitation, his eyes blinking, and the corner of his mouth twitching. The sweat was building on his forehead, and his hands were no longer trembling, they were shaking violently, but still, he did not budge.

"We will search your house, with or without your consent. Step aside." The magistrate deciding to push the man further.

Jameson began to shout, stepped back, nearly stumbling over a chair. As it crashed to the floor he wheeled around and ran toward the staircase swiftly ascended them with Childs on his heels.

The three men closed the distance between them as they found the second level. Childs gestured for them to slow their pace. He had no intention to intervene in the man's actions until he led them to the room where Leslie was being held.

Richard attempted to gain Sir Childs's attention, but to no avail. He had a gut feeling, and it was not a good one. In all his dealings, that feeling had never failed him. When they arrived at the third landing, Morgan's pace slowed as the old man fumbled in his pocket.

When he came to the door, he retrieved a key and quickly inserted it into the lock. As he twisted the key and prepared to enter, Childs quickened his steps, swiftly reaching the door, sliding his large leather boot inside the slab and casing.

Jameson pushed and swung his arm violently through the opening, hoping to dislodge the big man providing time to close and secure the barrier that separated them.

Childs placed his weight into the door. The other three men reached the magistrate's side, and another runner placed his foot against the hinge of the slab; it wasn't going to budge.

Leslie bolted straight up in the bed, clutching the pillow in front of her as a form of protection. She was confused and disoriented from being suddenly awaken and struggled to grasp the sudden chaos unfolding around her.

Jameson abruptly released the door, dashing across the room, making his way to the young woman, who was now struggling to reach the edge.

She detected a hand seize her arm and was precipitously jerked from her bed and dragged to the edge of the room, then hauled to her feet. She recognised her father, yet the madness surrounding her was confusing and illogical. She stood in silence as four large men burst into the room.

As the men were clambering through the doorway, she felt the small cold circle of steel press against her temple. "Oh God," Her heart stopped. The chilling truth descended upon her; it was a pistol. It dug into her temple, but it wasn't steady, it was quivering. "Oh, dear God!" She grieved.

As the activities around her deteriorated, she slowly emerged from the haze of being suddenly awakened, keenly aware her father held the weapon and wouldn't hesitate to use it. She was overcome by a wave of nausea and struggled to remain steady.

"Jameson!" the magistrate's blaring voice commanded, "do not be stupid. She is a thief and not worth getting yourself killed over."

Leslie's gaze flew to the man bursting in after her father, and curiously measured his countenance. She glanced at the other two men bewildered, struggling to understand what was happening. A thief? Did he just call her a thief?

She slowly and methodically surveyed each of the tall, brawny runners standing side by side across the floor, both rugged, sturdy, and strong, then her gaze met the fourth man... Richard! Oh Richard, she heaved a deep long breath, then locked her eyes with his. He nodded his head slightly as he stepped forward where the four stood abreast.

She was terrified as the cold steel of the barrel pushed harder against her, forcing her head over. She stared at the earl, seeking strength, guidance, and reassurance.

George Jameson's eyes were focused on the magistrate, who continued speaking calmly to the distraught man. Fixated on Childs, Jameson was unaware of the eye contact between the couple.

Leslie nervously moistened her dry lips, inhaled deeply, and bravely swallowed.

"She's no thief; she's, my… my…" Jameson was ranting unintelligibly while tightened his grip around Leslie's arm drawing her closer to him, shielding himself from the four intruders.

"Then you have no knowledge of what she has been up to." Sir Childs' spoke with a composed and authoritative tone. "Can you swear she has been in this house for the past several months?"

The wheels were spinning in Jameson's confused mind, his eyelids blinking rapidly.

"She is a thief! And I am here to apprehend her, and you are aiding her flight. You are now a party to this and will be arrested as well."

"Tell them, Leslie, tell them you are not a thief." He jerked on the arm he had bent behind her.

When she grimaced, Richard inhaled sharply, catching himself as his body instinctively began to lunge forward, knowing a misstep could prove fatal. Their eyes met; he was silently urging her to participate in the charade.

Leslie's heart was pounding, scarcely discerning the words being shouted and screamed around her. What was the large man in charge saying? She must concentrate. With fear gripping her chest and her breathing shallow and laboured, she stared into Richard's pleading eyes. What was he begging her to do? Who were all these men? She quickly deduced, he must trust them, or seemed to. She searched his countenance as she willed herself to calm. He would protect her and inhaled deeply… yes, she must participate in the deception; it was her only hope.

"I cannot papa. It would be a lie!" Her eyes remained focused on Richard, the slight twitch of his lip to suppress a smile, satisfied her the only safe way out was for to be the thief they sought.

"No," he demanded, "You are not!"

He jerked her arm and demanded, "what did you steal?"

"Jewels!" She blurted, the first thing that came to her.

"Don't be stupid, from where?" He pressed the pistol for capitulation.

"Rundell and Bridge." She had now become a part of the farce, and her mind worked furiously to think of appropriate responses.

The magistrate heaved a sigh of relief. She would say what was required of her. Until he had witnessed the pistol pressed against her temple, he hadn't fully understood the magnitude of the man's instability. Jameson was indeed completely unhinged. Morgan Childs had never expected to be standing between life and death due to a runaway child. He had to proceed cautiously if he was to keep everyone alive.

"I shall not permit you to take her! She belongs to me! You cannot have her." The old man was shaking and bellowing.

Richard was losing his patience with the delusional man but also knew the magistrate had been faced with similar circumstances. He was renowned as one of the finest negotiating runners in the history of Bow Street. He had to remain placid and patient for Leslie's safety.

"You have no choice, sir. She is sought after for crimes and has admitted to the theft."

"Who is claiming she is a thief?" ignoring the words of confession. "I will compensate them for the jewels. She is not leaving this house. Do you hear me? She is not." He was on the edge of hysteria at the thought of her being removed from his grasp.

"Jameson, be reasonable. She must be held accountable. You may very well settle your debt with Rundell & Bridge, but that changes nothing."

"I will ensure she doesn't escape again. I will hold her here whilst I resolved the matter with the jeweller and myself."

"It is no longer only between the jeweller and yourself. There is a charge made, now it is to be thoroughly investigated. I am obliged to arrest her and take her to Bow Street for questioning. There is no room on that, but you can bring her along."

"No! No!" He quaked, "She must not leave this house, this room, she cannot!" the old man was howling, shaking his head. He was clearly losing control.

"I can see no reason against us all proceeding to the station. That request is not unreasonable." Child's stated, then paused effectively, "Unless, of course, you plan to flee the country with her. We have no way of ascertaining that you have not been aiding her."

The magistrate realised he would have to take some risks; he truly did not wish to, but the man was not budging. He would need to push him further.

"Are you accusing me a thievery? Are you?" Everyone witnessed the pistol trembling in his hand, he directed it accusingly at the magistrate, before quickly returning it to his daughter's head as he became more unravelled.

"From my perspective," Sir Childs's voice remained steady, "your reluctance to accompany us to the station is because you intend to abscond with her yourself."

Leslie's breath was still shallow. She was determined to remain prudent. She was searching how to become more a part of the ruse and perhaps offer assistance in a situation spiralling out of control. She resolved to find a glimmer of sanity that might still abide within her father's mind.

"Papa do not take responsibility for my actions. I am akin to mama; I am not worthy. You do not deserve to bear the cost for my transgressions." She declared, stiffening, and straightening to appear confident and convincing.

The magistrate narrowed his eyes as he studied Leslie's expression. It was obvious she was attempting to think of some way to reach the madman, and she alone, might hold the information to do so. She offered him a reassuring glance and proceeded to taunt her father. Richard was exceedingly uncomfortable. In his opinion, the main was completely devoid of sanity.

"You know Papa, mama stole from you, just as I did. She ran away, like me. Neither of us valued your kindness or goodness. We both should be locked away. She resisted and you had to administer drugs to calm her during her illness. Is it not so? You knew she was wicked."

The uttering of those few words aloud, Leslie realised she must seek her own answers amidst the chaos.

Richard cringed as he witnessed the resolve that overcame her and concluded she sought satisfaction and closure. Dear God! He prayed she understood the consequences of those actions. It could be deadly, and he felt utterly powerless. He had to trust her instincts.

"No! She was not wicked." Her father's hand began to waver, and rested it on her shoulder, but pointed towards her neck.

"She loved me, she did." His softened sounding very much like a pouting child.

"No, papa, she did not. She was planning to elope once more; she told you so. That is why you administered the sedative to prevent her from leaving us. Isn't it so? She was going to abandon us. You know it to be true."

"Yes, but she didn't. I made her stay."

"With the drugs?" His daughter pushed for answers.

"Yes, yes," The man's shoulders slumped, and his voice quietened and whined, "but she kept requiring more and more. She continued to wak…"

He lifted the gun and pressed the knuckle of his thumb to his temple. Richard considered reaching for Leslie, but Jamison was too quick, bringing his hand back to her shoulder.

"It is all right, papa, you did it for me. So, she would not leave us."

"No!" he cried out and lowered his arm and the pistol to Leslie's waist, his voice regaining its vigour. "I did it because she had been with another man. Just like you were planning to do. You were not meant for that." He shook his head again, as if he were changing personalities again. "You wretched wench." He jammed the pistol into her side.

Leslie winced from the thrust, and it was almost unbearable for Richard. He curled his hand into a fist, but Sir Childs visibly flinched, jerking his head towards him, pleading with him to remain firm. He must allow this to unfold and knowing with a sudden move, Jameson would pull the trigger.

The man's ramblings continued directed to his daughter. "You were supposed to save yourself. I was the only one who was to touch you. I tried to make you understand, but you left with another man.

My dearest, dearest Mary, my love, I loved you with all my heart. I loved you." He tried to pull Leslie toward him, "Mary, say you love me." He pressed his lips to her cheek. She stiffened shutting her eyes to remain steady. "You told me once you loved me with all your heart. Please, say it, say it again." He abruptly moved the pistol to her cheek and forced her head towards him. "Mary, I love you! Say you love me. Say it, Mary! Say you will stay with me."

All four men stood paralyzed, afraid to break the old man's thoughts. But all fully aware the situation was headed towards its climax.

Richard inhaled and prayed Leslie knew what she was doing. This man genuinely believed she was his wife. He made a quick glance to the heavens praying to God, to help her choose her words carefully.

"Papa, I am Leslie!" Tears were streaming down her face. She was terrified, but with stalwartness and determination she continued. "I am not mama! Mama is dead. I am your daughter."

"No! You are my Mary!" he insisted, then paused, "but you can't be, she is... No!" he denied, "she can't be... You! But... you cannot be. No, no..." he howled. "She cannot be dead. I loved her. Oh God!" The wailing man was undone as he continued. "No! She kept waking and threatening to leave. I could not let her go, Leslie. I could not allow her to leave us. Oh God, why did she not understand," he was loosening his grip on his daughter, "I could not let her go. I couldn't..." It was the ramblings of a madman.

The old man's voice was out of control; he was no longer aware of his surroundings, but he still held the gun to Leslie's cheek. Everyone remained frozen as he continued his shrieking.

"Oh God, I... I... I killed her... Oh, Mary, I am sorry, I never meant to harm you. It was too much, I should not have... Oh, Mary, I did love you. I never meant to... I did not mean to... I only wanted you to stay with me. I'm sorry, so, so, sorry."

Leslie reached to take hold of the pistol, but Jameson pulled away from her. He raised the metal to her head once more. Everything and everyone inhaled and held it, including

281

Jameson. His head bobbed back and forth the gun still at his daughter's head. He was staring into her eyes, her tears streaming down her face.

"Oh God! Leslie! My child, my little Leslie." Her father dropped his head. "I am sorry Leslie, I am and… I love you."

Without warning, he abruptly lowered the pistol and shoved Leslie's small frame way from him.

Richard instinctively rushed to her dropping to the floor, shielding her with his body, as the thunderous sound of the gun exploded across the room; the sound was deafening. Leslie clasped her hands to her ears, attempting to protect herself from the vociferous, blood-curdling scream emanating, she realised, from her own lungs.

A mere second later, she felt Richard's embrace, but the screams persisted. She was trembling violently but managed to open her eyes, blood was everywhere, the walls, the floors. Richard was covered in it, along with her arms and face.

"Oh God!"

She struggled to free herself, but he drew her tightly against his chest, shielding her from the rest of the room. She was trying to pull away, but his grasped unyielding.

"Shhhhh," he whispered, "Shhhhh."

"You're hurt, Richard!" She was still screaming.

"Shhhhh!" He continued in a hushed tone and stroked her hair.

She pushed against him, but he maintained a strong hold, pressing her head to his chest, her face nestled in the V-shaped opening above his waistcoat. The commotion throughout the room took on a deafening quiet. People were scurrying about, but no one was speaking, was there a struggle?

"It's over, Leslie." She heard him say, her body still trembling. She was uncertain what had occurred, but Richard was drenched in blood.

"Oh God, please don't die, I beg of you do not die!" She was sobbing, attempting to control her breathing.

Then another woman's voice pierced the air with a blood-curdling scream. "Oh my God!"

She recognised Mrs. Jenkins voice, but Richard held her tightly to his chest.

"Get her out of here!" The commanding voice of Sir Childs bellowed.

Leslie turned her head just enough to witness the counterpane and sheets being stripped from her bed. It was all she managed from Richard's unyielding clutch. The sobs of Mrs. Jenkins were still ringing in her ears, but someone was leading her out of the room and down the hall.

"What is your name?" Childs' voice was unmistakable.

"Jenkins, sir." The voice of the butler answered.

"Get something to clean up this mess. We will remove him shortly."

"Hawthorn, we have things secure, you can remove Leslie now." Once more it was the magistrate.

He helped Leslie to her feet, still holding her against him as they walked into the hallway. There he finally released his hold.

She raised her head and felt the stickiness of her face. Her hair, cheeks, and neck were covered in Richard's blood. She seized his arm and drew him one way, then the other, searching for his injuries. He was shrouded in claret, as was she.

"Y-you are not h-hurt." She stuttered, before looking up at him.

"No," he said softly.

"Whose then…?" She attempted to glance back into the room; Sir Childs' hands were stained crimson. She turned her eyes to the other two runners, hunched over the blood-stained linens from her bed.

"Oh God!" She buried her head into Richard's chest again, and he wrapped his arms around her.

"I am sorry, Leslie. We tried…"

"I know." She cried softly, "I… I… oh Richard," she grasped his coat and buried her head into his chest, "somehow, I knew… I've always known… someday… one of us would never leave that room alive."

CHAPTER 26

Mrs. Jenkins immersed the bloody cloth in the large bowl filled with water and wrinkled her nose as it turned a bright shade of red.

"Thank you." Leslie sat motionless, still attempting to make sense of the past few hours.

"You're welcome, love." The housekeeper gestured for the maid standing nearby to remove the bloody mess. She reached for the dry towel sitting next to her and gently dried her mistresses face. "The dress is completely ruined, and it was a such a lovely colour of yellow."

"You think so?" Leslie tried to smile at her longtime confidant, who had become more like a mother to her over the years.

"I will purchase a dozen more just like it." A voice came from the other side of the room. The earl stood at the window in his blood-stained coat, staring at the street below.

The housekeeper approached him. "Might I fetch you something, my lord?"

"No, thank you, Mrs Jenkins." Richard held his gaze out the casement.

"My lord."

He realised the older woman wished to address him, and he turned to face her. Her eyes were kind. He recalled the look of desperation the previous time they had met. He smiled and the relieved face was filled with gratefulness.

"There is no need, Mrs. Jenkins."

"That is where you are wrong, my lord. We owe you a great debt. I can never express my thanks." She curtsied and quietly left the room.

He glanced toward Leslie, still seated and carefully drying each finger as if to remove more than the dampness. She never took her eyes from the exchange between her confidant and love. Then her gaze followed the woman as she took her leave.

"She was like a mother to me after my own... died, you know."

"I know, she told me."

"Richard?" She held the cloth still and lowered her hands to her lap.

"Yes, love." He retreated from the window and moved to the chair next to her.

"What happens now? I mean this evening."

Placated with no hint of sorrow or remorse, she only had a sense of relief. At long last, her ordeal had come to its conclusion.

"Once the doctor arrives, we will likely head to Bow Street. We will all have to give our statements."

"Oh." She said wearily.

"It won't be lengthy. But it must be done... whilst everything is still fresh in our minds."

"I understand. However..." She glanced down at her crimson splattered dress, arms outstretched. "And you are covered in... in..." Her eyes drifted over his claret stained coat, now drying a darker shade but left no doubt it was human blood.

"I know. Once we have finished at Bow Street, we will proceed to Gillford House and indulge in long, hot baths."

"What? I could not. I have no clothes; and… it would be most… most improper."

He longed to caress her face, embrace her, but thought better of it. They both appeared hesitant, neither quite certain how to manage their new circumstances.

Leslie had never suffered such violence. She was in shock, which accounted for her calm demeanour. This man had inflicted an unduly amount of pain, yet… he was still her father. Relief… grief… loss… a multitude of complex emotions overwhelmed her.

"We won't be alone." He assured her.

"What do you mean?" She looked at him curiously.

The last she remembered, everyone was at Westerham, or on their way. She had settled into her bed in the early morning hours for a brief rest before they were to travel to Scotland. She awoke to a shuffling sound in the darkness of her room. Then someone covered her mouth and nose with a cloth, plunging her into blackness. Regaining consciousness later, she found herself in a large canvas bag, which reeked of decaying vegetables, until she was unceremoniously dumped into her father's house.

His shrewd eyes mocked her, reminding her his wealth always provided success, no matter the duration. Then he had locked her inside the prison she had called home many months before. Now he was dead. She blinked back the memories and focused on Richard.

"Your grandmother is at Gillford House or will be by the time we arrive."

"My grandmama, in London?" she asked surprised. "She has not been to London in years."

"Well, it appears her granddaughter is worth the inconvenience."

"Oh, Richard, she cannot see me in such a state!"

"Rest assured, she cares only to see you and will be unconcerned with your appearance. I have conveyed the message; you are with me and are well. I provided no further explanation, so I dare say we can face that when you have rested and refreshed."

She quietly leaned into the corner of the sofa; her hands folded in her lap. They were still trembling, but she had managed the horrific unforeseen developments with quiet dignity and composure. She, indeed, was no frail female.

Recalling their first encounter, on the brink of death, Richard could hardly believe the transformation of the woman before him now. He was confident once the day's events fully penetrated, she would not be so placid, but neither would she be hysterical.

Resting in the corner of the settee, her eyes gently closed, as her head sank into the pillow. She inhaled a deep breath as she slipped into slumber. Discovering a thick lace coverlet draped across the sofa, he carefully placed it over her, hoping she might get a moment's rest. He tucked the throw around her, then reclined ardently guarding her sleep.

"Lord Gillford." Sir Childs filled the entryway.

It was unsettling to hear himself addressed in such a manner by this man. Sir Childs had never referred to him by any name other than Hawthorn. Now that he had finished his last assignment, he supposed this was to be his new life. He would no longer find the convenience of hiding behind plain Richard Hawthorn. He had then, and only then, realised it was over. His last assignment was indeed complete.

"Sir Childs!" Richard rose from his seat and crossed the room to meet him.

"The doctor and undertaker have arrived and will oversee the remainder of what is to be done."

The magistrate cast a glance at Miss Jameson, her eyes still closed and breathing steadily. "How is she?"

"Better than she ought to be. I have been a steadfast companion for several months, and she is a courageous, resilient young woman. I daresay she will be fine in time."

"I hate to ask it, but if you can bring her to the station tonight, we can dispense with any further need of her. Since we were all present, there will be few questions."

"I have prepared her, and she is anxious to be done with it."

"Gillford, I am not at all certain how much of this I can keep from the newspapers, but I will do my best."

The magistrate was eager to assist the young earl, whom he greatly respected, but this situation was bound to be an unavoidable scandal.

"I know, and here we are at the end of the season; most everyone still in town." Richard quipped.

"Considering all the recent scandals among the nobility, perhaps a wealthy merchant will pass unnoticed." Childs shrugged.

"It may very well be the reason it will not." The nobleman susurrated.

***

Lord Gillford handed Leslie into the carriage, apologising for its lack of luxury. She gave him a slight smile and assured him that as long as she was not forced to ride in a putrid canvas bag, she would make no complaints. The magistrate glanced at the earl as if to acknowledge the courage and strength of this young miss.

Upon Lord Gillford's arrival at #3 Bow Street, a palpable disordered ensued outside. When he entered the building, the clerk was overwhelmed with demands. Darcy peaked up and nodded him toward the back.

Richard passed the magistrate's closed door, heading directly to the kitchen. The counters had been wiped clean, with only a small candle glowing in the middle of a small wooden table casting eery images along the walls. He silently watched them dance around the room by the flickering flame and followed the shimmering shadows. Noticing the kitchen entry into the office was ajar and the room bright with candlelight, he stepped to the door. A large man peered out the window at the street and bustling crowd below.

Hawthorn tensed, his blood turning to ice, his hands mutating into unyielding fists until his knuckles paled. He burst through the doorway, moving swiftly and catlike across the floor giving no consideration to consequences or ramifications.

The abrupt disturbance caused the man to reel from the window, his eyes widening at the instant recognition. A smug short laugh escaped him as his lips curled into a sneering expression of gratification. However, before he could further exploit the satisfaction of his triumph, he felt a sudden tightness at his throat.

With one hand, Hawthorn snatched the man's neckcloth and slammed him against the nearby wall, jamming his forearm hard into the jugular of the smug adversary.

"Hawthorn!" the man coughed, gagged, and clawed at the earl's arm. "You're choking me!"

"I hope to kill you." The earl said in a low growl and buried a swift, solid knee into the man's groyne.

Weber made an effort to double over but found himself unable to budge held firmly in place by the powerful forearm. Gasping for breath, he fought the nausea rising from his gut. With a surge of determination, he mustered enough strength and delivered a blow to Richard's midsection. However, to his dismay it neither fazed nor weakened his opponent's firm grip.

The nobleman seized the flying appendage with his spare hand and forcefully twisted it toward the runner without yielding an inch from the man's throat.

Weber had severely underestimated the nobleman. The loss of air, strike to the groyne, agonising ache in his elbow and the constriction at his throat were having an impact. The thrashing ceased and he began to dangle lifelessly.

The noble earl had vanished, and the dangerous agent of the Crown had emerged. "Weber, I trust you have your affairs in order."

Immovable, unyielding and gasping for air, Weber precariously hung by the mere forearm of the highly skilled military spy. Accustomed to the rough brawls of Fleet Ditch, he found the finesse and quickness of a skilled professional beyond his abilities.

"Hawthorn!" A thundering sound echoed from the kitchen door. "Let him go! We've had enough killing for one night. The murder by an earl would hit the scandal sheets before daylight." Sir Childs boomed.

His voice was strong yet devoid of agitated or aggression. Sensing he had Hawthorn's attention, he lowered his voice and casually strolled to his desk and again addressed the earl.

"Let the son of a bitch go. He's not worth the effort, my lord." The justice sat in his chair and reached for a cigar.

He stooped to a candle and squinted as the flame sparked, flickered, then settled. He hurled his feet onto his desk and crossed his ankles before taking a long draw from his smoke.

The magistrate gazed curiously at the pair in the corner of his office. Hawthorn's body relaxed as he removed his forearm and Weber instantly dropped to the floor like a ragdoll, curling into the foetal position while the earl loomed over him.

"Good God, man, where on earth did you learn to fight?" Sir Childs glanced down at his finest runner curled on the floor with one hand on his throat and the other between his legs, embracing his manhood.

"A Shaolin monastery in Henan." Hawthorn raked one hand through his hair, pushing the chestnut locks back into place, shaking the other vigorously, attempting to ease the cramp from the tight fist. He tugged at his bloody waistcoat, straightened his topcoat, and turned to the magistrate.

"I've witnessed first-hand why the war department refuses to acknowledge nor accept your resignation." He said lifting the box of cigars offering the earl.

Lord Gillford shook his head in refusal, then glanced toward the doorway.

Miss Jameson stood, quietly watching the scene unfold with no sign of agitation or surprise. Her eyes on the slouched figure struggling to pull himself into a seated position.

"You gonna live?" The magistrate mumbled through the smoke from the thick cigar he held between his teeth as he dryly looked at the man still on the floor.

Unable to make a recognisable sound, his hands still at his throat, he only gagged and coughed.

"I've warned you, Weber, your main flaw is placing greed over ethics."

The gammy man's bloodshot eyes sought out the magistrate in disgust. Sitting up and leaning against the wall. his normal breathing had not yet returned.

Sir Childs stood and gestured Miss Jameson into the room and offered her a chair, motioning for Hawthorn to take the adjoining one. Nonchalantly, he withdrew writing paper from his drawer, placed a metal nib onto his quill and dipped it in the inkpot, noticing Leslie's curiosity.

"Bryan Donkin is a friend of mine. Gave me this a while back. He's unable to garner any interested in investing, but I like it. I am not the neatest at sharpening my quills, so my housekeeper is pleased." He smiled and redirected his focus. "Pray, why don't you tell me briefly from the beginning. I have a distinct impression Hawthorn and Weber have purposely omitted valuable information. It is not necessary to include mindless, unimportant details. Just tell me your story, Miss Jameson."

Before she began, a loud cough and vulgar clearing of a throat breeched the room. Sir Childs held up his hand, halting her and glanced to his runner, who was attempting to rise from the floor.

"If you can manage Weber, pick your filthy a…, I mean, take yourself off to the kitchen and find something to ease down your gullet and do not return. The site of you repulses me."

He stood and looked toward the desk at the three occupants for the first time noticing their blood-soaked clothing.

Barely audible, scratchy, and seemingly painful, he whispered. "What the bloody hell happened to you two."

The magistrate grinned. "Not that it's any of your concern… oh wait, perhaps it is." He laughed. "Have you secured the Jameson contract?"

"Tomorrow." Was all he could manage to blubber.

Tersely and dismissively, Sir Childs lowered his head over his paper as he spoke, "No need for you to waste your time. Jameson is dead."

He lifted his eyes to catch Weber's stupefied and sickened response. Childs felt the urge to burst into laughter at the runner's countenance but thought better of it. After all, this was the dead man's daughter sitting before him.

"I suggest you settle with your ruffians and move along to your next assignment. I trust your priorities shift somewhat. Perhaps, you should place greed a bit lower. You never know what might happen."

Weber staggard out of the room closing the door behind him.

CHAPTER 27

Weeks passed as they waited for the scandal to erupt, but it appeared a deranged nabob held no interest in the upper society of the *haut ton*. Sir Childs had kept his word, and the file remained locked in his personal desk. It seemed, as time went on and with another London Season months away, the nightmare was truly over.

Richard Hawthorn had completed his assignment and bid farewell to the war department, closing that chapter of his life. The new Earl of Gillford was at last assuming his rightful position. He was dedicated and determined to become an effective member among the powerful yet ageing gentlemen in Parliament.

Leslie Jameson sold the house on Seymour Street that had once been her prison. Her grandmother persuaded her to purchase a lovely townhouse on South Audley. Her father's solicitor and banker had the pleasure of informing her that despite her father exhausting an enormous fortune to locate her, several times more remained to support the lifestyle of her choosing.

She and Lady Merrick established their home together in a grand four-story dwelling, filling it with fine luxurious furnishings and making it their own.

The Jenkins, who had dedicated the past years to protecting Leslie refused to leave her and found themselves in charge of the new domicile. They were requested to seek and provide positions for as many domestic servants as deemed necessary for a well-run household.

Lady Merrick, a well-regarded member of the Ton in her own right, regained her spirit and eventually sold her cottage in Westerham to remain full-time in Town with her granddaughter and to properly introduce her into the beau monde the following season.

Once Leslie's inheritance was settled, the townhouse procured, the Westerham cottage placed up for sale, her grandmother whisked her off to the continent, leaving the Jenkins in charge to complete the setup of their residence.

Mary believed her granddaughter required a change of scenery and time away before dealing with the demands of London's *haut ton*. Where else could one possibly refine the skills of navigating high society better than in Paris? Following the drum with the admiral, she was well-connected in the French aristocracy.

Leslie and Emily remained as close as sisters, and letters flowed constantly across the channel. Lady Merrick and Lady Gillford agreed that upon their return, the young ladies would make their come-out together in the upcoming spring season.

***

After six months away, they returned to find their townhouse in perfect order, and a cast of servants to oversee all that was necessary. A closed carriage pulled by matched bays, had been acquired in her absence, along with a barouche for sunny afternoon promenades and soirees Leslie and her grandmother would be attending. Lady Merrick's staff from Westerham, who wished to remain with her moved to London and settled in with the Jenkin's. At the age of eighteen, it appeared Miss Jameson had come full circle, and could finally attempt a somewhat ordinary existence.

Emily sighed, making a backward flop onto the counterpane in Leslie's bedchamber. "Can you believe it? It is almost upon us. Not that I have been waiting for this moment all my life, but very nearly most of it."

"Don't be absurd, Emily Grace. You *have* been waiting for this your entire life." Leslie gave her a perfunctory nod.

She giggled, rolled to her stomach, propped herself up on her elbows, and rested her chin on her laced fingers, grinning at her friend, "True, but Mama insists it is not at all proper for me to say so. Did you have a pleasant journey to France with your grandmother? I overheard her conversing with Mama. It appears she had a splendid time."

Leslie ceased folding the wrap in her hand, lowered her arms and gazed at her friend. "I suppose I did, but everything is so incredibly strange."

Emily perched on the bed and stared at her. "Strange? How so? If I were in you, I would be the happiest female in the world. Mistress of your own home, furnishing it exactly as you wish, doing whatever you please, whenever you choose to do so."

Leslie seated herself next to her friend. "My life made more sense when I had no memory at all than it does now, which is nonsensical. Oh, I...I find myself at quite a loss for words to explain it. I felt lost before, but I had direction. Now I still feel lost but with no direction."

She had been back in London for a fortnight and Emily had visited her almost every day. They had gone shopping and explored her new home, but neither had mentioned Richard. She supposed it was time.

"Is it..." she hesitated, "is it Richard?"

Leslie lowered her head, "Oh, I don't know, but it is of no consequence."

"Good gracious, it most certainly is." Emily snapped. "I have watched his portentous manner around the house for months, attempting to hide his melancholy. He has become a tyrant and not an agreeable one, I might add." The girl protruded her lower lip in a pout. "I have always been able to charm whatever I wished from him, but now, I am not given half a chance, before being cut-off. Initially, he was only doleful, but after you left London, he became irritable and annoyed with everyone and everything."

"I do not understand." Leslie stared at her.

"He misses you," She asserted, "do not be so foolish."

"But he is the one who said I needed time and appealed to Grandmama to take me away."

"But he didn't intend forever. He might have said so, but he didn't mean it." Emily could see Leslie was perplexed. "He divulged to Mama one night at dinner you deserved time to discover yourself and live life. I was not at all certain what he meant by that. After all, in the few months surrounding your arrival at Gillford House, you had lived in a missionary in Ireland, sailed from there to England, almost snatched off the streets of London, embarked on a wild trip to Kent, travelled alone from Whitton Park to Westerham, kidnapped and driven over twenty miles in a canvas bag, then rescued by your hero. You came into a fortune, purchased, furnished, and staffed a Mayfair townhouse, took lessons from some of the top London tutors, travelled to France and God knows where else on the continent." She paused only long enough to catch her breath, then pressed on. "And now, back in England, you have a French modiste working day and night fashioning you a wardrobe for the upcoming season. All in little more than a year, if that isn't living, by God, I do not know what is!"

"Emily, do not use such vulgarities." Leslie scolded her.

"I beg your pardon, but really. What else do you need to discover?" She huffed.

Miss Jameson lifted her chin and stared at her friend. "Emily Grace Hawthorn, you are right!"

Leslie leapt to her feet, tossed the wrap to the chair, and dashed across the room to her closet, snatched a pair of walking boots and a bonnet.

The reserved, shy, once submissive young woman abruptly transformed into a force meant to be reckoned with as Emily in astonishment asked, "pray, where are you going?"

"To see your stubborn, obstinate, pig-headed, overbearing, domineering…"

"Do not waste your vocabulary on me. Apply it to him!" She laughed and sprang from the bed, clapping her hands gleefully. "I left him in his study, and by all appearances, he means to be there all afternoon."

"Good!" Leslie hastily slipped into her walking shoes and tied her bonnet. She headed to the door, donned her cloak, and pulled on her gloves, pressing the soft kid leather in place between each finger. She swiftly turned with an authoritarian glare at Emily. "Well, are you coming, or do you intend to just stand there?"

The earl's excited sister snatched her bonnet, cloak and slipped into her gloves as she rushed out the door following the exasperated mahogany-haired tigress. "Oh, I'm coming!"

She marched as closely behind her friend as she could, but Leslie was clearly on a mission, and she did not wish to interrupt the wrath that was building with every step.

Upon arriving at the townhouse on Upper Brooks Street, Leslie never missed a stride. Emily paused at the foot of the steps, observing with delightful giggles as Carson opened the door. His eyes widened in surprise as Miss Jameson, who he hadn't seen in months slapped her reticule and bonnet into his mid-section and, in an angry and methodical tone, snapped, "Good morning, Carson, I trust you are well," as she strode right past.

He glanced to his young mistress, who had rushed in the door laughing and rubbing her hands together mischievously. "Oh, this promises to be quite delightful!"

With haste, she took to the staircase, the butler close behind, as the two hurried up them in Leslie's wake. As they reached the landing, they stood in silence as she flung open the study doors, entered and slammed the heavy mahogany slab shut, with a rumble loud enough to awake the dead.

The parlour door opened, and Clarice looked puzzled. "What the... where are you going?"

"It is Leslie. She is about to give Richard a proper set down!"

"Well, it is about time!" She said as she fell in line with her sister and the butler. By the time they reached the study, the housekeeper and a maid had joined the convocation.

The countess walked up behind the group each with an ear leaned against the door and cleared her throat. "Might I ask what is going..." but was interrupted by a loud crash in the study. "Good Lord, who is in there?"

Emily giggled and whirled to her mother giggling. "It is Leslie... and Richard."

"Oh..." Then she grinned, "Well... do not all of you have somewhere to busy yourself?" She raised her eyebrows and nodded slightly.

"Oh, Mama!" Clarice and Emily retorted in unison.

The countess, raising an arm, pointed down the hall with a look of no argument. The butler and housekeeper slipped away quietly returning to their positions. Lady Elizabeth Hawthorn marched directly behind her daughters chastising them with every step in the direction of the saloon, attempting to hide her grin of satisfaction. She winced, then smiled with every crash she overheard from the study. Her silent prayers urged Leslie onward, hoping she did not back down for a second to her son.

The entire way to Gillford House, Leslie recollected all the reasons she had been miserable over the past several months. She had been the one initially to propose there was not the least necessity for them to marry. She contended that she was now safe and no longer required a protector. However, she had not expected the earl to concede quite so readily.

She recalled every word of his declaration in her grandmother's garden. All the moments they had shared, prior to and after she regained her memory. She remembered the conversation after she had come into her inheritance and had no need of anyone in her life.

The words of the aforementioned gentleman passionately conveyed his belief that she had been held captive for years and that he would be damned if he would shackle her so hastily. Especially now that she was finally liberated to pursue her desires and live life on her own terms for the very first time with the resources to do.

In her brief but brisk bolt from South Audley to #6 Upper Brook Street, Leslie concluded that all men were idiots and entirely ignorant regarding the fairer sex. With great force, she slammed the heavy wooden slabs shut and, in full-blown fury, cried, "I dare you!"

Richard's head flew up from his writing. "Leslie!"

His face lit up and he rose to greet her, only for the expression and movement to cease immediately when he saw the wrath in her eyes as she stormed towards him. He was prompted to meet her halfway, but reconsidered and retreated behind the safety of the imposing desk that separated them. He dropped his quill onto the parchment at the sight, he had not seen since she left for the continent. My God, did this woman become more beautiful with each passing day?

"Do not Leslie me!" She barked as she stomped towards him. "What gives you the right to direct my life?"

"What?" Richard, still fearful of moving, was trying to decide if he might possibly survive the leap from the second-floor window behind him. He backed away from the desk, closer to the glass and glanced down... no, not an option... "I haven't directed anything of yours in...in..."

"Exactly so!" She jerked her cloak off and threw it across the chair in front of the desk, "You dictated my every action, everything I ate, every place I slept, every person I met, even the decision to haul me off to Scotland, everything for months!"

"Well, yes, but... I... only..." Richard, by now, was gathering his wits about him and realised he was so happy to see her, he didn't care why she was standing there. She was looking more radiant than he had ever seen her. She appeared to have fully recovered, from the shipwreck, her memory fully restored and had moved past all the horrid events that followed. He also had to admit, she was absolutely stunning when in a full-blown rage.

Attempting to suppress the smile that continually crept onto his countenance, he raised his eyebrows and listened with undying affection, monitoring her pace back and forth across his study. She was slinging her arms about her, occasionally stopping long enough to extend one of those accusatory slender fingers towards him, only to start yelling and pacing again. He found it delightful.

When she exhausted insults to hurl, she began picking up items around the room. She hurled a rather heavy paperweight, which Richard caught, causing her to huff in disgust and stomp her foot. She easily located several vases of fresh flowers, which she threw at him with abandonment. He dodged most of them fairly easily, trying hard not to chuckle as they shattered haphazardly behind him, water soaking the rug. Spotting a large leather-bound book of Shakespearean plays, she retrieved it but hesitated, "You are not worthy of

Shakespeare!" She blustered, laying it aside and throwing a novel by Henry Fielding instead.

After dodging a few other smaller objects, Richard attempted to physically restrain her. The consequence of that foolish deed was being narrowly missed by one of the matching Cauldon Chinoiserie vases.

Of course, that may have been more a result of his unrestrained mirth than anything else. Following the unsuccessful attempt to control the situation, the Earl chose to wait out the fracas at his desk, taking refuge behind the tall leather back chair, which he found to be a nice cover from flying projectiles. He also began to understand the wisdom in Shakespeare's words - discretion is the better part of valour.

The anger finally waned, and the familiar look of anguish swiftly lapsed into tears. Richard took advantage of the brief respite, embracing her before she collapsed under the proliferating exuberance of her hysterical tantrum. Of which he would never accuse her.

He coaxed her onto the small sofa, her chest rising and falling as she regained her composure. Even in this state of agitation and distress, she was beautiful, and God, he had missed her. She inhaled deeply, then exhaled, shuddered a bit, and released a ladylike hiccup. Richard brushed the fallen locks away from her face and tucked them behind her ear.

He had a sudden urge to nibble on the exposed lobe but thought this probably was not the best time. He let out a small groan and grinned sheepishly.

Only inches apart, she snapped her head around to face him. "What?" She asked breathlessly.

"Nothing." He lied, attempting to repress a grin.

"Oh, it was something." She pulled her head back a bit to see him more clearly.

"I was admiring your ear lobe."

303

"I beg your pardon?" Bewildered she squinted suspiciously.

Richard began stroking her back.

She heaved another sigh, "That does feel wonderful. You used to do it when I was upset or had a nightmare." She gazed at him. "I remember."

"I hope it was a good memory?" His strokes became longer and deeper, from her neck down her spine to her waist.

She tucked her head and softly whispered. "Oh, Richard, why did you let me go?"

Richard lifted her chin with his forefinger. "I had to."

"What does that mean?" Her eyes searched his.

"Why are you here, Leslie? You've been back from France for weeks." He held her still.

"I thought you would come, but you did not." She turned her head, and he released his hold. "I had to know."

"Know what?" He asked, dropping his arm.

"How you felt, how you feel... I do not understand what happened. I suppose I was so confused for a while." She said, "But now, I cannot move forward, nor can I move backwards." She shook her head and dropped it into her hands.

"The last thing you said to me, Les, was, I will not hold you to your offer of marriage. It no longer signifies. And you were right about it. You were also correct that I had dictated everything regarding your life. At the time, I thought it necessary, and it was to keep you safe. I discovered, too late, it was not the only reason."

"I believed to protect me was the only reason you wished to marry me. I did not understand anything about people, relationships, feelings. I had been a prisoner in my own home with no social skills except from a book. How could anyone care for or love someone like that?"

"I don't know how one does." He said facing her. "No one can explain why they fall in love with another. But we are all born for love."

"Does one ever fall out of love?" She looked up at him; her eyes were moist, fearing the answer.

"I suppose one can if it is left unnurtured. But Leslie, there are various kinds of love."

"I do know that, and it frightens me. You told me once mine was not the right kind of love."

"I was an idiot!" He said bluntly.

"You were?" The corners of her lips turned up, hopefully.

"I was, and I am."

"Richard." She hesitated, fearful to inquire, but compelled herself on. "Do you think perhaps we can... I don't know... start over. I mean, truly begin again?"

"I can't do that, Leslie."

"Why not?" She said dismally, a tear trickling down her cheek.

"Because... I would have to fall out of love with you." He moved his hands to her shoulders, "And, I cannot unlove you."

He gently cupped her face with his hands and set his lips to hers. Softly at first, then as he sensed her surrender, he devoured her mouth with his. He felt her arms come around his neck and pull him closer. Experiencing the familiar burn course through him, Richard latched onto the copper sable locks pulling her closer, as they slid from the small sofa to the Aubusson rug.

Leslie began pulling and tugging at his shirt, recalling the heat of his bare chest next to hers at Whitton Park, and longed for his touch once more. In an instant, the sensations that had risen up and down her spine that night returned.

His tongue persistently explored, parting her lips, and delving between them. He released her hair and pulled at her clothing, tugging at the morning dress that covered far too much. His adeptness with tiny buttons did not fail him, stripping them open and pulling at the corset, skilfully revealing the alluring bosom he could not forget.

She arched her back, anticipating his indulgence, and he wasted no time satisfying their mutual desires. As his tongue caressed the firm nipples, he murmured inaudible words that were of little consequence. Weaving her delicate fingers through his chestnut hair, she held him tightly to her breasts.

"Oh, Richard!" She had forgotten the titillation of his touch that night in Whitton Park, but it all came flooding back, along with the sudden remembrance of their present location in his study in the light of day. This behaviour was quite improper, as anyone could enter at any given moment.

"Richard." endeavouring to gather her wits and put a halt to this loss of control.

"What?" He released her, and she sat up, attempting to catch her breath.

"We... must... not do this." She breathlessly stammered.

"Why not?" He grumbled, knowing full well why not.

"We are no longer betrothed." She tugged at her bodice, covering herself.

"Oh... right." His countenance revealed disgust and irritation, while other parts chastised his ignorance of their carnal need. He bent a knee and sat up impeccably straight.

"Forgive me for my lack of control." He reached out to assist with her dress. "But damn it, Leslie, I have nearly lost my mind over the past months in your absence."

Bowing her head, she whispered. "What now?"

"Pray, do you still hold affection for me?" He softly caressed her cheek.

"You know I do." She said, her eyes filled with tears.

He stood and pulled her to her feet.

"Do you still wish to marry me? As I still very much wish to marry you. At this instant, I wish nothing more than to whisk you up to my bedchamber to ensure this damn wedding takes place quickly without delay or interference."

"What! You must not! You cannot!" she shrilled.

"That is not an answer, and I do want an answer... now." Richard stood straight and stepped to her, nearly touching but not quite. "Do you love me?"

She glanced downward, her cheeks turning a rosy hue. "You know I do, with all my heart."

"As I love you and give you my whole heart and all that comes with it. Now, make no mistake, we will find a quiet place outside London and will be married with a special license in the next two days. But now, I intend to ensure there is no doubt to whom you belong."

"But Richard, you mustn't!" She looked at him in shock, remembering that Emily had followed her there.

"Oh, but I will." He seized her arms, took a mischievous step toward her, and grinned down on her.

"You see, as I mentioned once before, I am the Earl of Gillford. This is my humble home, and I will do whatever I damn well please within it. If I wish to claim my betrothal and bed her two days prior to our wedding to prevent any thoughts she might take into her head of running off to France or elsewhere, I will do so."

Leslie snorted a laugh.

"I beg your pardon?" The earl laughed at her.

All Leslie could do was grin.

"Leslie Jameson, will you marry me?"

She blushed from her head to her toes.

"Yes," she said breathlessly, "if you will still have me, I do wish to marry you."

He snatched up her small frame and tossed her over his shoulder, as he had done on the jetty at Waterford.

"Richard!" Leslie protested with a screech of delight.

Flinging open the doors to the study, he discovered the house to be quite empty, not a maid or a footman within sight. It appeared his mother had cleaned house in her own manner. The earl ascended the stairs two at a time as Leslie bounced and giggled the entire way to the master bedchamber.

EPILOGUE

Richard and Leslie were married, not two but three days later by special license and in a small chapel in London. The new countess of Gillford discovered her life to be as normal as anyone's, living under the quizzing glass of the beau monde.

At times Richard missed the adventures of his prior life. But Leslie eased most of those urges. They talked of other places to venture and experience together, which sounded far less dangerous.

Emily Grace was presented at court, enjoyed her first season to the fullest and found many things to enjoy within the upper society. The events of the past year had lessened her interest in searching for adventure and, indeed, settled her mischievous ways… a bit.

By the season's end, Viscount Wyndham approached Lord Gillford for her hand and was given approval to court his youngest sister. Emily and George were betrothed, with the caveat that the wedding would not be rushed, and a sensible engagement period would be heeded. Both mothers insisted upon it, as they had been waiting for this betrothal since the two were just out of leading strings and their wedding would be a huge affair.

Before the end of the summer, the dowager countess and Clarice relocated to the dowager house at Whitton Park and chose to forgo the following season in London. Clarice abandoned the hope of securing a husband and accepted her fate as a spinster, focusing on the care of her mother and anticipating the joy of spoiling her nieces and nephews that were sure to come. And indeed, the arrival of one or the other was expected by early spring.

The dowager countess and Mary Merrick frequently found opportunities to visit one another in London. Lizzie shared stories of the mischief she and Lady Merrik's daughter had discovered in their youth. It brought such joy to the elderly woman, who had lost so much and had come remarkably close to losing it all if it had not been for her beloved new grandson.

The earl doted on his new grandmother-in-law. Leslie's townhouse was retained for Lady Merrick. However, her grandmother joined her at Whitton Park when her confinement arrived. Where she would remain as long as Leslie would permit her to do so. Of course, the countess had no intention of allowing her to leave at all.

On the thirteenth day of March, Leslie lay in the countess' bedchamber in Whitton Park. It was the first time she had actually been in the bed of that chambre. She had used the room for her toilette, a change of clothes, and to closet those items. But today, she was propped up on pillows, surrounded by her grandmother, the Dowager Gillford, a local doctor, and a nurse. Her copper-brown locks were damp with sweat, her knees bent, and all she really wanted was to release blood-curdling screams.

However, at this precise instance, she preferred to be given the ability to breathe. With only a few more short breaths, she could once again start shrieking for someone to bring her husband into the room where she could kill him.

After enduring several hours of the same scene over and over, Leslie was exhausted and in tears. The dowager was holding her hand, telling her it was almost over, and with shuddered pleas that were barely audible, she whimpered. Her grandmother had moved to the chaise near the window with her hartshorn and was practically in tears herself, unable to bear witness to her granddaughter's suffering.

"Oh God!" With the strength of Hercules, the countess hurled herself off the pillows and clutched the dowager's hand so tightly she grimaced.

"This is it, Lady Gillford." The doctor declared. She heard the words, but he was no longer within her sight.

The nurse was standing to the side, encouraging her to push... she did.

After what seemed like an eternity, Leslie collapsed into the pillows and breathed in the air around her. She closed her eyes and sensed that the world around her had fallen into a deadly quiet. The sounds of movement surrounded her yet silence prevailed. She perceived activity, but the room was engulfed in an uneasy hush.

Unexpected tears began to trickle from the corners of Leslie's eyes, mingling with the sweat in her hair. She attempted to catch her breath, struggling to breathe and smile simultaneously, finding it impossible to do so. She glanced up at the dowager still holding her hand, and their eyes met, both drowning in tears.

"Is it... is that..."

"Yes," The dowager chortled.

It was all her mother-in-law uttered as they listened to the soft but demanding cries of the tiny baby the doctor had only moments before passed to the nurse. She was cleaning and wrapping the tiny creature into swaddling.

The door suddenly burst open, and Leslie attempted to raise her head but was entirely too exhausted. The dowager's hand slipped from hers as her mother-in-law drifted from the bed, allowing her son to assume her place. Gently clasping Leslie's hand, he lifted it to his lips and held it there for a moment then eased it to his cheek.

"I must look dreadful," She whispered, staring up at her dishevelled husband.

"You are the most beautiful thing I have ever laid my eyes upon." He said softly returning her hand to her side.

311

Leslie smiled as they both noticed the nurse approaching from the far side of the bed.

"Lord and Lady Gillford, I would like to present your daughter." The nurse placed the tiny babe into her mother's arms and discreetly moved away.

The earl smiled but struggled to find his speech.

The countess glanced up at her husband and brushed a tear from his cheek as he marvelled at their newborn daughter. He tenderly caressed the delicate hand resting upon the loosely wrapped swaddling. He gasped as the tiny hand gently curled around her father's finger. The parents were overcome with emotion as their tear-filled eyes met and Richard choked with affection, stammered. "Never again dare to inform me that you were not... Born For Love.

We hope you enjoyed "Born For Love"

The Born For series continues with Born For This, the story of Thomas Worthington.

A Match for the Marquess will be available in all formats soon. Follow Thomas, who, at the age of nine and twenty, learns he has been betrothed since childhood. He is determined to escape the contract until he meets the stubborn, free-spirited Mediterranean French beauty.

Until then, follow S.K. Snyder on Facebook, Instagram, and YouTube.

If you enjoyed Born For Love, please let us know by leaving a review on Amazon or Goodreads.

Made in the USA
Columbia, SC
14 October 2024

43544731R00174